SECRETS &
SABOTAGE

JANE ROSE

Book Cover created by Jane Rose Publishing, LLC

Published by Jane Rose Publishing, LLC

1st edition 2026

Print ISBN: 979-8-9907251-8-8

Ebook ISBN: 979-8-9907251-7-1

TWILIGHT KINGDOM
KASTOFF
THE RUINS
THE BANISHED
CITRINE CITY
KRYSTAL MOUNTAIN PASS
KORIN
ALICANTO STABLES
MAREEN
LUAR
REFLECTING POOL

THE ISLANDS OF LOCH
SUNSPARK KINGDOM
SPHINX FIELDS
OLYRIUM
N
W
E
S

*To those who became a different version of
themselves to protect the broken child inside...*

*May you find the strength to love both versions,
knowing each played a role in who you are today.*

*And to the reader:
Let's see if your favorite characters survive another book*

CONTENTS

BOOK ONE
RECAP

I f you're anything like me, you read a book and instantly mind dump to make room for the next story. In case you may have forgotten what happened in book one, here is a brief recap of events!

The scene opens with Aliyah and Saraphena being totally awesome and stealing cake together. This crap sack Cyrus whipped Aliyah on the post for being late on their rent and when that wasn't enough, he forcefully took her virginity from her. Aliyah got her back stitched up by Saraphena before passing out and waking up to her entire village being burned down by skeleton creatures called The Kalari, who wear human skin for fun.

Let's jump over to Olyrium where Enzo and his band of witty sidekicks are living it up in Korin, totally unaware their life is about to be changed forever. Fast forward to Enzo deciding they need to go to Luar to save the villages from being burned, the group fails to understand if they bridge "on three" or "after three" and ultimately end up separated from each other during the fight. It's probably for the best though because Enzo gets saucy during a fight with a strong- willed Aliyah in an alleyway. Deciding he wants to keep her forever, Enzo kidnaps her intent on bringing her back to Olyrium. Unfortunately, Aliyah gets an ax to the chest which later becomes a hilarious talking point when Enzo gifts her a necklace with a battle ax on it to remind her of the day they met.

Aliyah finds out she has actually always been fae when Saraphena drops the bomb on her that she is actually Aliyah's Soul Guardian since birth when an old hag came to her and bound their lives together. Aliyah was marked with a moon scar and Saraphena with a sun scar to signify this bond. Saraphena can't be mated while their souls are bonded, so that's a real bummer for her and Gunnar, who is her lost love from before she escaped with Aliyah to the human realm.

Let's fast forward again to the tavern where Enzo killed a man for touching Aliyah without her consent by making him drink shards of glass. Aliyah then matches with a beautiful alicanto she names Mirage due to her color changing feathers from maroon to indigo. Then a bunch of other crazy stuff happens with her and Jade connecting, the enchanted book of names goes up in flames when Aliyah touches it, and she finds this sword that belonged to the queen that she can touch, but not pull from its protective bubble.

After Aliyah destroys the ancient relic which has survived hundreds of thousands of years before she came along and touched it, they decide to go to SunSpark to have her float in the Reflecting Pool. Hopefully doing so would show her an image of her past or her future, but when has anything ever worked out for the hero in books?

Aliyah discovers the others have powers when they fight in training. Saraphena can disappear, Duncan can teleport, Gunnar has fire magic, Enzo can manipulate objects/people with his mind, and Jade can predict her opponent's next move before they even know they're going to make it. Technically this isn't a real power since she was low borne, but it may as well be for how good she is at it! Oh yeah, and Jade's parents were traitors from SunSpark selling secrets to the Banished King so they were hung and Jade was sent to the military academy where she met Gunnar and Enzo.

Enter Liliana. Gunnar's younger sister and a ball of sunshine. She has the ability to read and change another's emotions. She has an instant connection with Duncan. Much to his dismay, he can't seem to pull himself away from her either. After his first love died, he never expected to fall in love again, but his grumpy personality is no match for Liliana's sparkle.

They decide to have a huge ball in honor of Gunnar coming home. Kaleron, Gunnar's older brother, makes a deal with Aliyah to come with him to the ball and makes her swear to not tell anyone about the threat he made against her in order to get her to comply with his demands. But Saraphena overheard and told Enzo. Naturally, Saraphena had to go. Kaleron tries to poison her, but Marigold rushes in at the last moment and attempts to save her.

A fight breaks out and the whole ballroom goes up in flames...literally. Marigold tells Aliyah she needs to get out of there and will send the rest of them to find her. That was right before she got beheaded for helping them. Oh, I almost forgot, the Queen of SunSpark gave Aliyah a ring she brought with her from Twilight when she was a girl. The queen saw herself giving Aliyah the ring in her vision from the Reflecting Pool, so she knew Aliyah was meant to have it.

Where was I? Oh yeah. Aliyah flees to Krystal on the back of a sphinx. Saraphena is likely dead because Aliyah had to leave before she knew if Marigold saved her. She hikes through Krystal forever and has a dream where Enzo tells her to keep walking north and he will find her. Well, ten days pass and he still hasn't found her. She is out of water and food and is basically on the brink of death. She has a super heartfelt goodbye, but then right at the last moment, Enzo finds her. Also, SURPRISE, Saraphena lives!

They decide to go to Twilight since Kaleron marked them all as traitors, so they can't go back to Korin. Duncan brings them to his home, which he hasn't been to in ages since his father killed the love of his life. They find charred and skinless bodies littering the villages and discover the Twilight palace has been completely overtaken by The Kalari.

Plot twist! Duncan's older brother, Aramot, aligned himself with the Banished King and killed their parents before letting The Kalari wear their skin like a warm, bloody blanket. The group meets Aramot on the battle field and surprisingly, due to Jade's amazing battle strategy, win! The mate bond awakens between Aliyah and Enzo and it is this super cute moment where Aliyah tells Enzo she loves him! Everything is happy, Aramot is dead, and The Kalari are retreating. And that's it! That is the end of book one!

Wait....I feel like I'm forgetting something really important. Let me think. Let me think. OH! That's right.

Right before Aramot died, he stabbed Aliyah through the heart...killing her.

Okay, now let's get into book two's events!

BOOK TWO
RECAP

S o you are all caught up from book one and now you need to remember what happened in book two! Where to even begin!

Let's see...

Enzo was on a warpath to get Aliyah back. The hunt first started with the lost relic of Twilight Kingdom, which we later learned was a ring that was forged from a fallen star, said to grant wishes.

That hunt ended because Kaleron found pages from an old diary made by the previous rulers of Twilight detailing that in order to get the ring to work, one has to eat the heart of an innocent person. Well, based on how Enzo had been acting (you know, destroying an entire village of innocent people to get a spell to bring Aliyah back) the others decided not to tell him. But I'm getting ahead of myself here.

Let's back up. So Saraphena and Gunnar went around to three islands looking for the fallen star. They came up with nothing, but did learn the heir to Krystal Kingdom may, or may not, be a girl. They came back empty handed, but Saraphena came back sporting a new engagement ring and found out her and Gunnar are mates. I'd say Gunnar and Saraphena are sitting pretty right about now. Well except for the fact that her best friend is dead but...semantics.

Flip over to Liliana and Duncan who were off traveling Twilight checking on the people and trying to find information about the fallen star. There was this old man, who happened to love Marigold by the way, who told them the star was formed into a ring. Duncan and Lil formed a relationship and they were super freaking cute, right up until they broke up later in the book when she asked him to be his soul bonded and he decided to take the throne in Twilight instead...no comment.

Jade started calling herself Aliyah when Enzo was having his nightmares or uncontrollable rage in order to calm him down. To say that the others were taken back is an understatement.

Enzo and Jade were recruiting soldiers for the coming war back in Citrine. Enzo was boarderline an alcoholic at this point, but he was functioning so it's fine (lol not). He met Barley, Gwynavere, Felicia, and Rory...poor sweet, sweet, Rory. Everyone fell in love with his sweet spirit and knowledge of what it means to truly love. Every reader gave a piece of their heart to this sweet baby boy...so naturally I decided to kill him off. He died trying to get in contact with Aliyah in the afterlife, but he wasn't strong enough so he burned out his power and died.

This pushed Enzo to do the unthinkable...bargain with the Banished King to try and get a spell that would bring Aliyah back. Surprise, surprise, he couldn't be trusted and told Enzo to slaughter an entire village of murderers in exchange for the spell. It wasn't until after Enzo killed everyone that he realized the town was filled with innocent people...yikes. He raced back to the Banished King intent on killing him, right up until he saw Aliyah. BUT IT WASN'T ALIYAH. It was Tyros, the Banished King, who was giving him a vision of his worst nightmare. The power of the Banished King is to know and create your worst nightmare. Enzo saw every version of Aliyah dying until it sent him into a depressive spiral and he blacked out.

Rewind one second to when Enzo was killing everyone in that village, Jade was left behind with the Banished King as collateral to make sure Enzo came back, but really it was just the Banished King's ploy to get her to spend time with him...her father! He had an affair with her mother, who, if you remember, was a spy for the Banished King in SunSpark. That fact blew up Jade's world. While Enzo was having visions of Aliyah that drove him mad, Jade made a deal with Tyros to come back to him when she was ready to claim her power. When they shook hands, black snakes wormed their way through Jade's veins, a curse that she would later find out about. THEN! Jade took Enzo and fled from the Banished Kingdom when Gunnar and Liliana showed up to save them.

Let's rewind one more time. When Enzo and Jade were in the Banished Kingdom, Gunnar and Liliana were summoned to SunSpark to see their brother, now the king of SunSpark, Kaleron. He became king after his father died during the ballroom fight scene...they were super broken up about his death...lol nah not really. So now Kaleron is king and needed to pick a bride. Well let's just say, he only has one bride in mind, and she is in a coffin so...

Kaleron meets up with his siblings and informs them that he found the missing journal pages from the old kings of Twilight, detailing the events after the fallen star was found. They learned how the ring works and all the terrible wishes it granted. Turns out, you have to eat the heart of an innocent person in order to make a wish, and let's just say, some kings and queens had no issues killing innocents for the sake of a wish. This is when they got a message that Enzo and Jade were in trouble and headed off to the Banished Kingdom!

Now, while all that craziness was happening, Saraphena and Duncan led the training of the recruits back in Citrine. Saraphena had a super heartfelt goodbye to Aliyah and officially let her ghost be at rest. Mirage, who at this point had completely graying feathers due to lack of nutrition and grief, came to see Saraphena and Daisy brought Mirage a crystal in a super adorable moment between the two alicanto best friends. Then Saraphena and Duncan went to oversee the games they set up for the recruits and everyone had a blast.

When Enzo, Jade, Gunnar, and Liliana returned to Citrine after leaving the Banished Kingdom, Duncan and Liliana broke up, Gunnar got vulnerable with Saraphena about his feelings, and Enzo fell into a deep depression. Jade was getting sicker and sicker at this point and eventually fell into a coma, the blackness in her veins taking hold.

Liliana and Duncan share a moment in Jade's room while trying to find a cure, and Duncan tells her he wishes they never met in SunSpark. Lil decides enough is enough and turns off all her emotions. Lil and Duncan both try to convince Enzo to get out of bed and go see Jade in her dying moments, but Enzo won't have it. Duncan yells at him and reveals the story about how he had to kill his mate with his bare hands and this is why he feels he can't be with Liliana, because being king means you have things that can be held against you and he won't lose her.

Enzo finally goes and sees Jade in her room and she is looking *rough!* In a last goodbye, he kisses her on the lips and BAM! True love's kiss brings her back from the brink of death! They are each other's true love! Jade is healed and all is right in the world! Jade and Enzo share a super romantic moment when she takes off the ax necklace from around Enzo's neck and after he leaves, drops it out the window into the water below.

Turns out that Enzo and Jade almost had a thing back when they were teenagers, but that was ended because Jade killed Enzo's abusive father who was forcing him to kill off fae for practice with his powers and would make him cut the word "unworthy" into his arm over and over again. Enzo never forgave Jade for killing his father because he had hoped one day his father would be proud of him and stop hurting him.

But now they are together again! Yay! Jade decides that Enzo needs to fully let Aliyah go, so she wants to go back to Korin to have his final goodbye so they can move on and be happy together. Upon their departure, they say goodbye to their friends. Gunnar and Saraphena decide they want to get married officially when everyone is together again and Duncan and Liliana share a moment.

Enzo and Jade arrive in Korin and things start heating up. Kisses are exchanged, shirts are about to come off...but then a knock at the door. Kaleron stands on the other side, but it isn't him who catches Enzo's attention...

Aliyah stands there with Kaleron, but not the Aliyah who died all those months ago. No, this Aliyah is sporting some HUGE red, orange, yellow, and black wings...

And gosh is she pissed.

CONTENT WARNING

Welcome back, you little masochist you. Ready for more heartbreak? It's almost as if you *like* getting your heart ripped into a thousand pieces. If you're reading this, it's because you tortured yourself reading through the first two books. You were hoping I'd patch your heart back up after shattering it once again after book one and then praying to the Maker the entire time during book two.

But surprise! I only left you with more questions than answers. Well, welcome to the party! The first two books were filled with heart break, gut wrenching plot twists, and multiple occasions when you wanted to throw the book across the room...nothing has changed. Book three will likely leave your mouth agape, staring at a wall, and if all goes well, stuck in a reading slump for days.

This book is structured around the steps of a perfectly thought out plan, because like the evil genius I am, I have concocted the perfect plan to crush you once again. I'm not going to sit here and monologue my diabolical plan for book three because frankly, where is the fun in that? But I will be nice and supply those normal people out there with a list of potentially distressing things that are about to come in this book. So all you sane people, step right up and read through the triggers, I'll wait...

Okay, for those of you who are left, I just have one question...who hurt you?

If you said me...well I'm honored! Now do yourself a favor, call up your therapist and let them know you're going to need a double session this week! Let's get started. *insert evil laugher here*

Oh, and P.S., keep in mind that even the most well thought out plans almost always go right to hell, taking you with it...or was that really my plan all along?

P.P.S. This book contains violent themes that I in no way, shape, or form, condone in real life. This is a *fictional* book, so if you are sensitive to morally gray characters, unhinged actions, violence, or the like, please do not read this book.

Have fun ;)

!!! SPOILERS AHEAD !!!

This is your last chance to turn back...

<u>Triggers may include, but are not limited to:</u>

Animal cruelty

Anxiety

Childhood trauma (mentioned)

Closed-door/fade-to-black sexual content

Domestic violence

Graphic surgery scene

Graphic violence/Gore

Nightmares

Non-consensual bondage

Post Traumatic Stress Disorder

Throwing your book/kindle across the room

War

PROLOGUE
KALERON

I stand on the cliffs overlooking the ocean. The wind blows through my hair, the sun shining on my face. I see now why Enzo picked this location. I look to the sword sticking out of the ground above her grave. It shines in the light of day and I feel tears brim in my eyes. This is the first time I have visited Aliyah's grave since her passing. I sit on the grass which now grows over the packed dirt.

"I'm sorry it has taken me so long to come and visit you, Aliyah. In part it was because I did not want to step foot in Luar. Humans are not my kind of people, but I figured it was time. I know the last time you saw me, I did not behave like a gentleman. I needed you to hate me though. I promise you everything had a purpose. You needed to leave SunSpark. There were people there— Well let's just say, it wasn't safe for you at the time, but I never thought it would lead to your death. I've made it safe for you now though, if only you could be there to enjoy it."

I breathe out a sigh. "I feel I should explain myself, even though I will never be able to get your forgiveness. I had to poison Saraphena. I needed you to hate me and to leave and I knew that would be a sure way to make it happen. I made sure the guards spoke openly about it around Marigold and I made sure the village healer had the antidote. I didn't mean for Marigold to die, but I knew I couldn't let her live either. I have a part to play in this life. A life you were supposed to be a part of. I thought our fates would be intertwined forever. Maybe my vision was wrong. I hope in your death you can forgive me. I truly wished Enzo could have brought you back. I would have shown you who I really am. I'll see you in the next life, Aliyah. Maybe I can beg your forgiveness then."

I lay back in the grass and place my hands under my head. Staring up into the sky, I watch the clouds pass for a few moments. Tears drip from the corners of my eyes onto the dirt beneath me. As I move to sit up, a muffled scream breaks through the silence. I look around to see if anyone near by, but there is no one to be seen for miles. I lean down and place my ear to the dirt, listening. Banging ensues, mixed with muffled screams. My heart races as I start to dig. I use all my strength to dig as fast as I can.

When I reach her coffin, I see Enzo has buried her in traditional iron, etched markings depicting symbols of love and to help her pass on to the afterlife. The banging is clear now. I use my strength ability to lift the coffin out of the hole and place it on the grass. Pulling at the top, I break off the iron nails one by one. I stand over the box and throw off the lid, blinking down at the woman before me. Aliyah lays there, burned and bloody with tears streaming down her face and her nails torn to shreds. I note the massive wings protruding from her back, the lush feathers and polished horns cresting at the tops. My brain is barely keeping up with the information pounding into it. Her eyes remain closed as she adjusts to the light from the sun she has clearly not seen in months.

"Aliyah, oh my Maker!" I pull her from the grave and lightly cradle her in my arms, careful not to grip the burns on her body too hard. She cracks open her eyes and looks up at me before gripping my chest and sobbing into my clothes. I stroke her hair and rock her back and forth as she sobs. I look into the coffin, blood covers the inside, along with several broken off nails. My heart breaks as I think about everything Aliyah has been through in the last three months. Questions flood my brain, but the one the screams the loudest is, *how?*

"Kaleron— how long— has it— been? How long— have I— been down— there?" she says, her voice clearly strained from screaming.

"Three months." It's all I can manage to say as I stare down at the girl who was supposed to be dead.

"Where— is— Enzo?"

"Back in Olyrium."

"I need— to see— him— now."

PART I:
CONCEPTUALIZATION

Chapter 1
ENZO

"Aliyah?" Disbelief laces my words as I stare at the woman before me. The tether connecting our souls pulls me toward her. After what happened with Tyros in The Banished Kingdom, a small part of me doubts she is really standing here before me.

"Enzo, who's at the—" Jade's words cut off as she takes in the sight of Aliyah. *Transformed Aliyah.* I can't seem to pull my gaze away from her. Her once gray eyes are now a dark shade of blue and a solid gold ring surrounds her iris. Her hair is pulled back into a long flowing ponytail with cascading waves. I note the golden swirls that line her face and ears in a beautiful pattern and trickle down her neck, following her hairline. The same swirls crest over her collar bones and dip between the curve of her chest. Her exposed arms are covered in the same shimmering pattern, starting at her fingers and trailing up toward her forearms.

Her wings shift behind her, the red, yellow, orange, and black feathers reflecting in the light. The polished horns at the crest of her wings are short, but curve into a sharp point. She's mesmerizing. Aliyah still wears the blue tunic she was buried in, but now, it's hanging in tatters off her body. Blood coats the fabric in blotches and two lines rip down the back, accommodating her wings.

I don't even want to imagine what she must have looked like when she was first pulled from the grave. Was she bruised? Bloody and torn up from months alone, left in the dark? How did she survive for months down there? She should be dead, if not from the wound to her heart, but from starvation and dehydration alone.

I can't move. My feet can't seem to find the will to move toward her, but horror strikes when I feel Jade's hand slip into mine, her other hand wrapping around my bicep protectively. Aliyah's eyes track the motion as the world around us slows.

"So this is what you've been doing this whole time?" Aliyah's eyebrows drop with anger and her lips purse together. I quickly shrug out of Jade's grasp and move toward Aliyah.

"No— I just— We just—"

Aliyah steps toward Kaleron, her fists clenched. *What?*

"You left me..." She trails off. Hurt coats her words and I can't help the agony ripping through me. "That whole time you just...left me."

"Aliyah, please can we just talk?" I plead. She eyes the woman next to me and I turn to see Jade's hands on her hips and mouth pulled into a scowl. "Alone," I add, turning back to Aliyah. I can feel Jade's expression morph into one of shock, but I don't have time to deal with what *almost* happened between us.

Aliyah hesitates, her eyes roaming up to Kaleron who gives her a short shrug. *Why is she looking to him for confirmation? What has he done to earn her trust?*

"I'll be just outside," he smiles down at her. Aliyah lets out a breath before she steps around him and into our home, her giant wings bumping into the doorway. She whips around and glares at them as if the massive appendage chose to hit the wall.

"Out, Jade. Get out."

"Ugh!" Her tone is clipped, but she moves toward the front door and follows Kaleron out into the village. The moment the door shuts behind them I wrap Aliyah in my arms. Her body stiffens against mine in shock.

"Please let go of me."

"Aliyah, I—" I can't let her go.

"Please, Enzo. Get off of me. You're suffocating me."

I bury my head in her neck and hold on for just one last moment.

"I said get off me!" Golden light shimmers down her body, her irises glowing. I immediately release her as she places her hands over her eyes, her chest rising and falling rapidly. She mumbles something under her breath and I risk a step closer. "I'm safe. I'm alive. I'm *free.*"

"Aliyah, I'm so sorry. For everything, for all of it."

Her eyes flash open, the shimmer burns brightly in those resplendent golden rings around her eyes.

"You're sorry? That's it? Enzo, I was trapped in that iron grave for *months!* I kept waiting for you to come get me! Praying to the Maker you heard me down the bond! You even responded to me! I would have thought you would have visited my grave at least *once* and heard me screaming for you! Every day I woke up in that grave— alone and burning alive over, and over again, because of that iron. I needed you, Enzo, and you weren't there. No amount of words are ever going to fix that."

"Aliyah—"

"And then, to top it all off. I *finally* get set free and who do I find waiting for me? *Kaleron!* Of all the people I wanted to save me, I did not think it would be Kaleron! Where was Saraphena? Where was Duncan or Lil, or hell, even Jade? Why did no one come for me?! You all left me there. But now...now I know where you were. You were here...with *Jade!* You already moved on! Did you...did you leave me there on purpose? So you could be with Jade?"

"No! Aliyah, no!" I force another step closer to her, but she shoots her hand up between us stopping me in my pursuit. I just want to hold her and make everything okay. "I don't want to be with Jade! I never wanted to be with Jade! I only ever wanted you! I did hear you down the bond, but it was so soft and when I saw you in my dreams, I thought it was just my mind playing tricks on me. I thought I was going mad.

"The entire time, I only ever wanted you, but then...Jade got sick and you were gone. I couldn't lose her too. So when I went to see her on her death bed, I...I kissed her...and suddenly she was completely healed and everyone was talking about true love's kiss and I thought— I don't know what I thought, but I didn't think you were ever coming back, that maybe I needed to move on. So much has happened since you died."

"And what about me, then? If Jade is your true love, where does that leave me?" *Am I no longer your true love?*

"You are more than my true love!" *You're my mate. My one and only.*

Apparently not anymore. Aliyah moves to head toward the door.

"Where are you going?"

"To see Saraphena."

She storms out of the house and onto the busy streets of Korin. Kaleron pushes off the side of a building he was leaning against and makes his way over to follow Aliyah up the marble path toward Citrine City. I call out for Ruby and Jade signals for Reyla. If we are going to Citrine, it's going to be a long walk on foot. The alicanto come racing through the village to catch up with us.

"I take it the conversation didn't go well?" He smirks at me.

"Can it, Kaleron. How did you even find her?" I grunt. I follow Aliyah as she storms up the path, mumbling to herself as she goes. Her wings drag on the ground behind her and she keeps glaring back at them, clearly frustrated.

"I was in Luar." Kaleron shrugs as if him going to the human realm was just another day.

"*Why* were you there Kaleron?" I kick a gem in front of me, watching it bounce around on the road. Jade falls into step behind us, her presence beginning to irritate me.

"I went to her grave to apologize for everything. To explain what happened in SunSpark."

"You tried to kill her best friend and us. What else is there to explain?"

Kaleron huffs. "I explained this all to Aliyah already, but I needed her out of the palace and I knew what I did would push her away. My father was growing suspicious of Aliyah. His working theories were another spy for The Banished King, or something else he feared even more. A child of The Banished King was rumored to be somewhere in Olyrium. Both theories are completely ridiculous of course, because who could ever love that traitor? Either way, he planned on killing Aliyah after the ball in her sleep. I couldn't stand by and let that happen."

"But you could kill her best friend? And Marigold, what about her life? Did she mean nothing to you too?"

"My father grew weak in his old age. Abusing his ability and turning down a path which followed the Kings of Twilight. I was not about to let my people fall under a ruler who would so easily kill without evidence or question. Marigold was an unfortunate necessity. If I spared her life, my people would think I betrayed them for endangering their lives with that bomb she set off.

"I don't expect you to understand, Enzo, but I had to do what was right for my people...for Aliyah. I made sure the healer in the village had the antidote and I made sure a few trusted guards spoke about my plans in front of Marigold. Saraphena was never in any real danger. I just needed Aliyah out...and I needed my father dead."

"You do realize you just confessed to murder in front of the General of Citrine's army, right?" Jade quips from behind me.

"I do. I also know that your *General* has done far worse to those far more innocent than my father, so forgive me if I don't shake in my boots."

"Kaleron, do you know what she is? How her wings came to be? What has she told you?" Nerves fray the edges of my voice, fearing that she confided in Kaleron.

"What happened to her in the grave is not my story to tell. As far as what she is, I believe Aliyah has an ability similar to immortality. It would explain why she was able to remain alive for all those months. Dying and coming back again, and again. However, I have no explanation for the wings."

"Immortality? I knew fae lived a long time, but immortality? Surely it is only a thing of myths and legends."

"Of course she would be something rare." Jade rolls her eyes and clicks her tongue in disgust. "Leave it to some lowly fae to have rare abilities *and* be Enzo's mate. I mean what is this? Some oh-so-special prophecy crap?"

I scowl at Jade before turning back to Kaleron, but before I can ask further questions he strides ahead, keeping pace with Aliyah.

I watch their interaction, noting how Aliyah visibly relaxes in his presence, while my body coils tighter as Jade runs her hand down my arm. Fear grips my chest and I pull away, praying to the Maker Aliyah didn't see.

"Enzo, talk to me." Jade's eyes plead with me to change my words from before.

"There isn't anything to talk about Jade. We are done, over, never going to happen. What happened back in the village was a mistake. Aliyah is back now. My *mate* is back now."

"She wants nothing to do with you Enzo!"

I pull her arm harshly, forcing her to stop beside me. "Keep your voice down, Jade! I am only going to tell you this once more. We. Are. Over. It was a mistake. *We* were a mistake. One I will spend the rest of my days making up to Aliyah."

"Enzo, please—"

"Enough, Jade. Stop acting like a spoiled child who didn't get a sweet at the candy cart. I forgave you for killing my father all those years ago, telling everyone except our chosen family that he died in the war to protect you, but I will never forgive you if you stand in the way of my future with Aliyah. I have a second chance at a life with her, and I'm not going to throw it away for *you*."

Jade stumbles back, clearly shocked by my words. I don't mean to be harsh with her, but I need her to understand there is no future for us any longer. I need to fix things with Aliyah and if that means crawling on my knees every day for the rest of eternity, begging her to forgive me, then so be it.

Chapter 2

ALIYAH

I absolutely did not think this through, but I'm committed to this choice on principle alone. Walking to Citrine City takes far longer than I thought it would. A half days ride on an alicanto is turning into a full day's walk, minimum. My wings feel heavy at my back and my shoulder blades ache with the added weight. What I wouldn't give to be able to fly there, but I have yet to learn how to use these monstrous things.

I swear, as if knowing my thoughts, my wings get heavier on my back, dragging on the ground. I huff an irritated breath. My left wing shoots around me, smacking me in my face. I punch the center of my wing in retaliation. "You stupid bird ball! Knock it off," I mutter under my breath so no one hears me talking to a pair of wings.

I tip my head left and right to relieve some of the ache building there from the strain on my back muscles, but it only helps so much. I need to find out where the hell these things came from because I did not wake up in that box with them originally.

The first few times I died and came back were excruciating. I cringe at the reminder of what it was like to wake up and feel the scathing burn of iron on my body. I thought the bracelet Marigold gave me was bad, but this was immeasurable. When I came back with wings however, the small space of my iron grave became even more suffocating. I shift my shoulders again, trying to find a comfortable position for my wings to ease the ache.

My wings begin to purposefully sway side to side, causing me to stumble. "I swear, when we get to Citrine—"

"Hello, Olyrium to Aliyah?" Kaleron bumps into me with his shoulder as he catches up to me.

"Hey," I smile, pulling myself from my fight with my new appendages. "Sorry, I'm not sure where my mind went."

"You doing all right?" Concern pulls at his features and it shoves an uncomfortable feeling into my heart. I was in complete shock when Kaleron found me, yet simultaneously happy to have someone finally come for me. I had been down there for so long...screaming...clawing...trying to break free. I thought that was going to be my fate forever.

"As long as the sun is shining, I'll be fine," I smile.

"Are you going to forgive him?"

I turn behind me and watch as Enzo and Jade follow. I look back ahead and think over my response. Ruby and Reyla walk behind us all, Enzo apparently choosing to walk with me in solidarity despite the protests from Jade.

"I don't know if I can. I don't know if I can forgive any of them right now, but I want to hear Saraphena and the others out. They must have had a good reason for not coming to get me."

"And Enzo? What about his reasons?"

"He left me there. He was the only one with a connection to me. He literally heard me screaming at him day and night to come get me. He heard me die over and over again through our bond, but he didn't come for me. I'm not sure any reason can overshadow that fact."

Kaleron had explained everything to me on our way to Olyrium after he pulled me from the grave. The night in SunSpark, poisoning Saraphena, everything. I don't know why it felt easier to forgive him than it did Enzo, but what I do know is that Kaleron was the only one who showed up, and that had to count for something.

"He was looking for a way to bring you back."

"Kaleron, stop. Don't defend him. I didn't need to be brought back. I was already *back*. What I needed was for him to *listen* to me. He ignored me, pushed me out, gave up, and then went on and got with Jade. I can't forgive that. Please, just drop it."

"For you, anything." His smile eases some of the tension in my heart. "So do you want to try out your wings today?"

"I honestly don't think I could even if I wanted to. My shoulders are burning under their weight. I don't know how anyone could ever carry these around with them all the time. They are so inconvenient! I keep knocking into things with them and I'll have to alter all of my shirts now!"

Kaleron huffs out a laugh. "Only you would complain about being the only fae in history with wings. You're special, Aliyah, and yet you complain about the gift."

"Hey! I didn't ask for these," I laugh. Talking to Kaleron feels easy. I'm not fighting with him or upset with him, even though I probably should be. Kaleron is...Maker dare I say it...my *friend*. "Are you sure it's okay for you to be away from SunSpark this long? If you need to go back, I completely understand. I know I've thanked you a thousand times over for saving me, but truly, I can handle it from here."

"I made a promise to myself that if I had more time with you I would show you the man I really am, not the one who you saw that night in SunSpark. My kingdom will be okay without me for a little while longer. Right now, where you go, I will follow."

I smile and look down to my boots as I kick a loose crystal in front of me. "There really has been no other fae with wings?" I ask.

"None I have ever heard of. I am in awe of you, Aliyah." His eyes sparkle with something almost handsome.

"Well right now I am no better than an alicanto," I laugh. "Beautiful wings, but bound to the ground."

"Don't worry. I know one day you will soar amongst the clouds." He smiles down at me and I'm transported to the first day I flew on the back of the sphinx going to the Reflecting Pool. I had dreams of flying through the sky ever since that day, and one day soon, I would.

Night falls on Krystal Kingdom as we finally reach the gates of Citrine City. My nerves are on edge as the darkness around me creeps in. "I'm safe. I'm alive. I'm *free.*" Nervousness flares in my chest at the thought of seeing Saraphena again after all this time and an uncomfortable feeling shifts awkwardly in my veins. I've never been angry at her before like this and I can't help the irritation crushing my sanity at the thought of how she left me there, too. I'm uneasy waiting for the answer to all my questions.

The sound of running reaches my ears a moment too late as something collides with my body, throwing me to the ground. I land with a thud, catching a glimpse of the large creature above me. "Mirage!" I throw my arms around her long neck as she leans down to nuzzle my face. "Oh girl, how are you?!"

I take in her dulled feathers and anger once again joins the mix of emotions. "Who let her get like this? Why was no one making her eat something!?" I push her off me and glare at Enzo, waiting for an explanation as Mirage inspects my wings behind me. I pay her no mind, but I feel her shoving her beak into the plumes and shifting each wing around my body.

I feel a pull at my back and watch as Mirage goes tumbling across the ground, a squawk bellowing out of her. I move to ensure she is all right, but she leaps up and takes a charge at my wings, knocking into them and taking me to the ground once more.

"Both of you enough!" I yell. I don't miss the confused looks on the other's faces as I right myself. Enzo moves to help me up, but I swat his hand away.

"You can't make an alicanto eat, Aliyah. We tried, but she just wouldn't go to feed. Saraphena said Daisy got her to eat a few crystals, but she refused to leave Citrine," Enzo shrugs.

"So just another thing you neglected then?" I mumble, turning back to my matched. "I missed you so much sweet girl. I'm home now. I'm home."

Making my way toward the palace doors, I look back as Mirage takes off running in the opposite direction, headed right for the Twilight boarder. I smile as I note the excitement in her step. After crossing the large bridge over the light blue water, I push open those extravagant crystal doors and am met with a sight so foreign to me from the last time I opened them. Fae are racing all over the palace, some casually talking to one another, some running around in some sort of game, and others sitting on the steps lining the walls of the palace.

"What's going on?" I ask.

"We started recruiting again," Enzo says stepping closer to me.

"Recruiting?"

"For the coming war," Jade rolls her eyes.

"War? What war?"

"Honestly, Aliyah, think! We were battling The Kalari when you died. The Banished King...ring a bell?" Jade snaps.

"All right, all right! Maker, Jade you don't have to be such a dick about it. I know we were fighting The Kalari, but clearly you don't remember that I've been trapped in a box for the last three months! I didn't know it had escalated to a full out war!" The golden light swirling beneath my skin starts to illuminate as I try to reign in my emotions.

"No need to get all hot headed about it, *Aliyah*. We had no clue you were alive. Looks like we're even. Now get over it."

"Get over it?! Get...over...it?!" Iridescent pools pulsate under the swirls on my arms and my wings flex in response, stretching out and growing twice their size as a show of force. I look down and take in the bottom feathers that have turned to crystals as my right wing wraps around me protectively. If I'm going to face off against Jade, I can't say I'm mad about having back up.

"Ladies! No need to fight," Kaleron's cool voice washes over the group. He steps between us and puts his hands up to stop us from getting closer to each other. "We will have plenty of time to squabble about *who* left *who* to die later. Let's not forget, it was Jade's plan you all were following in the first place. Who's to say she isn't to blame for Aliyah's death?" Kaleron smirks at her before lowering his hands.

My light fades out, my wings dropping from their protective position. As I turn, I hear a soft thud as my left wing knocks Jade into the nearest wall before returning to their relaxed position. I roll my eyes, but can't help the small smile pulling at my lips. I reach out and touch the shoulder of a young boy chatting with some other fae. "Excuse me, what's your name?"

A smile spreads onto his face as he takes in my features. "Barley, ma'am. I don't think I've seen you around before and I would absolutely remembered if I had! What's *your* name?"

"Aliyah." I give him a soft smile, but it falters when his eyes shoot wide.

"You're— Holy— You guys!" Barley stares at me in shock while reaching behind himself to grab his friends attention. Two girls appear at his sides. One with striking ocean eyes and another who grips her gloved hands tightly around a book. "This is Aliyah."

The girl's faces pale and something shifts uncomfortably in my chest. "Do I know you?"

"No, but we know you. I'm Gwynavere and this is Felicia. You might know our friend...Rory."

A shock ripples through my system. "You— You know Rory? Is he here?!" I look over their shoulders to see if he is standing near by.

The girl, Felicia, looks around to the others before speaking. "He— He passed."

"What? How? When?" What could have happened to such an innocent boy? The war was obviously not here, but had they gone into battle already? He was so young, so much life left to live.

"I don't know how to say this, but...it was the day he contacted you. His power burnt out. He wasn't well trained in using it and he pushed himself too far." I bite back the tears welling in my eyes, not wanting the children to see me cry. I had taken their friend from them. I had been the reason for his death. Rory's blood was on *my* hands. I felt my lip quiver, but I shoved that emotion deep down inside to be dealt with later.

"Please don't be upset, Aliyah. Rory was honored to be the one to contact you," Felicia says. "Every day and every night he worked tirelessly to reach you. He would be so happy knowing you made it back. It's all he ever talked about. Trying to find a way to help the General get his mate back."

"He was a good friend," Barley says. "The best of us."

"I'm sure he was lucky to have friends like you," I say, trying to find the conviction in my voice.

"We were the lucky ones," Gwynavere says. "Rory showed us what true friendship means."

"Um, speaking of friends," I say, trying to change the subject before I lost my control over the tears threatening to spill. "I am looking for one of mine. Do you know Saraphena?"

"Aliyah?!" My best friend appears at the top of the steps cascading down the right side of the entryway. "Holy— Oh my Maker! How is this— What is— Oh my Maker!" Saraphena can't find the words as she scrambles down the steps, pushing everyone out of her way as she descends. I turn, seeing the group of children walking away and part of me feels relief I don't have to face them any longer. I can't handle the knowledge that I took their friend from them right now. As Saraphena reaches me, her arms fly around my neck in a tight embrace. My body tenses at the contact.

"How is this possible?" She finally questions.

"I was never really dead," I answer flatly.

"What?"

"Can we go somewhere to sit? I've been walking for hours," I huff.

"Walking? Why would you be walking when you have *these*?!" She runs her hands down the feathers and a line of sparks let loose as the feathers transform into sharp shards of crystal like feathers. "Maker, Aliyah! I'm sorry! I didn't mean to!"

I take in ragged breaths and try to calm the fraying nerves in my body. "It's all right, they are just...protective." As my breathing calms, my wings transform back to their feathery state.

"What in all the realms is happening down here?" Gunnar's voice breaks through the shock of the room. His eyes snag on me and shoot wide before settling into a smirk. "I always knew evil couldn't die so easily. How the hell are you, Aliyah?"

"Hi, Gunnar." I laugh as he steps into my space, but makes no move to hug me.

"I'd offer you a hug, but I tend to like my body intact. But hey, talk about making an entrance!"

"What can I say, I like to keep you on your toes," I wink. "Can we *please* find somewhere to sit down?" I plead.

"Maker, yes! Sorry!" Saraphena smiles.

"Wait, where is Liliana and Duncan? Did they get together yet? It's been driving me mad not knowing what has been going on around here."

"Ummm, why don't we just find somewhere to sit in the library and I'll fetch them." Gunnar makes for the stairs and I risk a glance around the room.

Enzo stands with his arms crossed, closed off defensively from the group. Jade stands directly next to him with her hand lightly brushing his hip. I quickly snap my head away from the contact. *I can't believe he's been with her this whole time.* I make my way up the steps to the library and like the first time I passed through these halls, my eyes snag on the picture of Queen Dione. Maker, she was beautiful. I wish she were here now to see her palace be restored to its former glory. I can't help the warmth that spreads through my chest at the sight of the halls being filled once more. Pushing open the doors to the library, I let my gaze drift over to where the relic of Krystal was once housed, now burned to ash. *Whoops.*

I make to sit down in a high back chair, but then remember the giant protrusions attached to me. Looking around at my other options, I find a small footstool that will allow plenty of room for my wings. Every other chair or couch has a high back, making sitting rather awkward. Enzo follows in behind me and watches as I sit on the footstool. A low growl erupts from his throat and a loud crack ripples through the room. My eyes flick over to the sound and notice the couch now lacks a backing. The section of couch is thrown across the room and Enzo nods his head in the direction of the seat.

"No mate of mine will sit on a footstool meant for holding up someone's feet."

I shake my head, standing and making my way over to the now perfect seat. I won't deny the cushion is far more comfortable than the footstool was. Enzo sits across from me and Jade plops down right next to him...*again.*

Seriously, Enzo? I'm gone for a few months and now you have a little lap dog?

Jade's body is suddenly thrown off the couch slams down on a chair clear across the room. Enzo's eyes never leave mine as he tosses Jade far away from him.

Better, my dove?

I roll my eyes and watch as Saraphena stares at me. I wish I could hear *her* voice in my head right now. I know she would be making some hilarious quip about the interaction between Jade and Enzo. I can't help but wonder though, did she approve of their relationship? Did she betray me, too? I shake my head at the thought.

Duncan pushes open the doors to the library and his eyes go wide as they take me in. "When Gunnar said he had something to show me, I never expected— Welcome back from the dead, Aliyah." This is arguably the best greeting I could get right now. Just a normal, unsurprised welcome. It's almost refreshing based on the way the other greetings have gone thus far. Duncan makes his way to the broken couch and drops down as if this is the most normal thing in the world.

"I swear you all keep dragging me into these dang libraries against my will and I'm really getting sick of it." Liliana's voice carries through the hall as she approaches the room. "Every time you do this, no one bothers to tell me what is going on and I'm going to stop being so compliant in the— ALIYAH!"

Liliana shoots across the room in a dead sprint. I stand right at the last moment before she crashes into me. Her legs wrap around my waist and we go flying backwards at the impact. My wings instinctively wrap around us as we tumble across the floor. "Hi, Lil. It's nice to see you, too."

Liliana places kisses to my face in rapid succession and she doesn't let go of my body. *Okay, it's getting to be a little much.* More kisses rain down on my face and Liliana's giggles fill the air.

"Okay, Lil. Thank you, but please get off now."

"Oh, Aliyah, I'm never going to let you go again! You just look so beautiful sporting these new accessories!"

"Lil...please." My wings flex on my back and I try to keep their temperament at bay. "I don't want you to get hurt."

"You could never—"

Horror grips my throat as my wings spark with those familiar aureate flames and the once lush feathers are replaced with crystal daggers. My left wing shoves its way between me and Liliana, throwing her to the side and off my body.

"Oof!" Liliana lands with a thud.

"Lil! Maker, I'm so sorry! I don't have control over them," I plea, scrambling up and making my way over to her.

"Don't worry about it! Enzo had the same reaction to my hug the last time we all got back together again. I know the risks when it comes to hugging you two," she laughs.

"What do you mean when you got back together?" I ask.

"Aliyah, why don't you sit down. There's a lot to cover." Saraphena gestures to my spot on the couch and I take it reluctantly.

A flicker in my chest wishes that Kaleron was here right now to help ground me to this new reality. He opted to skip this whole thing and retire to his room to write letters with instructions for his council during his absence. Liliana starts at the moment I got stabbed through the heart.

Chapter 3

ENZO

"I — I can't believe all that happened during the months I was gone. I'm a little confused though. Duncan and Liliana broke up because he is afraid she is going to be used against him, even though we all know he still loves her, so she could be captured at any moment and used against him whether they are together or not?"

Gunnar bursts out laughing and Duncan cuts him a glare. "That is exactly why I wanted Liliana to go back to SunSpark where she can be protected." Duncan shakes his head.

"And I told you to just screw right the hell off because this is my home and this is where my family is, so I'm not going anywhere." Liliana rolls her eyes and turns away from him. Aliyah decides that line of questioning is a dead end, dropping it and sighing.

"I need to ask you all something, and I want the truth. Even if the truth hurts, I need to hear it." The group hangs by a thread of anticipation, knowing this can't be an easy question.

"Did any of you even think about coming to visit my grave?"

Silence.

"That's my fault. From the moment we buried you I was so caught up in finding a way to bring you back, they would not have had time to visit your grave. If you are going to blame anyone, blame me. I take full responsibility." I know this is going to set my relationship back with her even more, but she needed to know and I was not going to let her friends take the blame for my actions.

"It isn't solely Enzo's fault," Saraphena adds. "I don't think any of us were in the right head space to visit you. It would have made it real and none of us were prepared for your death to be final. We all share the blame."

Saraphena's eyes snag on mine and I give her a small nod of appreciation.

"Did you approve of Enzo and Jade?" Aliyah's fists clench in her lap and I know the answer is going to cost her everything.

"Aliyah—" Liliana starts. Jade huffs across the room in annoyance, apparently waiting for me to step in on her behalf. I simply look away from her.

"The truth." Aliyah's eyes search her friends for the answer, but I think she already knows in her heart what they are going to say.

"Yes." Saraphena's voice cracks at the confession and a small tear drips from Aliyah's eye. My body burns in protest at the sight and every shred of my being wants to take all her pain away, but I know when she looks at me, all she sees is the source of her agony.

She sucks in a shaky breath before continuing. "Thank you for the truth. I'm not going to sit here and pretend like it doesn't feel like a betrayal, but only one of you in this room had an open connection with me. All of you thought I was gone...all but one."

"Aliyah you're just jealous your friends supported the person who is *right* for Enzo. I was there for him this entire time. I saw every dark and ugly corner of his being and loved him anyways. Yet here you are, unwilling to forgive him after everything he has done for you," Jade spews.

The room falls silent leaving only the harsh crackle of the roaring fire. Flames flicker in Aliyah's eyes as she stares at Jade, though I'm not certain they come from the hearth.

"Oooooooo, you are so dead, Jade," Gunnar laughs.

Aliyah's fingers fist in her tunic, restraint burning in her eyes. I open my mouth to stop Jade from spreading any more lies, but Aliyah holds up her hand to me.

"My relationship with Enzo is *none* of your business, Jade. What I choose to forgive him for and what I don't is between him and me. You were my *friend,* and yet the moment I was gone you latched onto him and clawed your way into his mind." Aliyah rises from the broken couch, the golden swirls on her arms shimmering, her power flowing like water right under her skin.

"Fight, fight, fight, fight," Gunnar chants under his breath and Saraphena slaps him on the chest.

"You aren't worth a second thought, let alone a drop of my power," Aliyah says, and pride flares in my chest at how strong she is before I remember what it took for that to happen. Aliyah takes her seat once more, but her eyes never leave Jade. The stare-off of the century is going down in this very room and I can feel the heat radiating off them from across the space.

Slowly, Aliyah's eyes break away, a clear sign she does not fear what Jade will do.

I turn to face her, noting how she is picking at her nails, spots of blood lining the cuticle. "Do you want to talk about what happened to you while you were in—"

"No. I— I can't talk about it. All that matters is that I'm out. Where are we now with The Banished King? What is he planning?"

"We don't know," Saraphena says. "Last we knew he was strengthening his army and with the pillar intact, he could Bridge over at any point, but yet he sits there...waiting."

"Waiting for what? He clearly has the forces he needs to take us," I say. "Jade, you were with him the longest. Did he say anything?"

"Why does everyone keep asking me that!? I don't know anything!"

"You know what Jade, I'm really getting sick of your attitude. I know I promised you I wouldn't hurt Enzo, but I didn't exactly plan to get stabbed through the heart. I get a lot has happened while I was gone, but I'm back now. There is no reason for you to be such a dick to me. I don't know why you feel like you have some claim over Enzo, but he is *my* mate. We might be on the rocks at the moment, but I'm not just going to sit back and watch as you paw at him like a lost puppy," Aliyah growls.

"Me?! How can *you* just come back here and ignore the fact that Enzo and I have a connection!"

"Actually," I start, "we don't have—"

"And furthermore," Jade cuts me off, "you did break your promise! You should have killed Aramot when you had the chance! You opened up the opportunity for him to stab you so really it is *your* fault you died you incompetent—"

"ENOUGH!" I shout. I can't sit back and let Aliyah fight this battle anymore. "I will not have you speaking to my mate this way. She was *merciful* to Aramot. Something you know *nothing* about Jade, or do I need to remind you what you did to my father. We are done, Jade. Aliyah is my mate which trumps true love, if it even exists. If I hear you speaking this way to Aliyah ever again, you will meet the same fate as my father, but I won't grieve your death."

"UGH!" Jade storms out of the room, slamming the door behind her. She has acted like a delusional child ever since she found out we are *true loves,* but that time is over. I will not tolerate her abuse of Aliyah when she has clearly suffered enough already.

"I don't need you to defend me, Enzo. I am perfectly capable of taking care of myself," Aliyah snaps.

"I know you can defend yourself. *Clearly*." I gesture to her wings. "But that doesn't mean I am going to sit back and let her speak to you like that. I've spent enough time sitting back and doing nothing to help you in the ways you actually needed me to. I won't make that mistake again."

"Look, clearly a lot has happened since I was gone. I think right now I really could just use some rest. Is there a room where I can stay?" Aliyah asks.

"You won't be—" I clear my throat awkwardly. "You won't stay with me?" I try to keep my voice even, but I can't help the crack at the end. Anxiety grips my heart as I wait for her answer.

"I think I just need to be alone right now."

"Oh, of course. Well let me show you to a room. All of them have been made up nicely since the recruits returned to Citrine." Aliyah stands from the couch, walking ahead of me toward the door. She doesn't say a word as we make our way through the hallways toward our wing.

"This is where you can stay. My room is just a few doors down, but Saraphena's room is right next door." I push open the door to her new room. White linens adorn the bed and a fluffy blue comforter tops it with several pillows at the head of the bed. The white crystal floors are topped with soft rugs and a reading chair sits nicely in the corner by the window overlooking the Krystal mountains. The bed sits along the right wall, across from the door to her bathing chamber. "Will this do?"

"It isn't a coffin so it will do just fine." Aliyah pushes through the doorway, her right wing bumping into the frame. She lets out a huff as she turns and glares back at the protrusion.

"Do you not like them?" I ask, stepping into the room.

"What?"

"Your wings. Do you not like them? I would have thought after seeing your face on the sphinx that you would have loved to have wings."

"They keep getting in the way of things. I'll have to rip all of my shirts now to fit," she gestures to the two lines ripped down the back of her shirt, "and I don't like how they have a mind of their own."

I didn't even think about how her wings might affect her daily life. I would have thought any fae would kill to have wings like hers, but clearly she is not the biggest fan of her new accessory.

"Enzo." Her voice pulls me back to the moment. I want to go to her, but I know the last time I tried, her wings had other plans. Tears brim in her eyes.

"My dove, what is it?" I take a step closer, but leaving enough distance so her guardian doesn't feel threatened.

"There is a lot to figure out between us." She wraps her arms around her midsection protectively and sits on the edge of her bed, her wings sprawled out behind her. "Can we just...talk?

Without yelling, without getting upset, just talk this out? Please."

"What do you want to know? I'll answer anything. May I sit with you?"

She nods her head toward the spot next to her. "I want to lay out some ground rules first, okay?"

"Anything."

"No lies. I want the full truth and nothing but the truth. No yelling, no breaking stuff, and no storming out. Deal?"

"Deal," I smile. She reaches out and takes my hand, lacing our fingers together. Feeling the heat of her palm in mine is intoxicating and every inch of me burns to lean forward and take her lips in mine. I have dreamed about this day for months, but it has not gone like I planned.

"Explain to me again what's really going on between you and Jade?"

"Oof. Starting out with the hard questions I see," I wink. She lets out a light laugh. "Jade and I had history long before you ever came into my life. She was my first crush, but my father would never allow me to find love. He thought it made you weak. Then, one night when I was a teenager, I almost kissed Jade. My father found us and dragged me away to...well, let's just say, he wasn't the kindest of fathers. Jade stormed in and killed him. In that moment, I never thought I'd forgive her.

"When you died, Jade was there for me. Through everything, the denial, anger, that stupid bargain with Tyros, and all through my depression, she was by my side. When she got sick, I wasn't even going to get out of bed when Liliana came to tell me that it was time to say goodbye. But she convinced me to be the man you fell in love with. So I went to see Jade. She was so sick, Aliyah. Black ooze creeping up her veins and into her heart. I had no idea when I kissed her she would wake back up. Everyone came flooding into the room saying it had to be true love's kiss. I didn't want to believe them, but what other explanation was there?

"She was the one who pushed me to go back to Korin and say my final goodbye to you. We...we almost...but then Kaleron showed up, and you were alive again. After everything I did, I thought I failed you again, Aliyah. I wanted you back so badly, but what it cost me— It started to become too damaging to those around me. I thought I had to let you go."

My gaze drifts up to meet her eye and a single tear falls. I reach out to wipe it away, my thumb connecting with her tear. She leans into my palm for just a moment before continuing.

"When you heard me down the bond, why did you never come to see if it was really me?"

My heart hurts admitting this to her, but she said she wanted the truth, even if it hurt. "Going to Luar...it was too painful. I knew I couldn't visit your grave or I would have dug a grave right beside yours and crawled into it to die. I thought I was going mad hearing you in my head. Words will never be enough to tell you how sorry I am for leaving you. I swear to you, I will do all I can to show you."

"I just have one more question. Where does this leave us?"

"I've said it before, but I'll say it as many more times as you need until you believe it. You are my mate, Aliyah. I am yours. I will forever be yours, even if you can't ever forgive me and our time together is over. I know the things I have done are unforgivable, but I will never stop being yours."

Aliyah lets my words wash over her for a moment, contemplation in her eyes. "I don't know if I can forgive you, Enzo. I never blamed you for my death, but I do blame you for not coming for me. Maybe that isn't fair of me, maybe I'm the one who is being cruel, but I came out of that coffin a different person. I'm not the same Aliyah who went into that iron grave. I think...I think I need some time to figure out who I am now. We will still have our bond, but right now, I can't be your mate. I need to just be Aliyah."

My heart breaks at the thought of losing her all over again, but this time she is sitting right in front of me. Aliyah is within reach, and yet her heart is still so far away. But I can't hold onto her. I need her to come to me in time. I know if I force her back into this relationship, I could lose her forever.

"Take as much time as you need. I will be here. Whenever you are ready, whenever you have questions or just need someone. I'll be here." I lift her hand up to my lips and when her flesh connects with mine, sparks fly across my vision. I shove the feeling down deep. If I let the fire that is Aliyah consume me, I won't be able to contain the inferno that blazes through the night.

I stand to leave, even though my heart calls me back to her side. I lean down and risk placing a soft kiss to the top of her head before heading for the door. As I reach for the door handle, Aliyah's hand lands on my shoulder.

"Enzo," she starts.

I turn around, my chest cavity bursting with that flame for my dove. "What is it?"

"Where is my axe necklace?"

Chapter 4

JADE

"How can Enzo be so blind!?" I pace back and forth in my room, pulling at the roots of my hair in frustration. "I've done everything for him! *Everything!* Yet the moment Aliyah comes back it's like I'm forgotten! As if everything I've done for him was a waste!"

I move to the window and whip open the curtain revealing the stars dancing across the night sky. I scream, letting the wrath boiling inside me mix with the night air. A bright light behind me casts a warm glow at my back and I turn just in time to watch the door to my room explode with golden sparks. "You cow! Where is it?"

Aliyah's massive wings burst through the entry, knocking me to the ground. I scramble up, preparing for a fight. I take my stance, watching her every move, calculating her next strike. I won't be caught off guard twice.

Enzo and the others appear where my door once stood and I hear them whispering about intervening, but Enzo holds up his hand in warning. Of course he won't defend me against his mutant harlot. Aliyah's grotesque appendages sharpen into their razor sharp form.

"I will not be taken down by some deviant with the wings of a clipped bird!" I spit.

"Where is my necklace, Jade?! I will not ask again!" The golden rings around her irises flare like molten lava threatening to incinerate my soul.

I can't help but smirk. "Gone. Just like you should have stayed."

I don't let her get another word in before I attack. I sprint at her, dropping to slide across the smooth crystal ground, swiping at her foot as I pass by. Her face connects with the ground, a grunt of frustration slipping from her lips alongside a few drops of blood.

"I don't want to kill you, but I will if I have to," Aliyah says, pushing off the ground. My eyes catch on her toes, twisting slightly, readying for a punch. Her torso turns, arm cocked. I prep to dodge, but it isn't her fist that connects. The sharp tip of her crystal plumes drag across my cheek, cutting a deep wound straight through until my teeth are exposed on the side of my face. Shock registers in my brain and blood slips over my fingers as I reach up to inspect the wound.

I hear the others gasp and Gunnar's familiar *ooo* as he sucks in a sharp breath. My eyes snap to their's in horror and when I gaze upon them, all I see is pity.

"I'd say I'm sorry, but you can burn in hell for what you've done for all I care." Aliyah stands with her hands fisted at her sides, her wings wrapped protectively around her.

"What *I've* done?! All I ever did was help Enzo! I helped him move on! He needed to let you go!" I scream, pain pulling at my cheek as it knits itself back together. I know it will never properly heal. I'll bear this scar for the rest of my life, but I won't let Aliyah leave this room without a reminder of her own.

I launch myself at her, hands poised at her throat. Right as I reach her, the back of her right forearm slices down across my hands and her left wing swoops in front of her, shoving me to the ground behind her. I quickly flip onto my back, preparing to take an assault from above. I raise my fists, but my eyes widen in shock as I look up at Aliyah's back.

As she turns, her right wing opens up and releases a barrage of piercing feathers that slice through my clothing, pinning me to the ground. Two land just outside my hips, two others capture my wrists by the hem of my sleeve and two more land just outside my throat. A clear warning that they could have embedded in the soft flesh of my neck if chosen.

Aliyah lands on top of my body, straddling my torso. "You are nothing but a leach! You fed off his grief and used it to satiate a longing in your belly like the parasite you are!" Fists connect with my face in rapid succession and I am powerless to defend myself.

"You." *Punch.* "Used." *Punch.* "Him!" *Punch.* "You made him forget me! You convinced him to give up on us! And what's worse...he *believed* your lies because that is what you do! You are a master at reading people and when you saw your opening, you took it!" More punches. More vile words being spit in my face.

Finally, the assault ceases. Aliyah's face is peppered in my blood and rage emanates off her like a beacon in a torrent storm. "And yet," she laughs ironically, "after everything he did, after everything you tricked him into believing, he still. Chose. Me."

Aliyah drags herself off my body, chest heaving, but through my swollen eyes I see it. Tears that cut through my blood dripping from her face. She turns, her wings returning to their soft feathers, and she pushes through the people who were supposed to be *my family.* I lift my head enough to see them dissipate from my doorway, leaving me beaten and alone.

Yet, despite the blood crusting on my face, the pain pulsating through my skull, I don't feel a single tear of my own threatening to spill. Instead, laughter bubbles up in my chest. Evil, wicked, unhinged laughter falls from my lips. I can't keep it inside. I let the sounds erupt out of me, villainy comforting me like a long lost love coming home. Today I lost the battle with Aliyah, but she has no idea the war she has just started. A war which will only end with one of us walking away alive.

She may be the mutant who rose from the ashes, but I am the nightmare that will haunt her in every life.

Chapter 5

ALIYAH

I lay in bed the next morning still fuming after my altercation with Jade. I wanted to kill her so badly. Every fiber of my being was screaming to cut her life short and I can't deny that breaking her face felt good. Like a small weight has been lifted off my chest. I pull myself from the comfort of my bed and pull some clothes from my dresser to change. I found it stocked with shirts, pants, and undergarments last night when I readied myself for bed after a much needed bath. I wanted to get that filth's blood off my skin as fast as possible. I can't *believe* I once thought of her as my friend.

I stand in front of my mirror now, ripping holes in yet another shirt. I adjust the band around my chest wondering how it has ever been comfortable for women to wear something without straps and expect it to stay up all day. Frustration is becoming my permanent feeling regarding my wings and a small part of me wishes I could just fold them up and tuck them away.

Sensing my thought, my right wing knocks into me, shoving me off balance. "Oh calm down, I know you aren't going anywhere!" I hike up the band once more and throw the loose tunic shirt over my head, adjusting the ripped flaps in the back to accommodate my wings.

"Well that looks positively dreadful."

I snap my head around, a smile instantly breaking across my face, my frustration forgotten. "Kaleron! I didn't hear you come in."

"That can't possibly be what you plan to do with all your clothes, is it?"

"I'm open to suggestions!" I laugh, gesturing to my back.

"I am hopeless when it comes to fashion, but luckily I'm related to someone who is quite skilled in that department."

"Saraphena if you don't hurry up and stop playing tug-of-war with my brother's mouth I'm going to strangle you!" Liliana's voice carries in from the hallway before her bright face appears in my doorway, right below Kaleron's arm. "Aliyah! Oh my Maker, what in all of Olyrium are you wearing? Kaleron, you were right, this needs fixing with much haste!"

"What's this?" I ask.

"Just a little shopping trip! On King Kaleron's coin of course!" Liliana beams with excitement.

"Um, I don't remember agreeing to—" Kaleron tries to correct his sister and I can't help but smile.

"Oh pish-posh, brother. What's the fun of being King if you can't flaunt your wealth every once in a while?"

"Once in a while?! Sister, you once gave the Master of Coin a heart attack when he saw the bills delivered from the shops in SunSpark!" Kaleron scoffs.

"Please, that was like, *one* time! He lived, didn't he?" Lil huffs. "Anyway, Aliyah you need one of everything new! I've heard there is a tailor in Korin that is simply the best in Krystal! We can get some food and shop 'til we drop! Which I suppose would only be unfortunate for Saraphena and me because you'll just come right back." Liliana can't help but laugh at her dark humored joke, but a small part of me cringes at the thought of dying again.

Saraphena comes into the room and Liliana immediately pulls her to the side, finalizing our plans for the day. Kaleron moves into my space and runs a hand down the crest of my wings. Something pulls in my belly and sparks fly across my vision at the contact.

"You're going to have to start accepting them as a part of you, you know?"

"I know. I just...they keep getting in the way of everything. I have lost all spacial awareness and suddenly now I'm a stomach sleeper. That is, when I actually find sleep," I laugh.

"Give it time," he smiles.

"Are you, um, coming with us today?" I know the question sounds desperate, but despite what I might wish, Kaleron brings me comfort. There is nothing complicated about him, nothing to figure out between us. Being around Kaleron means being able to breathe fresh air again.

"I thought you could use a day with just you girls. Minus Jade of course. I heard you had quite the little scuffle last night."

"Freakin' leech," I mumble under my breath. "A girl's day sounds nice. Thank you for arranging it. But, is it too bold of me to say that I might miss you just a smidge?"

"Only a smidge?" He smirks, leaning in to press a kiss to my cheek, his hand wrapped around the other side of my face.

I nudge him with my shoulder and turn to grab my bag from the chair. Shrugging it on my shoulder, I join the girls. Kaleron takes that has his cue to exit and I can't seem to tear my eyes away from him as he goes. I allow myself a moment to think on the mixed feelings swimming through my mind. I never thought Kaleron would be my friend, yet here I am laughing and joking as if our history was erased.

My dove, I heard you are going to Korin today for some shopping. Jerico is a tailor there, buy anything you like and have him send me the bill.

Thank you, but Kaleron has offered to cover the trip.

Silence. I almost think he isn't going to respond before I hear his voice once more through our bond.

That is very thoughtful of him. Have fun.

I don't have time to decipher the tone in his voice so I simply tune him out and focus back on my friends.

"So, how are we getting to Korin?" I ask.

"I know you decided to walk here, but I don't plan on wasting the whole day because you didn't think to call on your alicanto," Liliana winks.

"I had just gotten out of a grave for the last three months, I think a bit of walking did me some good," I laugh.

"I was wondering if it was too early to make grave jokes, but it seems you've already dug that hole." Liliana wiggles her eyebrows and nudges me with her elbow, willing me to laugh at her joke.

"Ha. Ha, Liliana. Very funny." I pull her into a tight hug and Saraphena wraps her arms around the both of us. The appendages at my back decide to join in on the embrace and push the girls closer to my body. "Okay, let's get going! We have money to spend!"

After dropping our bags off with a delivery person in Korin, the girls and I lazily walk around the streets taking in all this village has to offer. I think we have shopped at every possible store in Korin. My heart warms being back here, getting to explore more than I did the first time. The marble walkway gleams under the shimmering ribbons of light streaking across the sky above. We spent an astronomical amount of money today, but majority of that was spent on alterations to shirts the shop already had made.

Tunics with buckles, ribbons, buttons, and open backs filled my shopping bags to the brim and I even sprung for some new leather pants and a new thigh holster for my knives. After three months in the grave, I desperately needed to get back into shape. My blood has been itching for a fight and my spat with Jade wasn't enough to even begin to scratch that itch.

"Today was amazing. Thank you both for being here," I say to Saraphena and Liliana.

"I think we all needed this." Saraphena bumps my shoulder and I bump into Liliana on the other side of me.

"Kaleron is going to be so impressed with how much money we spent today!" Lil giggles.

"I'm not sure impressed is the word I would use. You bought four new ball gowns, Lil, and you don't even have anywhere to wear them," I laugh.

"Hey, you *never* know when you're going to need a new ball gown! It's for emergencies!"

"An emergency ball gown?" Saraphena asks.

"Like I said, you never know. You might be thanking me one day!" Lil smirks.

"If I ever have use for an emergency ball gown I will absolutely eat my words," I smile.

"Let's find some food! I am absolutely famished!" Lil states.

"Adryanna's should be around here somewhere!" I turn my head in every direction, trying to place myself directionally, looking for a landmark. "There!" I point to the old tavern with the windows still covered in grime, music pulsing from inside. As we approach, something pulls in my heart at the reminder of the last time we were here. Enzo dancing, well more like standing there while I danced, and then throwing me over his shoulder, taking me home, only to lock me in his room while he avenged my honor. I laugh to myself at the memory before pulling the door open. My hand instinctively reaches for my chest in search of the gift which should be hanging there. Three months without it and I still reach for it. Now it's gone forever.

The smell of ale and sweat greets my nose in a brutal assault, but I revel in the atmosphere because anything is better than the coffin. My wing catches on the door frame and I glare at them in contempt. "I'm starting to think you do that intentionally," I mutter to them.

Adryanna spots us walking in and a bright smile crosses her face. She pushes through the crowd, stopping before us. "Holy— What in all the realm happened to you girl?! Last I saw you, you absolutely did *not* have...these!" She motions toward my wings.

"The short version? I was stabbed through the heart by Duncan's older brother and then put in an iron grave for three months where I burned alive every day until these *things* sprouted from my back only making me die of starvation instead. Kaleron, Gunnar's older brother, found me and brought me back to Olyrium. All in all, it's been a grand ol' time." I give her a tight smile.

"Maker," she breathes. "Sounds to me like you could use a drink!"

"Or two," Liliana quips.

"I don't think we have met before, but I'd know those eyes anywhere. You're related to Gunnar, aren't you?"

"Unfortunately," Liliana laughs. "The name's Liliana, but you can call me Lil for short."

"Well, Lil, it is a pleasure to meet you. Welcome to my tavern. Drinks are on the house tonight. Order anything you wish and place it on my tab." The sound of a crashing glass rings behind her and she whips her head in the direction of the noise. "My apologies, but *clearly* my patrons have gotten out of control." Adryanna saunters toward the ruckus and disappears in the crowd.

"Come on, Enzo and the others had their usual table over here. Hopefully it's still open!" I call over the music.

I push through the crowd, but as they turn, the room parts for me naturally, my wings bumping into people along the way. "Excuse me. So sorry! Pardon me. Oops, so sorry!" *They are definitely doing this intentionally.* As we approach the table, I notice three fae males scurry out of the chairs, a look of fear in their eyes.

"Oh, it's okay! You don't have to—" My voice drops off as I realize they are already gone. I huff a breath and drop into the seat. The girls sit across from me, my wings taking up both seats on my side of the table.

They each give me a sort of lopsided grin, pity lining their eyes. "Am I really that scary?"

Both of them fire off comments at the same time.

"What?! No!"

"Of course not!"

"Why would you think that?"

"You're beautiful!"

"We love the wings!"

"You only horrify others! But we know the truth!" Liliana smiles reassuringly.

I deadpan. "Wow. Convincing, you guys. Thanks."

"Look, people just aren't used to seeing fae with wings, that's all! People fear what they don't understand." Saraphena reaches across the way to take my hand.

"Okay, enough of this sad talk! DRINKS!" Liliana stands to head over to the bar, shoving people out of the way. "SunSpark Princess coming through! Move people! Make room! Barkeep!"

We sit for a moment watching Liliana. "Gunnar and I are engaged," Saraphena says.

"What!? Saraphena! Congratulations! Why didn't you tell me sooner!?"

"I figured you had enough on your plate, but now since we are here just having fun, I figured there is no better time."

"Let me see the ring!"

She holds out her left hand, the dark purple stone shining in the light. "It is absolutely gorgeous! He did well! When did this happen? How did this happen?"

"When we were on one of the islands looking for a piece of the fallen star. Anyways, while I was gone, I would go out every day to the beach and talk to you. On the last day before we came home, I went out to talk to you and Gunnar was right behind me kneeling in the sand."

"Talk to me?"

"It's what kept me close to you. I would tell you about my day, update you on the search for a way to bring you back. I even got a sun tattooed where our bond used to be." Saraphena rolls up the sleeve of her shirt, flashing the sun tattoo in my direction. "When Gunnar and I found nothing on the islands and we got word from Jade that Enzo wasn't doing well, we decided to come home. I said yes of course, but then something even better happened. Gunnar is also my mate."

"What?! Ahh! This is amazing!" I stand, making my way around the table in pursuit of giving her the biggest hug I could muster, but my wings bump into several tables, knocking alcohol glasses to the ground. "Crap! I'm so sorry!" I turn, moving to pick up the mess, but as I whip my body around, my wings smash through another table of patrons. "Seriously!" I snap. The music cuts off abruptly at the commotion.

Patrons start yelling at me, embarrassment creeping up my neck. I feel my face flushing and every part of me wants to crawl back into my grave and die. "I'm so sorry. I didn't mean to."

"Didn't mean to?" One calls, wiping spilled ale off his shirt.

"I don't have control over them!" I plead.

"How do you not have control over your own body?" Another shouts.

Tears threaten to spill from my eyes. I make my way toward the door, needing to escape. "Not so fast!" A burly man steps in my path, throwing his hand up to stop me. "You need to pay for everyone's drinks you spilled tonight!"

"It was an accident!" I say through my teeth, forcing back the tears. "But I'm happy to pay if that smooths this all over."

"Leave her alone!" Liliana calls behind me.

"Yeah, back off." Saraphena steps up to take my hand.

"Or what?" Threat laces his tone and I know what happens next.

My wings flex and golden sparks flash down the feathers leaving behind crystalized plumes in their wake. Gasps sound throughout the room.

"Get this creature out of our tavern! She doesn't belong here!" Someone calls.

"Please, I don't want to hurt you." I try to will my wings into submission. They wrap around me protectively as the man before me draws a knife.

"If you can't get them under control, then I will have to do what is good for everyone and remove them from you!" He growls.

That is the final straw. In one swift motion, my wing shoots out a crystalized feather straight through his throat, embedding into the wall behind him. Blood spurts and curdles as it bursts from the wound. He drops to his knees, his head rolling clean off his body. Patrons scream and race for the exit.

Liliana, Saraphena, and I are left standing in an empty tavern, mortification occupying my very being. "I'm sorry. I'm sorry I ruined everything." I bury my head in my hands and let the tears fall. Maybe they were right. Maybe I don't belong here. I need to be away from everyone so no one else gets hurt. First Rory, now this man. How many more have to die because of me?

"Shhhh. You didn't ruin anything." Saraphena moves to wrap her arms around me in a tight hug and Liliana joins in. Their embrace makes me feel only slightly better, but I think Lil has a part to play in that. My wings flutter behind me before transforming back to their regular state and I swear they stretch out in pride at what they thought was the right thing.

The man lying dead before me was right about one thing though, I needed to get control of them, of *everything*. I just don't know how.

Chapter 6

ENZO

I toss and turn in my bed as the sun rises on Krystal, casting flecks of rainbow across my walls, the light refracting off the gem-encrusted mountains. Another restless night knowing I have Aliyah back, but I don't *have* her back. Worst of all, she seems to be drifting away from me. I know she asked for space, but I can't help the impatience creeping into my heart. I've wracked my brain on how to make everything better between us. Each time I've come up empty. Words don't seem like enough, but actions seem like I am forcing her to speed up the forgiveness process and I know I can't do that to her.

A soft knock at my door and my heart lurches in my chest. I want it to be her. *Please let it be her.* I stand from my bed, my loose pants falling low on my waist. I don't bother with a shirt. Why would it be Aliyah though? She is still in Korin on her shopping spree with the girls...set up by Kaleron. I try not to cringe at that fact.

I run my hand through the top of my hair, smoothing it out from the fight with my pillow. "Yes?" I pull open the door, and to my surprise, it *is* her. "Aliyah," I breathe. Tears streak her cheeks and I ache to pull her into my arms.

"Can I come in?" She sniffles with her request and wipes the tears from her eyes.

"Maker, of course! Please come in." I stand aside, making room for her to walk through the door without hitting me with her wings. She strides over to the bed, crawls inside, tucks her wings behind her, and pulls the sheet over her head. Silence passes over us and I'm unsure how to proceed. If I touch her, I risk her feathers turning into a weapon, but if I stay away, she might think I no longer care for her.

I already know she is worth getting impaled for. After all, she was impaled for me. I ache at the irony of my words. Walking around the other side of the bed, I crawl under the blankets and join her under them. "What are we doing here, my dove?"

"Hiding." It's all she says before rolling onto her side, her huge wings sticking out behind her, likely hanging off the edge of the bed. Her sapphire eyes sparkle with unshed tears making the gold ring around her irises dance in her gaze.

"Hiding from what? What could you have to fear my ferocious mate?" I reach out, risking my life as I tuck a strand of hair behind her ear. I run my thumb over the golden pattern on her face, starting at her eyebrow and wrapping down around her cheek bone. I never thought someone so beautiful could become even more enchanting. The pattern mirrors on the other side of her face, my fingers tracing each and every swirl.

She smiles, wiping her nose on her hand. "From reality."

I nod, understanding why she would want to hide from such a thing. "If we are hiding from reality, then this must be a dream. What do you see happening in your dream?"

"I see you," she breathes. My soul shutters at her words, hoping we stay in this dream forever. "There isn't this chasm between us. I don't have these hideous things tearing through my back. You can hold me without being afraid of me."

"Who said I was afraid of you?" I feel the darkness inside me surge forward, the promise of blood to anyone who would claim to be afraid of my mate because of her wings. They should fear her for the cunning, smart, beautiful woman she is, but never for the things she cannot control.

"I see it in their eyes. Everyone's eyes. They look at me as if one wrong move and they will be eliminated from this realm. The worst part is, they're right. One threat against me and the *things* burst into crystals and slaughter whoever stands in my way, even if I don't want them too. I feel like everything is spiraling out of control."

"Listen to me, Aliyah. I have done terrible things in the name of finding a way to bring you back, and long, long before that. It's one of the reasons I thought I had to let you go. I was hurting people, little dove. Innocent people who didn't deserve to die."

"Like Rory." Her lip quivers and my gaze falls from hers. "He must have been trying to contact me for some time based on the excitement in his voice when he finally found me. I guess we just needed to line up his magic with my death," she chuckles softly. "He told me you were coming to save me. He told me you were finding a way to bring me back home again. When he said his power was starting to fade, I begged him to go back, but he wouldn't leave me. Rory said he would stay with me for as long as it took for you to find me so I wouldn't have to be alone anymore. When he disappeared, I thought...I thought maybe he just went back to you."

"That's why he burnt out his power. To stay with you?"

"I think that's part of why I am so angry with you, Enzo. Rory gave me hope you had heard me and were coming...but then you never did. Rory died...and for what?"

"I know." I don't know what else to say beyond that. Saying I'm sorry didn't feel like it covered the ravine of atrocities I committed in her name. I can't meet her eye. I can't see the shame I know she holds for me. I don't deserve to be her mate. "That's why I stopped looking for you. I needed to let you go before anyone else got hurt. I'm— I'm trying to be a better man. A man worthy of being your mate."

"Enzo, for right now, under these covers hiding from reality, can we forget our past? For just this moment, can it just be you and me?"

I reach out my hand across the space between us and hers meets me in response. Our fingers lock together and I calm at the way her hand feels in mine.

"Kiss me, Enzo. In this dream, I need your lips on mine."

"You're sure you want this? I don't want to pressure you to—"

"For Makers-sake, Enzo. Just kiss me." She reaches forward, wrapping her hand around the back of my neck, dragging my lips to hers. I seize the opportunity, not wanting to waste a moment, knowing that even the best dreams have to come to an end. The moment her lips meet mine, I savor the taste of her, having missed it for so long. Her hands wrap around my neck, scraping her nails across my scalp. I groan in response, needing more of her, more of this. My palms find her waist and as I move her to straddle my hips, I shift my kisses down to her throat.

Heavy breaths make her chest rise and fall, meeting mine with each inhale. I've yearned to hold her for so long. Ached to kiss away every horrible thing that has happened to her. To erase all the pain I've caused her. My words may not fix what is between us, but maybe my kiss can be the glue that mends her back together again.

Her fingers trace over my chest and I feel the scorch of her touch with each movement. I let my kisses rain down over the golden swirls on her arms and collar bones, tracing the intricate pattern, memorizing the lines and committing them to memory. I slide my hands over her spine, pulling open the buttons at the back of her newly fashioned shirt. Her lips crash with mine in a desperate need to erase our past and just be here in this moment. To be safe...with *me.*

I trail my fingers up to the base of her wings, but the moment my fingers make contact with the feathers, they burst into flames, replaced with crystalline plumes. An irritated groan falls from Aliyah's lips as she sits up, pulling her body away from mine. The sheets have been burned away, our safe haven incinerated.

Aliyah scrubs her hands down her face and shifts off my lap. "Aliyah, wait."

"The dream is over, Enzo. It's back to reality now."

"We don't have to go back. We can stay here in this dream forever. We can forget the past and start fresh, here and now, just you and me." I scramble to the edge of the bed, desperation in my limbs. "I can be better. I *am* better. I have you back now. Nothing has to change between us."

Her lip quivers and my gut clenches at the sight wishing I could go to her. She backs up toward the door. "That's the problem, Enzo. Everything has changed. I'm sorry I came here. I know it isn't fair to you. I was upset and because of this bond between us, I felt *pulled* to come here. I just wanted to escape for a while, but I didn't think how it would affect you. I'm sorry, Enzo."

"Aliyah," I call. She hesitates at the door, but doesn't turn around. "Your wings, you said they shift when they feel threatened. Do you feel threatened by me?" Tension hangs in the air as I wait for her answer, begging the Maker above for her to say no.

She shifts her gaze back, but doesn't meet my eye, her hand placed on the door, ready to close it on our moment.

"I don't, but my *heart* does."

She steps through the doorway and closes the latch softly behind her. I stare at the opaque crystal door for far longer than I care to admit to myself. As I sit here staring at the wall, I think about what she said. Her heart feels threatened by me, and why wouldn't it. All the pain I've caused her, I don't blame her for a single second as to why she is acting this way. The push and pull between us is the bond forcing us together, but I need to show her that we are more than just an invisible tether. No matter how long it takes, I will show her she can trust me. I can't be the man plagued by the sins of my father any longer. That is not the man Aliyah deserves. I've been given a second chance with her and I'm not going to waste it. I just have to wait it out, wait until she is ready.

Chapter 7

ALIYAH

Saraphena, Liliana and I all sit in the library a week after I went into Enzo's room and got lost in the dream world I wish I could escape into forever, forgetting about reality. We're surrounded by open, discarded books, trying to find the answer to how I got my wings, and any other information we can find on the magic of the Pillars.

There isn't much about my wings and it looks like there is even less about the pillars. Just as much as the craps I have to give for Jade...*miniscule*. She hasn't joined in on any of the girls' nights we have had since I returned and I wish I could say I was bothered by her absence. Every time I look at her I can't help but think about how she kissed Enzo. I knew they had history, but I thought it was just that...*history*.

My heart and my brain are at war over my feelings for Enzo. Is he worth laying my heart on a silver platter, praying he doesn't cut it open? Everything has happened so fast since the day we met. Was what I felt for him ever even real or did the bond just make me think he was the man of my dreams? I had really screwed up that morning going into his bedroom when we returned from Korin. My hesitation had nothing to do with how he tried to get me back and everything to do with how he didn't even think to visit my grave and check if what he was feeling was real. I always seem to have a pile of questions with so few answers.

After hearing about the things he did while I was gone, part of me wanted to be so angry, but wouldn't I have done the same for him? If the others had asked me three months ago the things I would do to save Enzo, I would have said anything and everything, no matter the cost. But now— He gave up on me. He gave up on *us*. Even after I spoke to that sweet boy Rory and told him I was ready to come back. I thought he would have listened, but instead he just gave up. It isn't about the things he did while I was gone, it's what he *didn't* do.

What if I hadn't shown up that day in Korin? What would have happened between him and Jade? Sensing my emotions, my wings wrap around me protectively as if Enzo would come in and attack me at any moment and they mean to prep for the onslaught.

"You okay over there?" Saraphena asks.

"Huh? Oh, yeah I'm good." I close the book on my lap and stare out the window at the great crystal expanse before me. I itch to know what it feels like to soar over those gem-crested mountains, the wind whipping through my hair, and the feeling of being completely and utterly untethered to this world. Did it really matter how I got my wings? They were here and clearly not going anywhere. All I wanted to do was dance with the ribbons of color lighting up the sky and play with the stars over the open terrain.

"I know you're thinking about something. I know that face," Saraphena laughs.

"It's moments like this I wish we weren't so close," I laugh. "I'm just thinking about what it would be like to fly. I can't seem to get my wings to work properly, and to be honest, I'm kind of afraid. Based on how they respond to situations when I feel threatened, I can't imagine they would let any harm come to me, but what if this is the one time I'm wrong."

Sometimes it feels as if they are another being entirely, simply attached to my back. They change to crystal on their own, protect me on their own, and even have their own emotions at times. It's like I can feel them rolling their eyes, or bristling in rage or jealousy. Right on cue, my left wing shoots out and knocks the stack of books next to me tumbling to the ground. "That was unnecessary," I mutter to them, rolling my eyes.

"Have you tried to fly with them at all? Maybe we could find somewhere you could practice, I don't know...gliding?" Lil asks. My right wing brings itself in front of my face, shielding them from my view. I push down the plume, frustration budding under the surface.

"No. I'm afraid they won't catch me if I fall. I'm not sure I can trust them. They might be protective of me with others, but how do I know I can rely on them not to screw me over?" This stupid wing shifts back in front of my face. I shove it down again. "Seriously, stop." As my wing moves to create a feather wall between me and my friends once more, I shoot up, throwing my elbow into the center of the wing. The ball of feathers slaps me in the face, knocking me back onto the couch. "Ugh!"

"Sometimes you just gotta take the leap!" Lil smiles. She closes the book on her lap and stands. "Come with me, we need to find some strong alcohol for what I have planned. Try to keep your wings in check while we are in the cellar, would you? I don't want good alcohol going to waste because your *friend* decides to go on a smashing spree."

As we make our way out of the library, I swear I feel the guardian on my back snicker.

"Are you sure this is a good idea?" I ask, staring down at the endless drop below. The alcohol induced haze makes my depth perception waver in and out. This is definitely a terrible idea. We had raided the cellar in search of some liquid courage, but I think I underestimated how much courage I would need for this.

"Am I sure? No, but if it works it's going to be amazing!" Liliana is perched on top of her matched sphinx, Molly, and Saraphena is sitting right behind her, arms wrapped around Lil's waist.

"This feels like a bad idea," Saraphena says.

"I mean it's not like she can die!" Liliana smirks.

"I feel like that isn't the comforting statement you think it is," I huff. "I mean what if this is the time my powers don't bring me back?"

"Only one way to find out I suppose!"

"You realize Enzo is going to kill you if he finds out we are doing this," Saraphena adds.

"So then we just won't tell him until we are back! What he doesn't know won't hurt him!" Liliana gives Molly a nudge and she beats her huge wings a few times to push them higher off the roof. She flies out a few spans before turning back to face me, her huge white wings flapping hard to keep them level.

"Okay! So just watch Molly's wings. How they move, how they angle with the wind, how they flap. Just watch her!" Liliana yells across the gap between us. My feet are right at the edge of the roof. The same roof that Jade and I sat on not too long ago putting our differences aside. Oh how far we've fallen. *Yikes, Aliyah, poor timing for that statement.*

I don't dare look down, otherwise fear will slither up my spine like a snake, poisoning my mind with doubt. *I can do this.*

Aliyah, where are you? Gunnar said you would be in the library.

"Oh crap you guys, Enzo is looking for me."

"I guess you better hurry then! Gunnar is looking for me, too. If they catch us out here we are all in deep trouble!" Saraphena calls.

"Ugh!"

"You know what you have to do!" Liliana smirks. "Just count to three!"

"Do I jump on three or after three?" I joke. The laughter between us easing some of my nerves.

"One!" Saraphena calls.

"Two!" Liliana laughs.

Little dove, seriously where are you?

I'm on the roof. Catch me if you can.

The roof?! What in the Maker's name are you doing— Aliyah don't you dare!

"Enzo is pissed you guys! Luckily we have a little time before—"

Enzo and Duncan materialize behind me. "Aliyah, DON'T!"

"Three!" I leap off the roof, spreading my wings as far as they can go. My back *screams* in protest as I try to push them higher and higher.

"Aliyah!" Enzo yells from the rooftop behind me. I try to angle my body to turn back to them, but I struggle with the angle and suddenly drop below the line of the rooftop.

"Crap, crap, crap!" I will my wings to beat as hard as they can, but exhaustion in my back muscles starts to sit in.

"You're doing it! Go Aliyah!" Liliana cheers from behind me. Saraphena hoots and hollers, clapping her hands in excitement.

"I'm doing it! I can't believe I'm—" My excitement is cut off and anxiety creeps up my throat when I look at the ground beneath me. It's so far down and the alcohol burning in my veins is not helping. *Note to self, don't drink and fly.* Sensing my panic, my wings shift to their hardened form, the sudden weight pulling at my scapulas, throwing me off balance.

"Aliyah," Enzo's voice warns from the roof. "Come back to this roof right now."

"I— I can't. I can't seem to get the right angle!" I yell back.

My right wing dips with the down draft of wind. "It's okay, just stay calm," I say to myself. "I can't die. I can't die. I can't—"

Son of a—

The world spins above me as I'm caught up in the angles of the wind and the added weight of my altered feathers. I look up to the sky and see Molly descending fast, but not fast enough. My back is to the ground, wings spayed out behind me, unable to find the right angle to catch the wind. I reach my hand up to the sky, reaching for Molly and my friends. I know the ground is coming up beneath me. The wind whips past my hair too quickly and I know she is not going to make it on time.

I see Liliana and Saraphena's faces with a look of horror on them as they see the truth of the situation as well. They aren't going to make it. I'm about to test my power once again. This view is far prettier than the lid of a coffin though. Green and blue swirls flicker through the night sky, casting shadows as if there were mountains in the heavens made of light themselves. I close my eyes, bracing for the impact, hoping I die instantly.

At least this time I'm not dying in a coffin. This time, I'm dying free.

Chapter 8
ENZO

Duncan materializing us on the ground beneath her, I watch as Aliyah's small frame grows closer and closer as she falls toward us. I try not to let the anger I feel for her right now hinder my intention to catch her. How could she allow Liliana to convince her to do this? She hasn't ever attempted to use her wings to fly before, but suddenly she is jumping off roofs!

"I'll catch her." Kaleron comes racing down the path to where Duncan and I stand.

"You will do no such thing! She is my mate!"

"You aren't strong enough to catch her at this height! She is coming in too fast. If you drop her, she'll die! She shouldn't have to suffer that again because you aren't equipped to get the job done."

"Then it's a good thing I'm not going to drop her!" I yell.

Kaleron shoves me out of the way using his strength and I stumble to the side. "Move out of the way!"

I shove him back and his steps falter, tearing his focus away from the incoming Aliyah. I throw out my power, trying to halt Aliyah's body in the air, preparing to lower her to the ground safely. "Gah! Knock it off, Enzo! You aren't strong enough to save her!"

"Yes. I. Am!" My power over Aliyah falters as Kaleron's fist connects with my face and I shift my power to shove him back. He grunts in response and charges for me again. Duncan steps between us, getting caught in the chin from Kaleron's next blow. The three of us are thrown into a brawl over who is going to catch...ALIYAH!

Crack.

The three of us freeze, horror striking the group as Liliana and Saraphena land Molly next to us. Aliyah's wings are shattered into pieces on the ground, red, yellow, orange, and black crystals strewn across the marble walk way.

"You idiots! You let her die!" Liliana screams.

"Let her?! You were the one who convinced her to jump off the freaking roof!" I yell.

"She *what?!*" Kaleron growls, anger flashing in his gaze as he glares at his sister.

"I didn't convince her to do anything! She wanted to do it!" Liliana says, scrambling off Molly's back.

Aliyah's body lay on the crystal pathway on the outside of the palace, her blood pooling in a large red ring around her head.

Her eyes are closed and her face is almost peaceful, save for the awkward angle her spine has cracked into.

I close my eyes, not bearing to look at the sight any longer. I feel the tether tying our souls together sever in my chest. A feeling I now recognize so clearly. *The same feeling I had all those months while she died over and over again in that grave.* I thought it had just been my grief consuming me, but now I know it was my mate bond forming and breaking. How many times had I felt that feeling? A dozen? Two dozen? Too many to count, that's for sure.

Kaleron moves closer to Aliyah. "We need to get her inside." As he makes to lift her off the ground, her body disintegrates into sparks in his arms. Her blood still pools on the crystal, but her body is no where to be found. Each small gem stone that her feathers were once comprised of burst into piles of ash, sparks floating through the air in their wake.

"What the hell did you do?" I push him out of the way so I can get a better look.

"I didn't do anything! I just picked her up and she—"

"Where did she go?!" I ask.

"She'll be back." Gunnar walks out to join the group, a large tome open in his hand, and a casual way about him. "No one needs to panic like a bunch of headless alicanto. She survived three months in a coffin without you bimbos. I'm sure she can survive a little fall from a roof top."

"When will she regenerate?" Liliana asks.

"What? Suddenly I'm the group healer? How the hell should I know? I was just browsing the stacks when I heard all the commotion out here. Everyone started bickering like children so I figured I didn't want to miss the fight."

"Gunnar are you...reading a history book?" Saraphena smiles gesturing to the tome in his hands.

"What?! I read!" He shrugs.

"Not history books!" Liliana laughs.

"I know how important it was to Saraphena that we find answers, so I figured I'd lend my superior services. There isn't much to know about her powers since we don't actually know where they stem from exactly, but I do know why she sprouted wings," he smiles.

"Finally, someone with some answers." Aliyah's voice breaks through the group's focus.

"Aliyah!" Kaleron and I say in unison, a glare passing between us. We both move toward her at the same time, but she puts her hand up between us.

"I don't really want to be hugged right now. My body just fell from the highest roof in the palace and I went splat on the path. I think I just need a minute." Her wings flex behind her and the faint smell of ash hangs in the air.

"Aliyah, how are you? How did you come back so quickly? It used to be days before I would feel our bond awake again...now that I know exactly what I was feeling." I mutter the last part to myself.

"I'm not sure how long it was between when I died the first time and came back, but I know that each time it seemed to happen faster and faster. By the end, I think I would only be out for a few hours," she said.

"How did you calculate how long it had been?" Saraphena asks.

"I— I, um...I knew based on how dry the blood was on the inside of my coffin lid," she grimaces. Every inch of me burns to go to her, to make her forget what I left her to suffer all those months. "Anyways, moving on. What did you find out about my wings?"

The appendages flex instinctively behind her as if they know we are talking about them.

"Well, it's interesting that you should ask!" Gunnar replies. "I think it's quite fascinating actually. There was a study— Well not so much a study as a theory— And not so much a theory that was tested—"

"Gunnar, the answer please," Aliyah smiles.

"Right! Sorry, well I think your wings are a physical manifestation of your power. This book only says it could theoretically happen, but you can't exactly record something like this because well...let me just explain. It was theorized that in times of great distress, a fae's power could take a physical form. It might have looked different on everyone though. For example, for Kaleron here, it may have taken form through his massive ego! For you Aliyah, it appears to have transformed into wings. Which makes sense why they turn into those formidable crystals when you feel threatened. They protect you, almost as a sort of alternate version of yourself that is solely meant to protect you."

"Okay, but why can't I control them? Why can't I control the shift?" Aliyah asks.

"I think there is much to learn about your wings, including how to use them to fly," Liliana laughs.

Storm clouds cover the sky and rain begins to pour down from above. We all make a beeline for the entrance of the palace. Safe inside, we catch our breath and glance around at each other.

"Well I think it's safe to say that did *not* go as planned," Aliyah laughs. "I definitely need some more practice and maybe next time from a lower ledge!"

"What in the hell is going on down there? The recruits are sleeping and Eilith has them waking up extremely early tomorrow to fix another one of Gwynavere's training mishaps." Jade stands at the top of the steps, looking down at the group.

"Just a bit of flying lessons gone wrong," Liliana jokes.

"Well stop messing around. It gives a bad example for the recruits. The last thing we need is for them to be slacking off. In case you don't remember, there is a *war* coming!"

"Talk about a buzzkill," Gunnar says under his breath.

"Someone arrived from SunSpark and gave me this letter for you while you were out playing hero, Kaleron. I sent them to a room to rest and said I would get it to you."

"Ah, thank you! I'll see to it in my chambers." Kaleron makes his way up the steps and disappears down the hallway where his room lies. Personally I am thankful he is gone. This gives me time alone with Aliyah to try and gain some trust back between us.

"Care to go for a stroll?" I ask her.

"I suppose." She looks less than thrilled, but at least she agreed. I take her hand in mine and lead her away from the group.

As we make our way through the palace, I turn down the same hallway which contains the secret tunnel to the armory we took once before. This way no one can interrupt us. I push on the panel and watch the wall give way to the blackened tunnel. Memories of that kiss flash through my mind and I can't help the flare of excitement in my veins.

"I— I can't go in there," Aliyah says pulling my hand back.
"Why?"

"The tunnel, it just...it feels too much like—"

"Oh, Aliyah! I am so sorry! I didn't even think about that. Here let's go somewhere else."

"Actually, you know what. I think I am going to turn in. I'm feeling really tired and I could use the time away. Let's talk another time!"

Aliyah turns down the hall and disappears around the corner. "Enzo, you're an idiot of the greatest magnitude," I whisper to myself.

"She's never going to forgive you." My head snaps up as Jade rounds the corner.

"What?"

"She isn't going to forgive you for leaving her in that grave." Jade steps into me and runs her hands along the front of my chest. "But I've seen you at your darkest, Enzo, and I don't care. I love you for you, no matter what you have done."

Jade pushes up to her tiptoes and places a kiss to my lips. What once felt like possibility has now turned to resentment. I curse myself for ever giving up on finding Aliyah. I let *true love's kiss* blind me to what really matters most.

"Jade," I start. "This is—"

"No, it isn't. This isn't over between us Enzo. *I'm* your true love. I know you feel something for me otherwise the kiss would have never worked. Aliyah is your past, I am your future."

"Enzo, look I'm sorry. I shouldn't have walked—" Aliyah's shocked face comes into view as she sees Jade's arms locked around my neck.

"Aliyah!" I shove Jade back, but it's too late. Aliyah turns her back and walks away, anger etched into her face.

"Enzo, wait!" Jade pleads.

"No, Jade. This is over. You and I are done. There never was, and never will be an *us.* Kissing you that day in your room was a mistake."

"So...so you're saying you should have let me die?"

"I didn't want you to die, Jade, but I don't want to be with you either. Aliyah is my mate. Aliyah is my future. *Aliyah* is my *true* love. You are nothing to me Jade."

"You're a coward, Enzo. You string me along, making me think there is a future between us, and instead of standing up to Aliyah and telling her that there is something between us you hide behind this mate bond. Well then fine! Be alone, Enzo, because Aliyah is never going to forgive you and I am not going to be someone's second choice. But don't come crying to me when she discards you forever."

Jade storms off and once again I'm left standing in this hallway, alone.

Part II: Formulation

Chapter 9

THE BANISHED KING

The smell of fresh sea air wafts into my chambers through the open windows overlooking the ocean beyond. The door creeks behind me, a feeble attempt at breaking my good spirits, I suspect. It won't work, not today. I can feel the downfall of Olyrium in my bones, creeping closer and closer with each passing day. My daughter will return to my side, ready to to make them all bow, even if it means breaking their kneecaps to do it.

"Do you smell that?" I ask, a wicked smile playing on my lips. My three commanders stand in the doorway to my room. I know it's them without even turning around because they would be the only creatures allowed in this space.

"Sire?" one of the creatures asks.

"That's the smell of victory, my dear monstrosity! War is on the horizon, and I plan to sail right into her fading light. The time is soon upon us." I turn from the window, facing my hideous creation. Some old hags withered skin slips off his shoulder, his bony fingers grasping the delicate scrap like a fallen strap and pulls it back up on his shoulder. I'm not sure where they picked up this ridiculous habit, but it was certainly not taught by me. Children—you do everything you can to raise them right and they still find a way to forge their own sick path.

My daughter took that path as well. Aligning herself with the filth beneath my boots and claiming them as her family. She will learn soon enough what *real* family means.

"I can only assume you are here to give me news on the Olyrium front. It would be the *only* reason to bother me in my chambers as we have discussed."

"Yes...we...I— I'm not sure how...*We* are not sure how—" Powder plumes around us from the dust of his bones bursting into nothingness. My fist clenched tight as power ripples through me.

"Let's try again. What news do you have? How many more sacks of bones do I need to crush before I get an answer? Or have I not made it clear enough that you are *all* replaceable!" My voice rocks the very stone walls above us, some old pebbles shaking loose at the sound.

"The girl Aliyah is alive!" One blurts.

Rage.

Blinding, unfiltered, blood-curtailing rage bursts out of me. "*What?!* How?! Explain this *now* before this entire bucket of ruins feels my wrath and it will fall on *your* shoulders!"

"I don't know, your finest sire majesty! We were...out...keeping an eye on her grave site like you asked us to and well we...took a small break...and when we came back it just was...empty."

"Fools! All of you! Fix this! Fix all of this! You are to find out exactly how this is possible by any means necessary or our entire plan will fall to ruin!"

"Yes, Sire! We swear it!"

The two remaining creatures turn to leave...but it only takes one to send a message. I crush my fist tighter, the bone powder of my second commander mingles with the fallen particles from my decrepit ceiling. I slam the door shut behind my only remaining commander and stalk back to my window.

Looking out over the vast sea, the speck that is Olyrium sits in the distance. "You will not win, Aliyah. You will not be my downfall. My plan *will* come together. I have waited too long and worked too hard for some blonde *simpleton* to ruin everything! I am owed my retribution! I'm going to hit you where it hurts most and when you least expect it. My followers are everywhere and you will soon feel my wrath."

Chapter 10

KALERON

I pace back and forth about my room, reading over the missive for the hundredth time. *Captain Jonah is coming.* Jonah is the most infamous sea captain ever known from The Islands of Loch. The village that rests on the main island is home to some of the most notorious, ruthless sea fighters in all the realms, but they have *never* agreed to help in any war. It was forbidden for the fae of Olyrium to build a Bridge to The Islands of Loch and they would rather watch the world burn to the ground than help.

When I had requested a meeting with Jonah to try and find a common ground and secure his ships for the coming war, I never expected him to accept my request to visit SunSpark. Unease sits heavy in my chest. Why now? What has changed? Why *now?* Aliyah and I are finally getting closer. I can't leave her. If she is going to choose me, I need to stay by her side. I can't abandon her, but I *have* to meet with Jonah. If he arrives and I am not there, I might just as well surrender to The Banished King now.

A knock comes at the door. I stride over and when I pull open the handle, Aliyah stands there, wings comprised of sharp crystal feathers and tears line her cheeks.

"Aliyah! What's going on? What happened?" I ask.

"Enzo—" She sniffles and wipes her nose on her sleeve. "Enzo and Jade were kissing. I saw them. I knew— I knew she had feelings for him, and I thought *maybe* while I was gone he had developed feelings for her, too, but I never allowed myself to picture them *together* together, you know? I thought with me being back— Kaleron can I just come in instead of standing here sobbing in the hallway? I really don't want Enzo to see."

"Oh my Maker, yes of course! Come in. Sorry my mind was elsewhere before you got here and I clearly forgot my manners back with my brain," I smile.

"Thanks," she says, stepping into the room. I close the door softly behind her. "Anyways, I had seen them kissing and suddenly it was like my worst fears were confirmed. Is it me? Am I taking too long to forgive him? Is this my fault for not breaking out of my coffin sooner? I know I've been pushing him away, but I didn't want to push him *toward* her."

Tears pour down her cheeks now as her mind spirals with questions. I take a step toward her, but then remember her wings of crystal. *She feels threatened.*

I stand there awkwardly, not knowing how to comfort her in this situation. "Aliyah, if he thinks you are taking too long to forgive someone who left you to sit in a grave for three months while you begged him to come and save you, then he doesn't deserve you. If it were me, I— I would wait forever for you, Aliyah."

"Kaleron, can you please stop standing there and just hug me or something? I really need it."

"*Can* I touch you?" I ask hesitantly, nodding to her wings.

"Ugh! These stupid things. I don't know how to turn them off! I appreciate what they are trying to do, but everyone around me is afraid of them when they turn like this!" She throws her hands up in the air and huffs.

"I think it has less to do with the crystals and more to do with the piercing razor blades that tend to shoot off them when you are touched without your permission," I laugh.

Her eyes sparkle with delight even though they still brim with tears. Her smile is soft, but the sound of her laugh gets caught on a sob. "I suppose that's fair. Do I— Do I scare you Kaleron?"

"Only in the ways you should," I smile, stepping into her personal space. In reality, Aliyah terrifies me. She threatens to bring down everything I have built and everything I have planned for my kingdom. If she asked me right now, I would throw it all away just to be by her side. I've seen what lies in our future and I know the only way we are going to get there is if I remain here with her.

I reach out and risk running my hand over the sharp edges of her wings. She closes her eyes the moment my hand makes contact and as I run my palm over the crest of the wing, I watch as they transform from hard crystal, to soft, lush feathers. The transformation is like a wave cresting over the sands.

"There ya go, Sparky. No need to feel threatened here. I've got you now." I run my palm down the other wing, coaxing it to relax.

"Did you just call my wings Sparky?" She laughs lightly.

"I figured it was a fitting name," I wink. She shakes her head softly, a small huff coming out of her nostrils. I continue coaxing her wings to relax. A soft moan escapes Aliyah as I trail my fingers over the spot where her wings connect to her back. Her eyes slip shut as I continue to explore her back. She tips her head to the left and right, relishing in the contact.

"Is this okay?" I ask.

"Yes." Her response is breathy and filled with want.

I trail my hands up and down her spine, feeling each and every knot of flesh under my touch.

"You're back is filled with tension."

"It's the wings. I don't think my back muscles have quite gotten used to carrying them around all the time."

I press into one of the knots and a breath escapes her plush, pink lips. She tips her head down in a stretch and her fingers clench at her sides. As I feel the pop of the knot releasing, I move onto the next one.

"May I?" I ask as I pull at one of the laces at the bottom of her shirt.

"Please," she practically whimpers.

Hearing her give that one small word of acceptance could cause a man to combust on the spot. If I died right here and now, I will have lived a full life knowing I got to hear Aliyah beg for me. I pull the ribbon and watch as it falls to the floor before moving onto the other one. Once both ribbons are loose, Aliyah pulls the back of the tunic over her head, leaving her exposed skin to me. The band that covers her chest is comprised of black leather and clasps over her spine and again at the top of her neck, leaving plenty of room for her wings.

I gaze upon her skin and am in awe of what I see. Several scars line her back, raised flesh giving away the years of torment she suffered in Luar, but that isn't what my eyes linger on. Starting where her wings connect to her back, golden swirls spread throughout her skin, swirling over her scars before cresting up to meet the golden swirls on her neck and collar bones.

"They're beautiful," I whisper.

Aliyah huffs. "There is no need to lie, Kaleron. I know what they look like."

"Lie? Aliyah, the way these swirls have enhanced the beauty of your past— It's breath taking." I let my fingers trail over the golden swirls and Aliyah cranes her neck once more.

"They aren't beautiful, Kal. They are a reminder of— It doesn't matter where they came from. They aren't beautiful."

She spins in a circle, her wing catching me in the arm and a laugh falls from my lips as she strides over to the reflecting glass on the wall. Her eyes flick down to her shoes as she tries to hide the look of disgust from her face.

"*You* are beautiful, Aliyah."

She looks at me through the mirror. This moment between us seems to freeze in time as our eyes lock in the glass. I trail my knuckles over her flesh, goosebumps following in their wake. Her eyes remain locked on mine as I shift her hair over her shoulder, exposing her neck to me. I pause, waiting. Waiting for permission to take the next step.

I watch as Aliyah gulps, the movement of her throat enrapturing as her breath hitches in her chest. "Kal, *please.*" I can't help the smirk breaking through my features. I lean down, feeling her pulse kick up when she feels my breath on her neck. Aliyah's eyes slip shut, her head tipping slightly to the side, exposing more of her golden swirls to me. I lick my lips, praying to the Maker to let this moment last forever.

I watch her in the mirror as my hand wraps around her to the front of her neck, my index finger running over her jaw. Her lips part while mine move to place a kiss behind her ear. The golden liquid flowing beneath her skin begins to glow, casting a light across the space that rivals the most gorgeous sunsets in SunSpark.

"King Kaleron! Are you in there? I arrived earlier from SunSpark and passed a message along to one of your companions. I now must insist you return to court immediately. Your kingdom is waiting and the counselors—" I recognize

Clarence's voice immediately as one of my council members. Too bad they will be one short upon my return.

Aliyah's eyes fly open and when she blinks, the spell between us fades as she clears her throat. The light fades and the room dims along with it. She steps away and reaches for her shirt, throwing it over her head and quickly tying each ribbon through the holes. Another knock comes at the door, Clarence insisting he see me immediately.

"I'm sorry. I don't know what came over me. This is inappropriate. You're a king and I have a mate and we are just—" she whispers. I can hear the dead man speaking on the other side of the door still, rambling on about duty and responsibility as if my duty is not standing right in front of me. "I should go. Please forgive me, Kal. I never meant—"

"Come with me to SunSpark."

"What? I can't just—"

"I have to return there for a business meeting and I want you to come with me. I know you struggle in the dark, I see the light from your room under your door every night. SunSpark is never dark. It's the perfect place to heal and as an added bonus, I'll be there," I smirk.

"I don't leave the light on at night, that's just—" She clears her throat, "Can the others come as well? I don't want to leave them behind."

"If that is what it takes for you to come with me, then yes. All are welcome," I smile.

"Then yes. If they go, I'll go."

"Start packing, we leave at first light." I move her toward the side door that leads to the other side of the hallway. I've never been more thankful for a corner room before. Aliyah sneaks out the side door as I storm to the opposite side of the room.

"Sir, I really must insist—"

I whip open the door, using the strength of my power, I shove my fingers through the front of his neck, wrapping around his esophagus and pulling him into the room. Shock registers on his face as he realizes his throat is being used as a handle for his body.

"The sound of your voice cost me far more than your life is worth. Now you will never speak again, never take a breath again, and never be able to *summon* me back to my court *again.* It's a shame you didn't take the night to rest before coming to see me tomorrow. By this time tomorrow I would have already been headed back to SunSpark. Now you've lost your life for nothing, yet cost me everything."

His wide eyes fill with tears, but he doesn't get the chance to beg for his life before I smash his organ in my fist and rip it from his body, tendons and muscles snapping like taunt strings being clipped. His lifeless carcass falls to the floor, blood pumping across the crystal. As I reach down to wipe my bloodied hands on his white and gold SunSpark attire my heart feels like it is soaring in the clouds. *Aliyah is starting to choose me.*

Chapter 11

ALIYAH

"So you'll come with me then?" I ask Saraphena, my fist connecting with her palm in a rapid fire motion. We are working in the outdoor training ring, Krystals dark gray sky open above us. Marble pillars create a large circle around us, a glass dome placed on top to keep out any rain that might come, and thank goodness for it, because today it is pouring. Large beads of water splatter against the glass roof and provide a beautiful symphony of sound. I have learned to appreciate the small sounds in life from my time underground. I think I have a permanent ringing in my ears from how silent it was in my coffin.

"Of course! Now that you're back, I'm not leaving your side again!" She laughs.

"Me either! I told Kaleron I didn't want to go without you." *Right, left, right, right.* Each punch lands with a solid hit.

"What's going on with you and Kaleron anyways? It seems like you're spending more and more time with him."

"I don't know." I slow my punches and flop down into the dirt of the training ring. "I love Enzo...at least...I think I do. This bond makes everything so confusing, Sara. I keep feeling this pull back to him, but is that real? How will I know when I have truly forgiven him? I just wish this stupid bond wasn't getting in the way of my feelings. I want to know what we have is real."

"I completely get that! When I was in Luar, I missed Gunnar so freaking much, and I knew what I felt for him was real *because* I didn't have the bond connection."

"I'm so happy you have that now." I reach over and take her hand in mine. "Would you forgive him? If Gunnar left you in a grave, would you forgive him?"

"That's a hard question to answer. I think so? I'm not sure. I can genuinely say I don't think anyone has been in that situation before."

"The only other person might be my parents if they had the same ability I do. Do you think this means they are still alive?"

"Can you try asking me a question I might actually know the answer to?" Saraphena bumps my shoulder with a laugh.

"It doesn't seem like anyone has the answers I need." I huff. "Maybe I just need to let the whole parent thing go. I have all the family I need right here." I lay my head on her shoulder and she takes my hand in hers.

"They always say your true family are the ones you choose," she smiles.

"Saraphena, can I admit something to you? Something I can never say out loud to anyone else?"

"Always."

"If I could find a way to break this bond with Enzo, I think I would."

Saraphena sucks in a sharp breath. "Maker above, Aliyah." Shock registers on her face, but it isn't mixed with judgment, just concern.

"I know. I just wish I could have a completely clear head. Just some time to decide if this is what I really want. To figure out if Enzo and I have a future besides the one constructed by the Maker himself."

"I can try and help you resist the pull of the bond if that is what you truly need."

"I think I have to. If I ignore the resentment sitting in my chest for the rest of time, I'll never truly move on from what happened. I just need some time to figure things out."

"Agreed. Are you good here? I want to finish up any last minute packing before we leave. Gunnar's idea of packing is throwing everything in a bag all crumpled up, but I refuse to let him do that to my fine tunics! After years of living in Luar with almost nothing, I treat my clothes like delicacies," she laughs.

"When I was in the ground and my wings appeared for the first time, I had to rip my shirt right down the back. It was freezing and I was heart broken at another ruined shirt. Oh how the times have changed," I smile at her.

As Saraphena leaves, I start up another round of exercises. It feels so good to move my body again. I've lost so much muscle during my time away and I know I need to strengthen my back. Going through the training routines, I keep falling off balance, my wings shifting awkwardly behind me. Frustration coils in my gut. Anger simmers through my blood. I just need control. I try one of Saraphena's breathing techniques, but the continued clumsiness starts to fray my nerves.

Something sparks in my chest as if a beast has awoken inside me. I have to let it out. It's as if my skin is ripping apart to make way for whatever is going to come out of me. My breathing grows rapid and uneven. Golden light races up my fingertips and past my chest before reaching my face. I clutch my ears, trying to block out whatever this feeling is inside me. I need it out. I need it out. I need it *out!*

Golden light explodes from the swirls on my body and a golden sphere bursts from my flesh. It smashes into the marble and I scream as the pillars come crumbling down around me. My wings shift into a shield and cover me as the glass ceiling shatters into pieces, falling from above.

Rain beats down on my skin as I take in the carnage around me. Tears well in my eyes, masked by the rain sliding down my cheeks. "I have no control. I'm losing myself." I grip my head, wet strands of hair slipping around my fingers. My wings wrap around me in a tight manner as if hugging me.

"Well that's new."

I whip around, my wet hair smacking me in the face as I turn. "Enzo. I'm so sorry! I didn't mean to!"

A low chuckle leaves his body and I'm thankful for it. "Trust me when I say, Gwynavere has done far worse with her water magic. She breaks something new each week. We will have the recruits come and rebuild the training ring. No need to worry."

"I didn't know I could do that. It's like it came bursting out from inside me. One more thing I can't control," I say more to myself than him.

"So let's work on what you can control. Hit me."

"Enzo, I'm not going to hit you." I cross my arms over my chest. Water slides down my black halter top and I just know my new leather pants are going to be drenched when this is all over. I left my feet bare today, hoping they would provide me with more balance, plus I like feeling connected to the ground.

I don't move from my position, afraid my feet will get cut up on the glass. As if reading my mind, Enzo uses his magic to sweep away the carnage I created.

"I want you to hit me. I want you to take all your frustrations out on me. Let the anger take over inside you and then expel it into me. I can take it, I promise."

"Oh you think you can take it, ZoZo? I've got powers now. You won't know what hit you," I smirk.

"I'll know what hit me. A fierce, powerful, strong woman who doesn't take crap from anyone. You've been holding onto too much. I know you're angry at me and if this makes it even a fraction easier on you then I would happily let you beat me until I am unrecognizable."

"I don't want you to hold back. If I'm going to beat you, I want to earn it." I wipe the rain from my eyes. It pours down around us now, puddles forming in the packed dirt beneath my feet. I squish my toes in the mud and quietly thank the Maker for a chance to feel the rain on my face again.

"I won't hold back, but I won't use my powers on you either."

"Enzo, it's—"

"I'm not using my powers, Aliyah."

"No powers then. A true hand-to-hand match?"

"Deal."

"Do your worst, my dove."

A single smirk is all I give him before launching myself at his body. I leap into the air, arm cocked for a right hook, but as I come down, Enzo dodges, grabs my arm and yanks it across his body, exposing my back to him. I stumble forward as I feel his hand push between my shoulder blades, shoving me to the ground. I land with a thud, but not before my wing clips Enzo in the face, forcing him back a few steps.

"Two against one? It's almost a fair fight," Enzo quips.

Frustrated, I push myself to my feet. Right on cue my wings shift to their crystalized state and I roll my shoulders back, adjusting to the weight. Enzo's eyes flash with mischief and I have to admit, it feels good to fight again.

Two steps toward him and I move into a rapid punch combination. Enzo blocks almost all of them, but he won't expect the leg sweep I'm planning. I worked on this move with Saraphena a lot in Mareen so I know I have it perfectly timed! I drop quickly into a squat, prepping my right leg to connect with his, but as I kick my leg out, my wings shift to the left too far and I lose balance, tumbling back onto my butt.

Enzo doesn't miss the opportunity to pounce. "Yield!" He yells, straddling my hips as my wings are pinned beneath me.

"That's not fair! I was sabotaged," I grumble back at my wings.

Enzo smirks, leaning down to press a light kiss to my nose. I close my eyes at the contact. Once again my body is betraying me. My soul aches to be joined with his, but my heart slowly fortifies itself with barbed wire and marble walls. A war rages in my chest, the bond against my mind and I'm not prepared to see who will win that fight. If the bond wins, then Enzo will be in my arms in less than a second, the past forgotten, but if my mind wins, I'll leave this training ring, the past remembered and forgiveness no where in sight.

I look into Enzo's eyes, the smile on his lips, and the comforting feel of his body on mine. I wish I could forget. I wish I could look past what he did. I wish— I wish we could start over again. "Enzo," I breathe.

"My dove."

"You're crushing my wings." I feel them shift back to their feathery form. Enzo moves to get off me and reaches down to pull me up from the dirt. Rain still pours down around us and I'm thankful for it. I turn to leave, knowing nothing has changed between us.

Enzo grabs my arm as I turn, but I don't dare look back at him. "Aliyah, wait. Please."

"I can't do this. I want to let it go. I want to start over with you, but I just...I can't. I can't forget what you did. I can't forget the fact that you just left me there. I know it doesn't make rational sense, because I know you were here fighting for a way to get me back, and I can't imagine what you must have been going through thinking I was dead. But I was there the whole time, begging you through the bond to hear me, to save me. I know why you did all the things you did and I know why you had to give up on me...on us. But knowing why doesn't make it hurt any less."

Enzo releases my arm, knowing there isn't anything more to be said. I leave him standing there in the rain. The bond in my chest screams at me to turn around, to go back to him and make everything right between us, but I ignore it. I shove it down as far as it can possibly go into my chest, because listening to it would mean ignoring the hurt between us, and ignoring it won't heal the carnage we have caused.

Chapter 12

LILIANA

I shove the remainder of my clothes into my satchel, knowing I'm already late for dinner. Tonight is the last dinner we will have with the recruits before we leave tomorrow morning and I want to make sure I get a seat next to Aliyah. All the fighting the boys have been doing over her is getting old. Kaleron clearly feels something for her based on the emotions I read from him whenever he is around her, but Enzo is her mate. He loves her deeply, but there is so much between them that needs repairing first.

I race down the steps heading toward the dining hall. I've felt lighter since Ali came back. I was in a dark place after everything happened with Duncan, something still pinching in my heart at the thought. But with Aliyah back, it gives me hope that our family can be whole again. Duncan and I are over, he made that perfectly clear, but I'd rather die first than let a man rule over my emotions. I planned to turn them all off, to hide inside my mind and let it slowly go dark, but Aliyah is back now and she needs me more than ever. I can be her light.

I slide into the grand hall, chatter from the recruits filling the air. We turned the grand hall into a sort of family dining room when the recruits moved in a few months ago. Three long tables fill the space with benches for everyone to sit on. Sconces line the walls, illuminating the space and the gem encrusted walls sparkle in the fire light. A large hearth sits at the back of the room, warming the air around us. It stretches at least two fae taller than myself and takes up almost the entirety of the wall.

I look around, seeing if I can spot Aliyah, but I don't see her anywhere yet. I find two open seats next to Saraphena as she pats them excitedly.

"Hey!" I say, plopping down into the seat next to her.

"Hi! I was saving you and Aliyah a seat, but I haven't seen her since training earlier today."

"Strange! I haven't see her either, but I'm sure she will be here soon." I spot Jade sitting two tables over with Eilith and Davion. She has barely spent any time with us recently, not that I blame her, but I miss my friend. We are supposed to be whole again, but there is this giant chasm separating Aliyah and Jade. I wish Jade could just see that Enzo and Aliyah belong together and not just because of some silly mate bond. He is the rhythm to her song.

"Saraphena, I need your help with something," I smile.

"Okay?" Her tone suggestions she knows I am up to something mischevious.

"Enzo and Aliyah need to move past whatever is between them. We need to formulate a plan to get them back together and I'm going to need your help," I smile.

"Liliana," she laughs. "You shouldn't meddle around in their relationship. They will get there in time."

"Ugh! Saraphena, they just need a little *push*. Just a lil' nudge. A tiny shove! That's all!"

"Lil," she warns, a laugh on her breath.

"Saraphena." I wiggle my eyebrows in response.

"Fine. I'll help, but only because I love Aliyah and I agree she does belong with Enzo. BUT! If Aliyah finds out, I'm blaming the whole thing on you."

"Deal! Her and Enzo just need to be reminded what it was like to be in love with each other! I have the perfect plan to do it, too."

"What do you need me to do?"

"Show up tonight at midnight in the throne room."

"And what will we be doing?"

"You'll see." I give her a quick wink as I see Aliyah coming in the doors. I throw my hand up and wave her over to our seats. Every head turns to watch her walk through the grand hall. She walks with determination, her head held high, as if she knows every eye is on her and refuses to crumble.

Murmurs ripple through the space, but they are quickly cut off by Enzo's booming voice. "Quiet down everyone! Quiet down!"

"Hi," Aliyah whispers, taking her seat next to me. "You certainly have a lot of recruits!"

"Our numbers grow by the day! I think we are almost at 300 soldiers! Not a ton, but hopefully more will come."

"Tonight is our last night together before some of us have to leave to travel to SunSpark," Enzo continues. "You will be in good hands here with Eilith and Davion. I trust you will be fine soldiers by the time we return. Please do try to keep the damages to a minimum," he smirks. "Let's eat!"

Others begin piling food onto their plates in heaping mounds. Thankfully we have been able to keep our supply of magical seeds well in stock to feed this many fae. Conversation starts up around us and I take the chance to turn to Aliyah.

"Let's have a girls night tonight. At midnight meet me in the throne room for a special surprise!"

"Liliana, what do you have up your sleeve?" She laughs, shoving a spoonful of mashed potatoes into her mouth. A smile slips onto her face and I can't help but smile too. "What?" She asks, knowing I am looking at her.

"It's nothing. I just don't think I've ever seen someone so happy over potatoes before."

"Well when you lie in a grave every day for three months straight, dying of starvation or burning alive, you tend to be thankful for any food," she winks.

"So it isn't too soon for grave jokes?" I laugh.

Aliyah simply huffs a laugh before spooning some peas into her mouth next. I dig into my own food, silence stretching around us and the only sound is forks and knives on plates. I finish my food quickly, knowing I have a lot of work ahead of me if I am going to be ready by midnight.

"If you'll excuse me, I have some things to take care of. I'll see you tonight, right?"

"I'll be there," Aliyah says.

"See you there," Saraphena agrees.

I dash from the grand hall. So much to do and so little time. I think I need to enlist some more help with this one.

Chapter 13

DUNCAN

"This is a ridiculous idea." I cross my arms over my chest.

"I didn't ask for your opinion, Dunca-doodle-doo. In fact, I don't remember asking for your help either. However, now that you are here, I might as well use it, but this help does not require speaking!" Liliana flicks me in the nose before shoving a basket of fire crystals into my hands. "Here. Set those up in two parallel lines. Do try to remember that you are only here by *chance*. A last resort of sorts."

"You can't force them to be together you know?" I lay out the fire crystals like she asked.

"Believe me, I know I can't force anyone to be together. I'm not trying to *force* them together. I'm reminding them what it was like being in love. Enzo clearly wants to be with her and she wants to be with him too, she is just struggling to move past things. I'm just giving them a little...nudge."

"More like pushing them off the dang cliff." I roll my eyes.

"What happened to not speaking?" She places her hands on her hips and a part of my resolve cracks just a little at how determined she looks.

"I'm just saying, how do you even know she is going to want this?"

"I already got the all clear! I spoke with Gunnar earlier and he was all for the idea! It's going to be great!"

"Well it's almost midnight, are you finished?"

"Just onnnneeeee last detail!" Liliana places her finishing touches on her plan and I have to admit, even I'm falling a little more in love with her though I'll never admit that after what I've done.

The smile plastered onto her face. The way her eyes sparkle in the fire's light. I never knew my heart could be so full after Zorellya, but seeing the way Liliana loves others so fiercely, how could I not love her? I just wish I could tell her, but to be the king Twilight needs, I can't be who she wants.

"You're coming to SunSpark with us right?" She beams at me across the room.

"You want me to come with you?" I ask taken aback. " I thought—"

"Oh, um, this is awkward. I didn't mean for me. I spoke with Gunnar earlier and he was hoping you would come. You can do whatever you want, I just told him I would ask you if I saw you."

Ouch. I don't know what is worse, the fact that she was asking on behalf of her brother, or the indifference on whether I came or not. I suppose I shouldn't be surprised.

"I do plan on coming. I will not return to Twilight until after we have this mess with The Banished King settled. No sense in me taking the throne if I am just going to die on the battle field, right?" I wink, trying to ease the tension between us. *Definitely not because I am seeing if she would care if I died or not.*

"Yeah, how embarrassing would that be for you! You finally come and claim your crown just to die in battle. That would really be a downer for the kingdom," she laughs.

Double ouch.

"Okay! I think we are all set up! Now I just need them all to get here! This is a night we are not going to soon forget!"

I look around to see how she has transformed the throne room. "No, they certainly won't."

Chapter 14

SARAPHENA

"I feel like Liliana is up to no good," I say, pinning a lock of hair up.

"She is always scheming, just like her brother," Aliyah laughs. I can't help but stare at her as she readies herself for our night with Lil. It's almost as if the last three months were all just a bad dream.

"True, but you don't think it is a little strange that we came back to our rooms only to find fancy dresses laid out and a note saying tonight we are playing dress up?"

"It's Liliana, this really isn't the strangest thing she could have done."

Aliyah's dress is a shimmering black silk that hugs her curves perfectly before fanning out around her ankles with a small train behind her. The dress is strapless with the back dipping low, leaving plenty of room for her wings. She piles her wavy blonde hair on top of her head in a messy sort of bun and pulls out a few face framing pieces.

"It's kind of nice I don't need to wear jewelry anymore because of all the golden swirls across my body," she laughs. "A small perk I suppose."

"You look gorgeous! Not like you lived in a grave for three months at all," I wink.

"You and Liliana are never going to let that one go are you? I'd say to stop, but honestly, finding laughter in the darkness helps me process through it all. Maybe if I can joke about it, the pain won't cripple my mind so much."

I move into the mirror next to her, my white dress a stark contrast to her black one. I lay my head on her shoulder, my black curls cascading over her arm as we stare into the reflecting glass before us. "So much has changed. You've changed. Black is a good color on you. The blue was nice, but something about black brings out the inner *you*."

"I couldn't agree more. It's strange, I never used to wear black. It felt so...depressing. But now it feels like I'm becoming who I'm meant to be, even something so simple as wearing black makes me feel...powerful."

"Then it's a good thing I got you this." I walk over to my dresser and pull out the large box from the bottom drawer. Aliyah hops onto the end of my bed and a frown crosses her face.

"What's this? I feel bad I didn't get you anything."

"You being alive and being here is the best gift I could have ever received. Open it." I place the large box on her lap and she cautiously pulls the ribbon. Removing the lid, her eyes go wide, her golden orbs sparkling in the fire light.

"Saraphena! Oh my gosh, these are...I don't even know how to describe them!"

Aliyah pulls out several black leather corset style tops; however instead of lacing up the back, they each pull on like a jacket and lace or button up the front. The backs dip low enough to sit under her wings, while the straps or sleeves crest up over her shoulders.

"I specifically had them designed so you won't have to wear a chest band. The tops are structured to function as both so you can be more comfortable with your wings. Jerico is truly a creative tailor."

"Saraphena these are absolutely incredible! Thank you!"

"And there are several pairs of matching black leather pants with built in thigh holsters for your knives," I smile.

"You really did think of everything." Aliyah wraps her arms tightly around me and her wings envelop me as well. "Liliana is going to kill us if we are late though."

"I was just thinking the same," I smile. Aliyah sets her gift on my bed to be retrieved later and we head for the throne room.

I smooth the satin of my white dress down wondering how Liliana always manages to pick such beautiful designs. My dress is a pure white that stops mid-thigh, leaving my legs exposed, but the A-line waist has a floor length layering of tule crusted with golden gems to form small swirls. The top of the dress has a square neckline and she paired my outfit with gorgeous golden earrings that hang like elongated tear drops from my ears. I feel like I am back at home in SunSpark with the white and gold that adorns my body and I am thankful for her thoughtfulness of my home kingdom.

Aliyah clasps her hand in mine as we make our way to the throne room. As we round the corner, Kaleron stands outside the throne room door with Enzo by his side. The tension in the air is palpable as we approach and I can't help the snicker creeping up in my nose.

"Aliyah, Saraphena, you both look absolutely exquisite on this fine evening," Kaleron smirks. Enzo offers his arm to Aliyah, but her hesitation to take it is only further noticeable as her eyes snag on Kaleron.

"I thought we were having a girl's night?" I ask.

"Change of plans," Enzo smiles.

"Are we going to go in, yet?" Aliyah asks.

"We are waiting for our cue," Enzo says.

"Cue? Cue for what?" I wonder.

"Just wait," Kaleron says.

Enzo pulls Aliyah in front of Kaleron and myself, the doors to the throne room opening and Barley and Gwynavere smile back at us. Time stops as I take in what is happening.

Will you marry me tonight, Saraphena?

Gunnar's voice in my mind brings tears to my eyes. *You did all this?*

I wish I could take the credit, but this was all Liliana.

Enzo and Aliyah walk ahead of us and pass through the aisle of fire crystals casting a red glow across the opaque floor. Liliana has completely transformed the throne room.

Rows of chairs are set up facing the back of the throne room where giant glass panels allow us to overlook the Krystal Mountains. The ribbons of color dancing across the night sky flick across the floor, illuminating the white of my dress. All the recruits are seated and staring back at me, smiles breaking across their faces.

"I know your father can't be here with you today, Saraphena, but I hoped it would be all right to walk you down the aisle as both your soon to be brother-in-law, but also as your King." Kaleron's smile is genuine as he walks me toward my future husband.

"Thank you, Kaleron, but I'd prefer you walk me down the aisle as something else."

His head tips in question and I can't help but smile when I think of how he tried to kill me not so long ago, but is now giving me away to his brother.

"I'd hoped you would walk me down...as my friend."

Light beams in Kaleron's eyes as he gives me a short nod. Looking forward again, Gunnar waits for me at the end of the fire-lit walkway, his own smile beaming across the space between us.

Enzo breaks away to stand next to Duncan who waits behind Gunnar, while Aliyah waits for me across from him. I see Barley, Gwynavere, and Felicia giving me nods of encouragement. Seeing the children in their finest tunics instead of their normally dirty training attire brings a chuckle to my throat. This is not what I had envisioned for my wedding day, but seeing all of my friends and family here and having Aliyah back is all I needed.

As we reach the end of the aisle, a small group of musicians cut off their tune and wait for Liliana to speak, apparently the one who is going to marry us.

"Friends and family, welcome. Tonight, under the light of the moon and stars, Gunnar and Saraphena will tie their souls together not only through the bond they share, but through vows of love and commitment to one another. King Kaleron, will you please present Saraphena to her mate?" Liliana gestures for me to take Gunnar's hands and I do so eagerly.

You look absolutely radiant tonight, Saraphena.

You can thank your sister for that apparently. This dress was waiting for me in my room. She can be such a sly creature sometimes.

Gunnar's laugh fills my mind as we turn our attention back on Liliana.

"I told you those emergency dresses would come in handy," she whispers to me. "It has been requested that Aliyah and Enzo share some words about each of their friends as a memento of their love," Liliana says to the crowd. Aliyah steps forward first with a sly smile, shoots me a wink, and now I know she was in on this the whole time. How could all of this have been done without me knowing?

"When Liliana left me a secret note tonight that this was happening, every part of my heart lit up with joy. Not only because my best friend was *finally* getting her happily ever after with her one true love, but because without her, I would not have known what that kind of love felt like myself. Knowing what I know now, the love Saraphena had for me my entire life rivals that of this world. She taught me that love can be messy, and scary, and unsure..." Aliyah's eyes drift to Enzo as she continues. "But most of all, she taught me that love can face great challenges, and still come out stronger on the other side. She showed me that a love which faces the greatest obstacles and still shines brightly in the darkest of nights, is the kind of love one will only find once in a lifetime. I hoped I would never have to share you with someone else, but if I had to choose someone to share your heart with, I'm happy it's Gunnar."

Tears stream down my cheeks at her words and my heart feels so full it could burst. I don't know what I did to deserve a friend like her, but I will thank that old woman every day for the rest of my life for bringing her into my life. Aliyah steps back behind me and Enzo addresses the crowd.

"I'm not quite sure how I am supposed to follow that, so I'll keep it short. Gunnar was there in my darkest times, always willing to be my light. The brightest sun rays in SunSpark couldn't match how freaking full this man's heart is for those he loves. He is an example to us all of what it means to love someone unconditionally. I was there the day he came home and found Saraphena gone, and while he may have made some questionable choices to help fill the cracks of his broken heart," Enzo laughs lightly, "I know he dreamed of a day when she would walk through our door and be home again. Gunnar sets the bar when it comes to being patient and holding out hope for a better tomorrow."

Gunnar claps him on the back and brings his shoulder into his chest for a tight hug.

How did we get so lucky to be blessed with such amazing family?

Gunnar's reply is brought with a laugh. *I think they are the lucky ones. We are the only stable couple in here at the moment and I think they all could use a solid foundation for what true love really means.*

"Thank you Enzo and Aliyah for your beautiful words," Liliana smiles. "While I may have orchestrated a small scheme to bring everyone here tonight, it was Gunnar and Saraphena's love that opened the door for this chance to come together one last time before our paths must part for a short while. On that note, Saraphena, Gunnar, you will now recite the words to bind your lives together. Please place your in hands in each others and hold tight while you recite the words."

I grip Gunnar's hands in mine and my heart races with excitement. We recite each line Liliana says, magic crackling between us.

"From this day forth, my soul, is your soul. Through the darkest of nights, I will be the light guiding you home. When the Maker decides to take you from me, I will wait for the day we find each other again. From now and into eternity, I am yours."

Magic sparks between us and a small flame slips beneath my skin, racing up my forearm, and when I glance down at my sun tattoo, a small black flame has taken form in the center of the sun. Tears prick in my eyes at the sight, knowing that my bond with Gunnar will be as permanent as my friendship bond with Aliyah.

"Congratulations! We are now officially family for life! You're stuck with us forever!" Liliana cheers and Gunnar sweeps me into his arms, crashing his lips with mine.

You're my mate, my best friend, and now...my wife.

I won't tell Enzo you said that part about me being your best friend.

A smile pulls at my lips and I unapologetically kiss my husband while every recruit cheers and for this moment, everything feels right in the world.

Chapter 15

ALIYAH

Music blasts through the roof, vibrating up my spine, and making my sternum pulse in my chest as I look out over the expanse of Krystal. I left the party to change into a more comfortable outfit for my wings and somehow found myself walking up to the roof. I'm wearing one of the halter tops Saraphena bought for me and black leather pants with the holster built in. I know I might be over dressed, but I couldn't resist how good they looked. A new set of daggers rest along my leg and my hair is pulled up high into a ponytail. My new boots fit perfectly and their combat style only accentuates my new look.

Saraphena was right, I was transformed in that grave. I am no longer the light-hearted girl from Mareen. That girl died on the battlefield and as much as I wish I could return to who I was, it's not who I need to be. I need to be strong. I need to be formidable. I need to be *unbreakable*. The power inside me burns as bright as my golden swirls, and I too will rise from the ashes of my old self and with the strength of my Maker. I will become a weapon strong enough so no one I love ever gets hurt again.

Laughter breaks through my thoughts and grounds me back to my reality. The recruits are enjoying a much needed night off, but Duncan told me Jade plans to wake them up extra early tomorrow as some sort of mental test. I try to imagine what it was like here growing up for Enzo, how hard he must have had to train to survive all these years.

If I am going to go up against The Banished King I am going to need to step up my training regimen. Everyone else has had years more than I have and I'm not going to let the events with Aramot happen again. I won't be caught off guard this time. Looking out over the Krystal Mountains, I think about what my life could have been.

"Hey," Liliana plops down beside me. *Right on cue.*

"Hey." I try to sound happy, but it doesn't quite translate.

"Why are you feeling so sad? Is it because Saraphena got married to her mate and things are so difficult with Enzo and you?"

"What? No. I'm so happy for her. I've just been thinking about what life could have been like for me if given different circumstances. Speaking of, what's happening between Duncan and you? I don't think I fully understand what happened."

Liliana lets out a long sigh, pulling her knees up to her chest and resting her head on her arms. "I know my heart loves him and some part of me thinks I always will, but he wants nothing to do with me. Every time I think we are going to move past this and he realizes that pushing me away was a mistake, all he does is open the chasm between us further. I don't think anything will change his mind at this point so I'm choosing to let him go, as hard as that might be."

"I'm sorry, Lil. I wish there was something I could do."

"You being back is enough for me right now. Things were...dark...when you were gone. We almost didn't make it. Enzo wasn't himself, Jade was so wrapped up in her love for him, Duncan pushed me away, and I— I did all I could, until it hurt too much to keep taking it all on. I think Saraphena and Gunnar were the only stable people in our family, but even they struggled with losing you."

"Lil, it isn't your job to keep everyone together. You spent so much time taking care of everyone else, but at what cost? You all had lost so much already. They wouldn't have made it if they lost you too."

"She's right you know." Saraphena walks out onto our spot on the roof and sits down on my other side. "I lost my family 26 years ago, but the one I found brought me home again. I'm not willing to risk anyone else for the sake of keeping us together. From now on, we stick together. No matter what. Promise?"

Saraphena lays her forearm on my leg, her palm facing up, waiting for us to join her. I lay my hand down first, and Liliana happily follows.

"'Til the end," I promise.

"'Til the end," Lil swears.

A moment passes between us when a resounding boom blasts through the night in the distance. Flashes of red, yellow, and orange ripple over the expanse before us as flames lick across the inky sky. Smoke plumes in the distance and fear strikes into my heart.

Enzo, we have a problem.

Already on it. Word just came from the Flying Legion that The Kalari are in Krystal. We are rounding up the recruits now. They are changing into their fighting leathers and finding their Matched or pairing up. Meet us at the front gate.

I'm already changed. I'll meet you there.

Be safe. I love you.

I don't respond as Liliana and Saraphena race back inside. "I'll meet you there!" I call.

"Aliyah come on! We need to change and meet the others!" Saraphena calls.

"I'm already ready! I'll meet you at the town! Get the others and come as fast as you can!"

"How are you getting there?" Lil asks, pulling open the hatch to the hall beneath us.

"I'm going to fly," I smile.

A devious smirk spreads across her face and I wink back at her, definitely ignoring the fear in my chest at the thought. "I won't tell Enzo, but you better not die or else I'll have to wait 'til you come back to kill you myself."

"Liliana, let's go!" Saraphena calls and Liliana disappears below the hatch door.

I turn and face out toward the edge of the roof. "All right wings, don't let me die. If you truly mean to protect me, you'll carry me through the night until we reach that village. Don't embarrass me in front of the others by splatting on the pavement again. I'm trusting you. Don't make me regret it."

My wings snap out behind me as if in understanding. I nod once and decide that hesitation will only instill more fear. Swallowing my panic, I break for the ledge. My heart pounds, but a smile breaks across my face in excitement. I leap off the roof with a scream ripping from my throat, eyes closed, bracing for my wings to catch on the wind. I tighten my muscles, prepping for the rapid change in direction. I wait one second...two seconds...three seconds.

Nothing. I open my eyes, wind whipping through my hair, and the ground racing up toward me.

Chapter 16

ENZO

"**G**et a move on! This is not a drill, recruits! Move!" My voice booms through the entrance hall as over 300 recruits find their way down the stairs from their bedrooms. "Fall in line! Fall. In. Line!"

Voices cut off as the final fae find their spots. Liliana and Saraphena make their way down the stairs last, but Aliyah is no where to be found. She said she would meet me here. Where is she?

"Liliana, where is Aliyah?"

"Um..she already left. She said she would meet us there." Her gaze is avoidant and anxiety claws at my throat.

"But Mirage is out in the crystal field with Daisy. How is she— Liliana, how is Aliyah getting to the village *exactly?*"

Liliana only gives me a tight smile before slowly backing away to stand by Saraphena. Maker of the above and below, Aliyah is going to attempt to fly there. Would she put her life at risk again? *I hate this.* If I didn't have troops to address, I'd storm out there right now and hunt her down until I knew she was safe, but as much as it pains me to say, I have to trust she is going to be safe.

"Listen up! We have a serious situation on our hands. A village just over the southern mountains has been ransacked by The Kalari. King Kaleron of SunSpark received word The Kalari crossed into Olyrium and were headed for the villages in Krystal. For those of you who have matched sphinx here, you will be joining the ranks with the SunSpark Flying Legion who have just landed. You will take orders from their General and you *will* listen! If you have a matched alicanto, you will be riding in line with Jade and Reyla. If you do not have a matched, find someone who does and pair up. I will be riding ahead with Ruby to get a lay of the land before we attack. This is *our* land. These are *our* people! Stay focused, and stay sharp. I refuse to lose any lives tonight. If you truly feel you are not ready for this fight, please stay behind."

Not a single recruit moves. I don't believe for one second it is because they believe they are ready, but their hearts are strong. Pride flares in my chest at their commitment.

"Recruits, TO YOUR STATIONS!" I yell to the ranks before me and everyone bursts into action. Fae scramble around me, but I catch Saraphena's arm. "You are to find Aliyah as soon as you can. Search the skies, search the village, search everywhere. You will find her, is that understood?"

"I'll find her, I swear it." Saraphena takes off toward Daisy and I spot Kaleron at the top of the steps.

"You could use another hand."

"Any hand but yours," I sneer.

"Even though it would be two more hands protecting Aliyah?"

"Your hands will go no where near my *mate*."

Kaleron chuckles darkly, "We'll see about that."

Every inch of me screams to rip him apart, but I know Aliyah would never forgive me if I hurt him. Like it or not, she finds comfort in his presence and I promised I would do everything I could to show her that she can trust me. I grit my teeth and swallow down every instinct I have. It's more painful than swallowing the glass I put down that fae's throat not too long ago.

"Fine. You may join us just this once, but you take orders from me and that's final."

"Oh silly, silly ZoZo. I don't take orders from anyone and make no mistake, I'm not going for you or that village. I'm going because that is where Aliyah is and I refuse to let anything happen to her."

Before I can respond, he slips out the crystal doors and joins his sister on Molly, preparing to take off. He smirks back at me as Molly's giant wings shoot them into the sky. I whistle for Ruby and she bolts around the corner, ready for action.

"All right, sweet girl. Let's go save a village."

Chapter 17

ALIYAH

"Crapcrapcrapcrapcrap. You son of a— Why do you always work when I don't want you to, but when I *need* you, you literally let me down! Don't you know I'm going to die?! I thought you were here to protect me!?"

The marble path races toward me and I close my eyes once more. "I trusted you," I whisper. Tears stream down my cheeks and fly away in the wind. "I *do* trust you."

My stomach drops, everything goes black with the change of direction. I feel my wings snap out behind me at the last moment, catching the wind, and my feet sway inches above the ground. The heavy beating at my back raises me higher and higher off the ground, the marble path becoming nothing but a speck on the ground.

A laugh bubbles up in my chest as we break through the clouds and into the night sky. "This whole time you knew exactly how to fly and you just let me die!?" I yell back to them, but my words aren't harsh. They angle with the wind and loop us into a spiral, breaking back down through the clouds, clearly showing off. They burst wide again, leveling us out, and finding a steady rhythm.

"Well I have no clue how you work, but take me to the village!"

With a mind of their own, their angle shifts and we bank left, heading toward the rising smoke. I soak in the last few moments of flying free before the carnage from The Kalari comes into view below me. As much as I love riding on the back of Mirage, my wings fly far faster and when I land, the recruits and the others are no where in sight.

I'm here. How far out are you?

Coming up on the edge of the village soon. We will talk about your actions later.

A scream pulls me from my conversation with Enzo. I snap my head to the right and glimpse a woman and her husband standing outside their home, flames consuming the structure, and four of The Kalari walking toward them. "Help us! Someone, please!"

Sprinting toward them, I unsheathe a dagger and lock in on my target. Releasing a steady breath, I launch the dagger. Golden sparks release along the hilt, matching the cascade along my back, transforming me into a fierce weapon. When the dagger embeds into The Kalari's sternum, a golden orb surrounds its skeleton, bursting it into oblivion.

I knew I saw sparks fly that day in Mareen when I finally landed my dagger in the target. *So glad to know I wasn't going crazy.*

The woman shrieks behind me as another of The Kalari brings back their ax, preparing to strike. "Duck!" I yell. Pulling another dagger, it flies from my hand and burrows into the skull, consuming The Kalari in its wake. Two more stand before me now, the couple locked in place with fear behind me. I pull my third and final dagger from its place on my thigh. "Do your worst."

Mindlessly, The Kalari march forward, prepared to slaughter me, but I won't be leaving my family any time soon. Before I have a chance to strike, The Kalari's heads are ripped from their body, and while I expect Enzo to walk out of the carnage, Saraphena appears out of thin air, a smile plastered to her face.

"Found you," she says.

"Who knew you could be such a savage!? I mean you when *straight* for the heads, ripping them off with your bare hands!" I laugh.

"It seemed easier than waiting for you to do it," she winks.

"Where are the others?"

"Taking on a horde across the village. I had specific instructions to find you by one General ZoZo."

"Let's meet up with them and figure out a game plan. I assume Jade is already here putting one together?"

"She is riding with the recruits and their matched alicanto. The SunSpark Flying Legion is here being led by Kaleron and Liliana. We should have this situation wrapped up in no time."

"I have to admit, it's nice having it not just be the seven of us this time," I laugh. "We might just stand a chance after all."

"Beatrix? Marlin?" Saraphena walks around me toward the couple we saved.

"You know them?" I ask.

"Saraphena, it's lovely to see you again, though I wish it was under better circumstances. Why are they here?" Beatrix asks. She is a middle-aged woman with gray hair pulled into a tight bun and worn features. The man beside her looks as if he carries the weight of the world. Graying hair, sullen eyes, and a smile that doesn't quite reach his eyes.

"Aliyah, this is Beatrix and Marlin. They are the parents of one of the recruits," Saraphena says.

"Were," Marlin corrects. "We *were* the parents of one of your recruits. Rory was our boy, and if you truly are Aliyah, then you are the reason our son is dead."

A lump forms in my throat. "Words can never match how sorry I am about what happened with Rory. He was an amazing boy and I wish— I wish things had been different."

The man lifts his nose in disgust as he gazes upon me. The woman leans into his side and he wraps his arm protectively around her. "He would never have burned out his power if it wasn't for your mate trying to rip this world apart to bring you back. I see he has succeeded. If only he could extend the same courtesy to my family and bring me back my boy."

My heart breaks knowing it was no task of Enzo's that brought me back. "If there was anything in the realms I could do to bring Rory back I would, but it was not Enzo who revived me. It's my powers that burn in my veins which bring me back. I was never really dead, they just didn't know I was alive."

"Then I thank you for saving our lives, but after this night, I no longer wish to see you. I am plagued with the same ability as my son, but in solidarity of my wife, I refuse to contact my boy. It is unfair for me to be blessed with this gift when she cannot see him for herself. Save this village, then get out of my sight."

Saraphena grips my hand and gives the couple a soft nod. "I'm sorry," I whisper. A building crashes down in the distance and I'm transported back to my village in Mareen. Glass shattering from the windows of local shops. Screams ripping from throats before their lives ended. A stranger in an alley who would change my life forever. I let Saraphena pull me through the streets once more, but this time I won't be hiding away. I'll be fighting alongside my found family.

"Up ahead! Move! Three on your left, Enzo! Liliana, watch your back. You've got a group coming from the north!" Jade's voice carries over the sounds of battle. She is perched atop Reyla, several of the recruits mounted on their own matched behind her. "You lot, follow me! We will take the south quadrant of the village! Stay close or lose your life!"

Jade's glare pierces my very essence as she rides by on Reyla. I cast an irritated look her way, feeling my wings bristle behind me, then jerking back. A yelp cuts through the air and I whip around just in time to see Jade clasping her arm, a crystal feather embedded into the flesh of her bicep.

"Oh sorry, Jade! Misfire! You know, lack of control and all. Total accident!" I quip sarcastically. All she does is kick Reyla's sides, spurring her on faster away from me. I glance back at my wings who stretch with pride. "Feel free to misfire around her anytime you deem necessary," I laugh.

"Aliyah!" Enzo's gruff voice is filled with anger as he storms across the village square, heading directly for me. Three of The Kalari come around the side of a house, but Enzo doesn't even spare them a glance. His hand shoots out, blasting them to dust with his power. Dried blood splatters across his skin and coats part of his face, likely from healed wounds. I can't help how my mouth dries up at the sight, both in fear and dare I say, adoration.

I remember the day we met when he smeared his own blood over my cheeks while I held a dagger to his throat. My fingers twitch wanting to return the gesture now, but his creased brow and snarl make me think twice.

"You were supposed to meet me at the gate!" His voice booming across the distance.

"I don't remember agreeing to that. I believe my exact words were *I'll meet you there.* I just never clarified where," I smile.

He stands before me now, looking down his nose at my smirk with disdain. "You could have been killed."

"I can't die, remember?" I cross my arms and cock out a hip, a smile pulling at my lips.

"That does not mean you can blatantly risk your life on a whim and pray to the Maker you get brought back."

"I was in complete control the entire time...well, not the entire time, but close enough." I swear I see smoke pour from his nostrils. I don't know what comes over me, but I reach out and wrap my hand around his forearm. Heat races up my fingers at the contact, but my muscles tense even with just the lightest touch. "I'm not going anywhere, Enzo. This is my home. You all are my family. I may not be in the best headspace, and we might be...figuring things out...but this was the first place I wanted to be when I left my grave. I didn't blatantly disregard my life, I was just determined to save another's."

I try to give him the most confident smile I can. Another boom sounds in the distance and Liliana yells something to Duncan about not moving out of the way fast enough, but everything silences when Enzo stares into my eyes. I'm caught up in all that is him. The bond pulls me a step closer to him, breathing in the smell of blood and dirt. The connection between our souls sings a perfectly crafted harmony, and despite my wings bristling in their crystal form at how close I am to him, I let us have this moment. Enzo doesn't back down, his hand slowly reaching out to cup my jaw.

"Your heart may be threatened by me, my dove, but our souls belong together. I can feel it, in here." He moves his hand to cover where my scar lies from the day we first met. "Until the stars die out, the sun loses her light, and the moon cracks apart, I will wait for you, Aliyah."

"Enzo—" My eyes fall shut and the world falls away as Enzo's lips meet mine. There is desperation in his kiss and the bond between us explodes into a fury of need. I claw at his chest, trying to pull him closer. I grip the back of his neck and my fingers clasp around the locks of hair there. A low groan falls from his lips and his hands travel lower, gripping my thighs as he lifts me up. I know stealing this moment between us is wrong, especially given the circumstances, but I can't deny our bond, even if my wings know the truth of my heart. Enzo is risking it all holding me like this with my guardian in their crystal form, but he holds me tighter anyway.

I feel my wings beating hard, trying to pull my body away from his, but he grips me harder. A pained groan leaves his lips and he rears back from me, blood spilling from a surface cut on his neck. A grin plays on his lips as he gazes into my eyes, but irritation sits in my chest as I see the crystalized feather embedded into the ground behind him.

"You tried to impale him?!" I yell at my guardian. In response, they beat once more, trying to rip me from his grasp, and this time, I concede. I'm pulled away and placed what they must deem a healthy amount of space away from him.

He steps closer, our breaths still heavy and the sounds of battle falling into place around us once more. Our eyes stay locked until I see a three forms approaching from behind him. Time moves in slow motion as The Kalari notch three arrows, posed to strike. Sensing my panic, my wings curve in front me and I step toward Enzo. They shove him behind me right as The Kalari let their arrows fly. I glance back, ensuring Enzo is safely behind me and a smile crests my lips, taking in the sight of him. He reaches out in realization, but he isn't fast enough to stop three arrows from embedding into my chest. I don't take my eyes off him as I fall back into his arms and everything fades to black.

Chapter 18

ALIYAH

I 've learned to find comfort in the void between worlds when I die. It's always the same when I come here. I wake up in an endless sea of black, a shallow expanse of black water beneath me. Sitting up, I revel in the feeling of my wings being absent at my back. The lack of weight from their plumes a reminder of what life was like before them.

The tattered dress from my dreams blows around my ankles, threats of war and battle no where in sight. Here, in this place, there is no need for a guardian. No need to be protected. Here in this haven, I am safe. This is where I met Rory. His small face beaming with delight after finally being able to make contact with me. Our time together was too short, however. My heart aches at his sacrifice, all so Enzo could tell me he was coming for me, only...he wasn't.

Rory's message had given me the spark of hope I needed to survive another day in my iron grave, but as each day passed, I lost hope that someone was coming to save me. Seeing Rory's parents was an unexpected reminder of how far we go for the one's we love most. Rory told me how much he just wanted to make General Enzo proud, how he wished he could have found a way to bring his Nona back. Rory was so happy that Enzo would get another day with me. Why is it so hard to forgive him when so few have been gifted the chance we have?

Why does my heart continually war with my mind? One moment I want to be swept up in his arms, and yet the moment I have to become emotionally vulnerable with him, I pull back. Being physical with Enzo isn't the problem. It's when I have to open my heart up to him once more that my walls thicken another foot around me, guarding me from harm. I need my head freaking clear. I need my emotions to be my own...without the bond. *Wishful thinking I suppose.*

My eyes catch on a familiar pair of feathered wings soaring down from the darkness above. The golden light trailing behind them illuminates the onyx expanse and my heart oddly warms at the sight of them. Wrapping me up in their feathers, fire crackles down the plumes and in a burst of red, yellow, and orange gems exploding around me, the burning village comes back into view and Enzo's pained face appears above me.

"Hi," I whisper.

"I thought you said you weren't going to leave again?" He surprisingly jokes.

"I figured saving your life might take priority over that promise."

Enzo's forehead comes down to rest on mine for only a moment before he helps me to my feet. "You know, your golden blast that destroyed the training center might come in handy right about now."

I close my eyes, trying to concentrate on the power inside me, but all I find is a small golden orb glowing in my chest. "Hm," I say, frustrated. "Just one more thing that doesn't seem to want to work when *I* want it to."

"Don't push yourself. We can fight them off one by one if we need to, as long as we do it together," he smiles.

"Are you two done making out over there?! We do have a battle happening over here!" Gunnar calls.

"Struggling to handle it without us?" Enzo yells back.

"Ha! I've killed at least fifteen of these bastards while you had playtime with your mate!" Gunnar says, striking another of The Kalari in the chest with his sword.

"Well best take a break then and let the professionals handle it from here," I quip.

"I see how it is! You get super cool powers and suddenly you're better than everyone else?" He laughs.

"Yeah, that about sums it up!" I call.

"Care to show him how it's done?" Enzo asks.

"Let's put him to shame."

The battle goes on until the light of day breaks over the Krystal Mountains. Blood coats every inch of exposed skin on all of us, but The Banished King's creatures were no match for the Citrine Army. However, I am under no illusions that when it comes time to face Tyros himself we will be at an advantage. We need serious help, and not just from some young recruits. We need true, skilled, fearless, soldiers. I have no doubt it will take all of Olyrium, and likely even Luar, to take him down once and for all.

Chapter 19

JADE

"Faster! Let's go! Pick up your feet!" The recruits run around the training field trying to build up their endurance. This is the last training session I will lead before leaving them in the hands of Eilith and Davion, so I am making sure they are in prime condition. I want them to have at least a fighting chance. After lasts nights fiasco, they won't survive going up against my father. We won on luck alone, but my father is a far greater foe than his mindless creatures. Footsteps sound behind me, but I don't have to turn around to know who is coming.

"You're not coming with us are you?" Liliana asks.

"You don't need me in SunSpark."

"Yes, we do. We are a family, Jade. Despite what is going on between everyone, we want you there."

"Who is *we*? Because there certainly wasn't a *we* when your little mutant friend was beating me to a pulp. You just stood there, Liliana. You've chosen your side, even if you deny it."

"It's not about sides, Jade."

"It is! You're just standing on the wrong one and you'll see that soon enough."

"What's that supposed to mean?"

I huff out a breath as I stare out at the recruits. "Nothing. But I'm not coming with you to SunSpark. I don't want to be anywhere near Aliyah, and Enzo has made it perfectly clear there is nothing between us. I don't see the point in torturing myself."

"Will you be here when we get back?" I hear the earnestness in her voice and it almost makes me feel bad for moving forward with my plan.

"Where else would I be?" I give her a tight smile.

"I'm going to miss you." She wraps her arms around me and I feel the warmth in her hug, but it doesn't deter me from what I have to do. "I'll see you when we get back!" Liliana walks off and I see them loading up their satchels onto the backs of their alicanto and sphinx. No one else says goodbye, and I know I've made the right choice as I watch them run off into the distance.

"Bring it in!" I yell across the training ground. The recruits make their way over to me, Eilith and Davion bringing up the rear of the group. "You all did great today. The Banished King doesn't stand a chance with the lot of you! Keep working hard and don't forget everything you have learned. You're going to be training with Eilith and Davion until the others return. You will treat them with respect. I will see you all very soon, I promise."

"Where are you going?" Barley asks.

"I'm going to visit some family."

I stuff the last of my belongings into the satchel on my bed before taking a look around my room for the last time. I never had many belongings, but somehow packing up for this trip feels different...because it's final. I'm never coming back here, not until it's time. Walking through the palace, I memorize the details of every wall, every painting, every crack and crevice. This place holds so many memories for me, but the bad memories are easiest to pull from my mind. Enzo's father, almost dying from that curse, Enzo choosing Aliyah, all memories I wish I could forget. I walk out across the bridge leaving Citrine City and call for Reyla. I wish I could bring her with me, but she would never survive on an island with no crystals to feed on. She is the only goodbye I will make. She runs up beside me and I fling my pack over her and hoist myself up next.

"One last ride, girl." I pat her feathers in affection for my matched. As I set off toward the edge of Twilight Kingdom, I run over my plan again and again.

Step one: Journey to see my father.

Step two: Force him to unlock my powers.

Step three: Master my new abilities so no one can ever hurt me again.

Step four: Burn Aliyah's world to the ground.

Part III:
Proposition

Chapter 20

ALIYAH

My fists beat against the coffin lid, throat raw from screaming. I claw at the iron, the acidic burn of its components sending scorching fire over my skin. "Please help me! Someone help me!" Hunger churns deep in my belly. I claw at the lid and agony like lightning ripples through my middle finger. I suck a breath in through my teeth and snatch my hand back. In the darkness, I feel around my hand, noting the slick river of blood that surely pools from my nail bed. When my thumb dances across the tip of my middle finger, tears well in my eyes.

I place my hand on the lid of the coffin, searching. Something breaks loose from the iron and falls onto my chest. I pick it up and recognize the texture. My nail. Sobs wrack my chest. How did this happen? How am I here? I know what happened on that battlefield. I know the sword that pierced my chest was a killing blow. I remember my final words to Enzo as my life force drained out of me. This isn't real. It can't be.

I reach down, pinching the skin on my thigh. Wincing, at the feeling of my broken nails piercing my skin, I release. Okay, so I still feel pain. It's okay. Enzo will come for me. I just have to wait. He'll visit the grave and save me. It won't be too much longer now.

Blackness swirls around me. My mouth waters, hunger carving into my stomach like a knife. I'm so hungry. I don't know how long it's been, but I know I won't survive down here much longer. I claw at my skin, reminding myself that I'm alive. Wetness pools along my arms. I've spread my hair around me and tried to cover as much of my exposed skin as I can. I will not burn.

Time waivers and the black ink swirls around me once more. I'm clawing at my neck now. Panic surging beneath my skin. I need it out. I need this feeling to be ripped out of me. Clawed out of me if it must. Out. Out. Out. My heart beats too fast. The blood rushing in my ears and the sound of red rushing through my veins is too much in the silence. Out. Out. OUT! I need out! I claw at my ears, lines of fire burning beneath my touch. Fingers scratch fingers. Teeth tear into flesh to sate the hunger. Vomit burns in the back of my throat at the rejection of the only food available.

I scream and scream if just to hear something other than my own bodily fluids rushing through veins and intestines. "Please!" I beg to the Maker to end this suffering. To let me wake up in my soft bed, Enzo by my side, and Saraphena just a room away. I plead with Him for this all to be just some horrible dream.

My back aches. It's as if my skin is being split in two. Pure agony rips through my scapulas. The coffin gets smaller. Tighter. Darker. My palms press into the lid of the coffin, trying to find more room, but hands dig into several sets of embedded nails from past attempts to escape— as if I could simply claw my way to the surface.

Soft feathers wrap around me. The burning stops, but the panic only increases. "Enzo! Please! Enzo! Enzo! Enzo..."

"Enzo!" I shoot up in bed, sweat covering my brow. The reminder I am safe in SunSpark comes flooding in. Breaths come in rapid succession. The open curtains let light pool onto the white marble floors and I try to look out across the horizon at the blazing sun, but fear grips my heart instead. I bury my head in my hands. "You're safe. You're safe. You're safe." My wings wrap around me protectively, providing me comfort and companionship in this moment. We've been in SunSpark for just two days and the panic attacks still come at full force. The door bursts open.

The guardian's on my back snap into their crystal form and are poised to strike at whoever has come in. "Aliyah, are you okay?"

Kaleron. I note how my wings relax at the sound of his voice. "No. I'm not okay. I don't think I'm ever going to be okay again. I don't know what to do, Kal. How do I stop this? I needed Enzo. I needed him to come and save me and he wasn't there. Intentional or not, he hurt me Kal and I don't know what to do." My voice cracks as I lift my eyes to his. His face is blurred by my tears, but I know it's him.

Kaleron makes his way over to the bed, moving the covers back and climbing into bed with me. My wings shift to the side and I lay down with my head on his chest. His arm wraps around me and pulls me close to him. "It's okay, Ali. Feel what you need to feel. Let it out."

Tears slip from my eyes, leaving a large blotch on his shirt. I grip his tunic in my fist and let every feeling I have pour out of me. Time passes in a tear-filled blur. When I finally find the will to stop, I look up at him. "I'm sorry. This is so inappropriate. I just cried all over a king." I move to push away from him, but his hand wraps around my wrist, pulling me back down.

"I don't care about inappropriate, Aliyah. I care about you."

"You can't say things like that, Kal. Someone might start to think you have a heart," I smile. A soft chuckle comes from his lips.

"I won't tell if you don't," he winks.

"I'll take it to my grave," I promise.

"If I have anything to say about it, you'll never be in a grave ever again." He lifts my hand to his lips and places soft, tender kisses to the golden swirls there. "But you know, secrets are only fun if we both have one to keep. I can't have you gaining too much leverage on me now."

"You want to know a secret?"

"Only if you're willing to share," he smiles.

I lift my hand up in front of him and point to the golden swirls along my skin. "Do you know how I got all these swirls?"

"I assumed it had something to do with your abilities."

"You would be half correct," I sigh. "When I was in that coffin, I panicked. A lot. Everything felt too small and too confined. Sometimes my skin would itch with how much my body was panicking. I thought...I thought that if I could claw out the panic it would go away."

I feel him tense beneath me, but I don't take my eyes away from my arm. His hand reaches out, tracing along the lines on my arms. "The golden lines...they are where you tried to rip out the panic." It isn't a question.

"I didn't realize it until I was standing in front of the mirror looking at all the places the golden swirls touched. For every claw mark made, a golden swirl replaced it."

"But they cover your body."

"I know."

His fingers trail up my arm, interlocking with my fingers and bringing our hands down to rest on his chest. "The ones on your back—" he trails off.

"From when my wings tore out of me. There wasn't much space for them to maneuver in the small coffin. With how they sense my emotions, the shift wasn't always gentle." The feathers curl around Kaleron and me in an embrace I've learned to appreciate more with time.

"I'm sorry."

"You have nothing to apologize for, Kal. It's done now. I'm out."

"I know you don't want to hear this, but you're not out. Not mentally anyway. You left a part of yourself in that coffin and it's going to take time to unbury it."

"I will. One day I will be whole again," I smile.

"And I can't wait to be standing by your side when you do."

A moment of silence passes between us. "Can I show you something?"

"Any small part of yourself you wish to share I will take greedily as if it is the most precious thing in this realm," he winks.

"Okay well you don't have to be all dramatic about it," I laugh. "You said you always see a light on under my door, right? Close the curtains."

"Yes?" His eyebrow quirks, his interest peaked as he gets up to shut them before returning to me.

I close my eyes, feeling the small golden sphere in my chest and holding onto it's light. I feel the panic creeping in. I feel the horror of being trapped in that coffin. I let myself feel the need for the light.

"Aliyah." Kaleron's voice is filled with awe and when I open my eyes, golden light is streaking across the room.

From under the swirls on my skin shine a soft golden light, swirling across every inch of the room. Sparkles dance across the ceiling and walls, creating a pool of light that ripples around the space. Kal reaches out his hand, running it through the ethereal glow coming from my body.

"You are magnificent, Aliyah." Wonder laces his tone as his eyes drop back to mine. The golden light casting a warm glow across his features makes my heart pinch. His hand trails up to my jaw, pulling my face closer to his. My lips tingle, wondering if he is going to kiss me. Part of me wishes he would, but some small piece inside me knows it would ruin everything.

Can a heart be torn in two? Each piece belonging to another? My eyes close as Kaleron leans in, but instead of my lips, I feel his kiss on my cheek.

"Sleep. I've got you."

"I can't sleep with you in here!"

"Why not?"

"What would the people say?! The whispers, Kal," I wink, the moment passing between us. "Whispers are said to be the downfall of Kings," I say smirking.

"Just one more secret then," he says with a soft smile.

"You'll— You'll stay awake right?"

"I'll stay awake for as long as you need me to. I'm not going anywhere."

The rise and fall of his chest starts to lull me into a sleepy state once more. "Promise me you will stay awake."

"I promise. As long as I'm here, no nightmares will reach you. Sleep, Aliyah. I'll be here when you wake up." I feel a soft kiss planted to the top of my head as my arms curl tighter around him. The light from my skin continues to illuminate the room as I drift off.

"Just for tonight, I'll be better in the morning," I say, a yawn pulling at my lips. Sleep greets me faster than I expect and this time, in the comfort of Kaleron's presence, I have a dreamless sleep.

Chapter 21

ENZO

I race down the hall, intending to rip Aliyah's door right off the hinges to get to her as she screams out my name. I had jolted awake in my bed at the feeling of her horror coming down the bond. Agony had ripped through my very soul when she started screaming my name and I knew this was my moment to finally be there for her when she needed me most. But as I reach the door, I hear another voice coming from inside her room. *Kaleron.* Intent on tearing down the barrier between us, and opening the door as well, I stop as I hear Aliyah speaking. "—know what to do, Kal. How do I stop this? I needed Enzo. I needed him to come and save me and he wasn't there. Intentional or not, he hurt me Kal and I don't know what to do."

An uncomfortable feeling sits in my chest as she confides in the one man she hated so ferociously not so long ago. She was calling out for *me*. But was she? What if— What if her screaming was her asking for help...and again I didn't get there in time before *he* did. Every inch of my skin burns to intervene, but it's clear Aliyah feels comforted by Kaleron, and as much as it pains me, I've taken enough from her. She needs him. At the end of the day, Aliyah needs someone who she can feel safe around right now. I've seen the way her wings respond to Kaleron, not a single crystal feather in sight. Aliyah may want to work things out with me, but she *needs* Kaleron to make her feels safe in this world again. I leave them to their conversation and make my way back to my room, each step more painful than the last. A door cracks open next to me and my eyes turn, meeting the stare of Duncan.

"Fight for her, Enzo. Fight for her even when she can't fight for herself right now. Don't give up so easily."

"I don't know how," I admit. Duncan presses on, "It doesn't matter what you do, it's just a matter of you doing *something*. Don't wait around for her to tell you how to fix things. Show her the man she once fell in love with."

"What if that man no longer exists? What if I was the man she needed then, but not the man she needs now?"

"Kaleron was there for her in one of the most excruciating times of her life. He is there for her now, but he won't be her love forever. Aliyah and you were drawn to each other from the moment you first laid eyes on each other. It was fast, and messy, and unexpected, but it was yours. Kaleron has a kingdom to run, and that will always come first."

"That was just the mate bond pulling us together."

"Don't do that, Enzo. Don't down play the love you both had for each other and chalk it up to some bond. Aliyah fell in love with you long before the bond snapped into place. Zorellya and I were together for almost a year before our mate bond revealed itself. It did not make that year together any less special because it was designed by the Maker."

"Yet it still turned to hell, mate bond or not. You still lost her."

"I lost her because I didn't fight hard enough for her. I let fear consume me. I let my father's will play over my life out of respect or duty, or whatever the hell you want to call it. Because I was afraid of what he might do, I became a coward and it cost me the woman I love. I suppose history was doomed to repeat itself for me, because once again, fear ruled my life and I lost someone I never deserved to have in the first place. It's too late for me to fight for the woman I love, but you still have a chance."

"I'm not so sure. You didn't hear what I did." Duncan moves to close the door. "Those are just words. *Show* her." I make my way back to my room. I flop down on my bed, Duncan's words floating around in my mind. Insecurity creeps in. I know it's irrational and I know what the solution is, yet I can't bring myself to tear her and Kaleron apart. Aliyah deserves one good thing in her life and I'll be damned if I'm the one who takes it from her. Reality is like a vice on my heart when I come to the realization of my future. A future that is likely without Aliyah. I know at the end of it all, I'll lose her to Kaleron, and maybe it's for the best. I never deserved her from the start.

Chapter 22

KALERON

I sit high up on the dais, overlooking the crowd gathered below. All my council members have attended, along with several other powerful families that reside here in SunSpark. They couldn't resist the chance to meet Captain Jonah and his dastardly crew. The Islands of Loch are not a kind place to grow up, and the men who come from there are less than refined, but that is what will make them formidable in battle on the seas.

My hope is to bring the fight to The Banished King. To sail Jonah's ships right to Tyros' front door before he has a chance to prepare. If we can catch him by surprise, maybe we will stand a chance, but I have to first get Jonah to agree to giving SunSpark his ships and crew.

My knee bounces in anticipation while my eyes scan the room looking for...*her*. She isn't hard to miss, those giant wings catching every eye in the throne room. I see the members of my court whispering and glancing over to where she stands, completely unaware that all eyes are on her. How could they not be?

She is a vision. Her black silk dress pools around her feet and the neckline squares before cresting up to clasp behind her neck, her new favorite style of top. Her back is completely bare, showing off the golden swirls that highlight her past in such a beautiful way. She wears her scars proudly now, unashamed by her history, because now...now she is a force to be reckoned with. Her wings, an outward expression of the inner strength she contains. Aliyah, brilliant, indomitable, dangerously beautiful, Aliyah.

As if she hears my inner thoughts, her eyes catch on mine, and a bright smile breaks out across her face. She nods her head in my direction, flooding me with courage for the deal to come. This is why all those other women in that ballroom paled in comparison to her. Those women could never be my bride because I want more than just a Queen, I want a partner. A partner in life, love, and power. Aliyah rivals them all and one day, she will choose *me*.

Duncan, Saraphena, Gunnar, and Enzo are all on time, but of course Liliana is late. That girl can never get anywhere on time, even when given explicit orders by her king.

The doors swing open and our gazes break. Captain Jonah strides into the room, his deep bronze skin glows in the golden light of the palace. His fire-red hair is long, braided down to his waist, but his eyes— His eyes are what catch my gaze. The right eye is a light hazel while the other is as blue as the seas themselves. Scars line his exposed skin, the most jagged one running from the point of his left ear all the way down to his chin, following the curve of his strong jaw. Despite his deranged appearance, Jonah carries a light hearted way about him. He smiles at some of the court ladies as he strides toward the front of the dais.

I watch as his eyes snag on the only important woman in the room. He drinks in everything from the tip of her wings to the crest of the golden swirls across her chest. *Absolutely not.*

"Captain Jonah, welcome to SunSpark!" I stand, my voice carrying over the crowd. His eyes still linger on Aliyah, her gaze boring into him. Jonah stops and turns to push his way through the crowd toward her. I hear his soft "excuse me" as he pushes everyone out of the way and they do so happily.

Jonah walks right up to Aliyah, but she doesn't back down. She lifts her chin ever so slightly and stands at her full height, her wings stretching out to make herself bigger. Enzo steps closer to her back, wrapping a hand around her waist from behind.

Jonah's eyes snap to Enzo's before laying back on Aliyah. "Who's the bodyguard?"

"That *bodyguard* is none of your business. All you need to know is that it is in your best interest not to piss me off," she spits.

"You are a creature I have never before laid my eyes upon, and I have seen many, many creatures." Jonah reaches out and takes her hand in his, placing a soft kiss to her knuckles. Her body tenses at the contact and Enzo lets out a low growl. *That's at least one thing we can agree on.* Irritation pitches in my chest not only at the fact that he would so blatantly ignore the king, but also because he is touching *her*. I clench my fists and try to reign in the beast snarling in my chest. Aliyah doesn't need me to defend her, she can smite him all on her own if she so chooses, but it is taking everything in me not to run over there and pull his lips from his mouth.

Jealously burns in my chest at the thought that he has felt her skin on his lips. A feeling that my very being craves to experience for myself again.

The crowd all watch on as Jonah interacts with Aliyah, curiosity beating out what is an acceptable amount of time to stare at someone. Enzo's face is riddled with anger. He takes a step to move around Aliyah, but her left wing shoots out to stop him from proceeding with whatever plan he had to rid this world of Jonah.

"I am *not* a creature."

"Forgive me, my lady, I mean no disrespect," he smirks.

"Then if you'd be so kind, I'd like my hand back please."

"Of course." Jonah drops her hand, but lingers before her still.

"Can I help you with something?" She snaps. "Stop gawking at them. They are just wings."

"I have a tendency to stare at beautiful things far beyond what is considered decent. I wonder though..." His hand extends toward the wings, and a smirk crosses my face at what I know will happen next. The moment his hand connects with the feathers, golden fire cascades down the plumes in rapid succession as they turn to crystalized feathers. Her right wing wraps around her protectively and the crowd gasps in horror as Jonah snaps his hand back.

"Fascinating," he says under his breath. I start to storm down the dais, my resolve having burned away like the feathers on Aliyah's wings.

"Back away! I do not want to disrespect you as my honored guest, but if you irritate her a moment longer, I'll—"

He clearly isn't listening because he reaches out his hand again! *Idiot!*

"Captain Jonah!" I yell. "Don't—"

But it's too late. His hand connects with the crystalline wings and all hell breaks loose. The left wing swings around in a flash, releasing a flurry of sharp dagger like crystals. They land in a flurry at Jonah's feet.

Aliyah stands impassive behind the right wing, completely protected. "That was a warning shot. Reach for my wings again and they won't hesitate to give that thing on your face a friend."

I expect Jonah to back down. To bristle at her disrespect or storm out of the throne room, board his ship, and leave us all to fend for ourselves. Instead, he simply sits back on his heels, shoves his hands in his pockets and smirks. "I like you. This place may just be worth saving after all."

Jonah turns on his heel and makes his way back toward the dais. I return to my throne reluctantly, but the sooner this meeting is over the better. His crew members wait patiently, swords gleaming on their hips, mud tracked through the throne room from where they dragged it in from the sea. I'll have to get someone to re-polish the floors and next time, their shoes come off at the door. I take my seat on the throne and wait for him to approach the bottom step.

"King Kaleron. What a *pleasure* it is to make your acquaintance. I've heard so much about you, but I had not heard about your winged friend. If you had told me you possessed such a fine creature in this kingdom, I would have come much sooner."

"I do not possess anything and that *creature* is fae. A fae that you will not disrespect ever again in my home or I will not hesitate to throw you out of my kingdom and watch as you sail away to that piece of filth you call a home."

His crew draw their swords at my threat, but my guards are faster. Tension hangs in the air, thin enough it could snap at any moment. I don't stand and Jonah's eyes don't leave mine, even as our men prepare to slaughter each other. This is not a battle of steel, but of power, of will, and I refuse to back down.

The doors to the throne room clatter open, Liliana spilling into the space. The entire room falls silent in this moment, and every head turns to watch my sister slowly close the doors behind her, her face cringing at the sound. I shake my head. *Of course she would make an entrance at this very moment.*

She mouths the word *sorry* as she slips around the back of the crowd, making her way to her friends. Jonah's eyes track her movements.

"Sister," I warn. "Thank you for joining us. Please come and meet our guest."

"Oh, 'scuse me, 'scuse me. So sorry, 'scuse me." The room waits as Liliana weaves her way through the crowd. "Pardon me, so sorry I'm late!" She finds herself finally at the edge of the crowd, Jonah standing before her. My guards and his crew still have their weapons drawn, waiting for our command. "What the hell has everyone so on edge?"

"Princess, you are simply exquisite," Jonah inclines his head, but makes no move to bow.

"Oh, um, thanks. So is the deal done?" Liliana looks away from Jonah and up to me.

"No where close to beginning, it seems," I say. I rest my ankle on the knee of my other leg and shift down in the seat to show I am unthreatened by Jonah or his men.

"I had no idea the women of this kingdom were so mesmerizing. It seems every time I turn my head, another beautiful woman appears," Jonah smirks.

"Do you not have beautiful women on the islands?" Lil asks.

"None more beautiful than you," he winks.

A blush creeps up my sisters cheeks and I watch as her eyes flick to Duncan, who stands there, arms across his broad chest, biceps flexing in challenge. I know they aren't together anymore, but their love still shines clear as SunSpark's sun at mid-day.

This time, Jonah does kneel, but not before me, the King of SunSpark, but before my sister. Her eyes grow into huge orbs as she watches him lower onto his knees. "Princess Liliana, may I have the honor of bestowing a kiss upon your hand without the threat of being impaled by crystalline feathers?"

Liliana looks to Aliyah with a smile on her face. "There is never a chance that won't happen, but you can risk it if you'd like." She extends her hand toward his face and he takes it gingerly.

"You seem worth the risk." Jonah takes her hand, his lips connecting with her knuckles.

"Can we get back to business now? I do have a kingdom to run here," I grumble.

Jonah's eyes sparkle as he soaks up the rays beaming off my sister. Her and my brother were always the light in the room, a contrast to the darkness required to be a king.

"What is your offer?" Jonah straightens to his feet, resting his hand on the pommel of his sword. Liliana walks up the steps of the dais, plopping down in the seat next to me looking as if she would rather be anywhere else in the world. She picks at her nails and I try not to scold her in front of our subjects. Usually mother would join us for these events, but she wanted nothing to do with my summons of the conniving Captain Jonah.

"I want you to sail your ships to the gate of The Banished Kingdom in alliance with the SunSpark Flying Legion and cut our enemies off at the knees."

"And what benefit would I get out of this? If rumors are to be believed, Tyros has an army of vile, skeleton-like creatures that he can continue creating despite how many we cut down, making *you* sorely outnumbered."

"Well we wouldn't be outnumbered if you joined our forces. The benefit to you helping us is not letting the evil that plagues this land make it to your doorstep."

"The Islands of Loch would never allow such a fate to fall upon them," Jonah smirks. His crew nod and mumble their agreement, their chests puffed out in pride.

"What would you wish for your alliance?" I grumble.

"Hmmmm," he says, scratching his chin. "I wish to spend some time here in SunSpark. I want to see if this kingdom is worth saving. You will house and feed my crew for as long as we wish to stay here. I will give you my answer when I see fit."

"You do not command a king in his own kingdom!" I assert myself as the ruler I am. Standing, I make my way to the edge of the dais, looking down at the Captain and his men. "You have a fortnight to decide if you will join us. No more. Housing and food will be provided to your men, *pending* they can be civil house guests. If I hear even a *whiff* of hostility toward anyone in my kingdom, you will be lucky to leave here with your lives. You will start this civility by attending the welcome ball tomorrow night. You will have a chance to meet with the leaders of my Flying Legion and the other council members. These are my terms and as *King,* this meeting is officially over. Everyone, OUT!"

Jonah smirks and bows in a mocking posture before spinning on his heel and exiting the throne room with his crew in tow. I storm back to the dais and sit ramrod straight until the entire room has cleared, all except for one.

Aliyah saunters up the steps to join me. I rise, gesturing to the seat I just vacated. If I wish for her to be my queen, I want her to know what it is like to sit in the most powerful seat in the kingdom. When she chooses me, I will burn the current chair of the queen and replace it with one larger than even mine. A chair fit perfectly for *her.*

She sits, her wings shifting uncomfortably behind her as the high back crushes them toward her body. In one swift motion, they push away from her back with force and splinter the wood connecting the top of the throne to its seat. They shudder with the new space around them as if they are pleased with the fact they just broke the throne of the king.

"Better?" I ask.

"Apparently so," she laughs.

"How are you?" I walk behind her, running my finger gingerly up the crest of her wing, watching as the feathers ruffle under my touch. Aliyah's breath hitches and she tips her head to one side, soaking up the feeling.

"I'm adjusting. Sleeping is a bit of a problem, but I'm managing. Sleep doesn't come easily for me anymore. I used to relish in my dreams. The thought of falling asleep and seeing— Well, let's just say I am okay with a dreamless sleep right now. I'm still trying to...figure things out. My mind is so confused, so clouded with what I should do."

I settle behind her, rubbing that spot on her back that I know causes her the most pain. The place where she carries the weight of her wings most. With each muscle knot that relaxes at my touch, so does Aliyah.

"What do you want?"

"What do you mean?" she says, breathless.

"Don't think about what you *should* do. What do you *want?*"

"I...I don't know what I want." She pauses for a moment, thinking about the question. "No, I do know what I want. I want a clear mind. I want a mind and soul unburdened by fate. I want to just be the girl I was back in Mareen."

"You want to be a poor, filthy, thief?" I joke.

"No!" She laughs, elbowing me in the stomach. "I want to be able to do what is best for me without having the burden of someone else's thoughts and feelings tainting the waters of my mind. In Mareen, I didn't have the bond with Saraphena like I did when we arrived in Olyrium. I knew that we were close, but my thoughts were my own. I want that again."

"I wish I could give that to you, but know, with me, your thoughts are your own. Anything you wish to share with me, remains with me. I want to know the deepest, darkest parts of you, Aliyah. I want to know the parts you are afraid to share out loud, because..." I know what I am about to say is a risk, but it's a risk I want to take...for her. "Because I want to see those parts and hold onto every inch of them, because it is in that darkness where I can finally be your light."

"Kaleron, what are you saying?" Aliyah shifts, her wing practically hitting me in the face as she turns. Her dark blue eyes sparkle as that golden ring around her irises hits the light.

"I'm saying—"

A throat clears in the entry way and one of my guards opens the door for the celebration planners to enter. My eyes close, knowing this moment between us is about to end before I can tell her.

"I should go. Liliana is probably looking for me to start designing dresses for tomorrow's ball. You know how she gets about these things." Aliyah stands, shuffling down the steps quickly. She glances over her shoulder before she slips out the door and when our eyes meet, it's then I can see just how weary she's become. I make a mental note to send the healer up to her chambers later to help in any way he can.

Chapter 23

ALIYAH

My heart beats out of my chest as I make my way back to my room. I don't know why I decided to stay behind to check on Kaleron, but there is this part of me that feels safe around him. When he pulled me out of that coffin, I wanted it to be anyone else but him, but the feeling when he held me, the feeling that I was safe, is too strong to ignore. Every moment we have shared since then has made me rethink everything I know. Everything I wanted for myself.

You okay, little dove? Enzo. The man I'm supposed to love, but do I love him still? I can't trust that the bond between us is allowing me to see clearly. They say forgive and forget, but I don't know if I can ever forget what he did. Forgiveness used to come easy for me; Saraphena lying to me for 26 years? Forgiven. Enzo kidnapping me and getting an ax buried in my chest? Forgiven. Kaleron poisoning my best friend? Surprisingly, forgiven. But Enzo hearing me scream down the bond day after day and never coming for me? I don't know if I'm ready to forgive that.

I'm fine, just tired. Heading to find Liliana and Saraphena. I'm sure Liliana wants to get our dress designs in as soon as possible.

Let me know if you need me for anything. I love you, Aliyah.

Those words. Three little words that carry the weight of the world.

I love you, too. Can you love someone without being *in* love with them? When he speaks those words to me, they constrict on my heart like a vice and suck the air out of my lungs, the same as when my own breath ate up the oxygen in that coffin. I need to breathe air that Enzo doesn't share with me.

I run my hand down the golden swirled wall, and the similarity between the wall and the swirls on my own body does not go unnoticed. Maybe this is where I'm meant to be.

"How did you get them?" A familiar voice breaks through my thoughts. I whip around toward the sound, but my wing catches on a pillar stand that holds up the marble head of a previous king. It clatters to the ground and breaks on impact.

"Son of —" I move to clean up the pieces, my wing catching another pillar sending what looks like the realms most ancient vase careening toward the marble floor. "Maker!" I reach for it, but Captain Jonah beats me to it, catching the relic in his scarred hands.

"It seems you lack a basic awareness of what's around you," Jonah laughs, his hand brushing mine as he passes the vase back to me.

When my eyes find Jonah's the vase is back on the small pillar. When did I put that back? Haze sweeps across my mind as I try and place the events that just occurred in order.

"Yes, clearly they seem to have a mind of their own," I smile, masking my confusion of the moment.

Jonah laughs, the sound light and full of life. "Apparently so. They are simply remarkable though! One day you must tell me the story of how you obtained such a magnificent gift."

"I wouldn't exactly call them a gift," I huff.

"On the contrary! Your wings are something to behold. They are something that should be on display for all to see," he smiles. Jonah seems innocent enough, earnest even, but I can't help the prickle coiling up my neck.

"If you'll excuse me, I am meant to be meeting my friends."

"Oh, of course. I don't mean to keep you. I look forward to getting to know you better in the coming weeks." Jonah nods his head in reverence before disappearing down the hallway. As soon as he is out of sight, I note how heavy my wings feel on my back.

"Can't you pull it together for once?! One of these days you're going to get me killed with your lack of awareness," I mumble back to them. I walk down the hallway that holds our rooms, mumbling to my wings as I go like a crazy person. "Then again it isn't like I can die anyways so I guess you'd be off the hook for that one, but honestly can you just *pretend* to be normal for like five minutes."

My wings don't shutter, or quiver, or flutter in the normal way they would when I scold them, but as I push open the door to my room Liliana and Saraphena wait with sketch pads and wine, my wings current state forgotten.

"Just like old times, huh?" I ask, closing the door behind me.

"Let's just hope we don't have a repeat from last time! You barely got to enjoy the ball!" Lil laughs.

"I'm pretty sure I had the worst time at the last ball," Saraphena quips.

"Okay...true, BUT this time is going to be better! I can feel it in my bones!" Liliana's smile brightens.

I plop down on the bed beside them, my over protective body guard oddly cooperative behind me. "I think I'm going to need a bigger bed," I laugh.

"Yeah, yeah, we can talk about that later. I'll have Kaleron send for one. Right *noooowww,* we need to focus on our dresses!"

"Liliana, I have dresses already hung in the closet. I don't need anymore." Saraphena teases Lil, knowing it will get a rise out of her.

"*Those* dresses?! Absolutely not! You've already worn those ones! We need *new* dresses! It isn't every day we get to attend a ball together! Plus, I've already got the designs in my head and if I don't bring them to life I might just EXPLODE!" Liliana motions her hands like an explosion is going off in her head.

"All right, all right, but you know I can't draw for anything so I trust you to design me something spectacular!" I say.

"This is your big debut! Kaleron said this party was for Captain Jonah, but it's really your *surprise-I'm-not-really-dead* party! You have to look absolutely fabulous!" Liliana begins sketching something down on the pad and I take this opportunity to pour us all glasses of wine. Taking a sip, I practically moan at the taste of blackberry and melon as it rolls around on my tongue.

The three of us sit in silence as Liliana finishes up the sketches for our dresses. A few hours later, and several bottles of wine later, they are bounding out of my room and back to their respective sleeping quarters. A soft knock comes at the door and my heart wars with itself over who I hope it will be.

"Come in," I call.

"Ehhem," a throat clears. "Good evening, my lady. King Kaleron sent me to perform a check-up on you and provide any assistance I can."

"Oh, that's um, thank you. Please come in." I note the old man's robes and withered appearance. "Are you a healer?"

"Of sorts," he smiles. He places his bag down on the foot of my bed before pulling a chair over to his side. "Would you mind sitting here so I can inspect you?"

"*Inspect* me?"

"Apologies, apologies! I mean no disrespect!"

"It seems a lot of people are saying that to me lately," I mumble. Slipping off my bed, I make my way over to the chair, my wings heavy as they unfurl behind it so I can rest my back on the chair.

"Do I have permission to evaluate you, my dear?"

"I say yes, but Sparky behind me might have something different to say about it, so I make no promises." I roll my eyes as my wings shift lazily behind me.

"I'll do my best to keep them calm," he smiles.

"Do you have a name or should I just call you 'the healer'?"

"My name is Bairastyn, milady. You may call me as such," he smiles.

"Why did Kaleron send you here?"

"The king was worried about your health, my dear. My speciality is in potions, poisons, and all things mystical in nature."

"If your specialty is poisons, how do I know I can trust you to give me something safe?" I laugh.

"Oh my dear child, I much prefer my head attached to my body and I fear if I let any harm fall to you, King Kaleron would have my head on a spike by sundown," he quips.

"I suppose that's fair." I can't help the smile that creeps onto my face. Bairastyn reminds me of Marigold. *I miss her.*

"So what seems to be troubling you most?" His hands inspect the scars on my back before moving to check on my wings.

"I wouldn't touch them if I were you."

"I saw what happened in the throne room earlier. I wouldn't dream of touching them." His muffled laugh catches in his throat and he coughs a few times before continuing his exploration. "If you don't mind me saying so, you appear to have no physical ailments upon my evaluation. How are you *emotionally?*"

"That's a difficult question. I was locked in an iron grave for three months, burning alive every few days, begging my mate to come save me down the bond. My heart is conflicted on what I want most."

"Dear...that...I don't even know what to say to that. You must have been forced to do...unspeakable things...inside that box."

My mind shutters at the memories of the time in my living hell. *Clawing at the lid. Nails breaking. Starring at my own flesh, willing myself to rip a piece off just to have something in my belly. Never being able to bring myself to do it. Screaming until my throat was raw. Catching my tears with my tongue just to taste water one last time before darkness consumed me, again.*

"Yes...unspeakable things." I catch myself staring off beyond the healer. I snap back into reality and give a soft smile. "I'm afraid the thing I want most, you cannot help me with. I've spent hours combing the libraries, and what I wish cannot be done."

"What do you wish?"

"I wish...I wish I no longer had my mate bond."

The healer doesn't judge. He doesn't scoff or draw back in horror. He doesn't even bat an eye at the thought of ripping out a piece of me that others might hold so dearly. He takes time to consider my request.

"I believe it can be done."

My heart stops. "What did you say?"

"I think I may be able to find a way to break the bond, but it is not scientific in nature, but more...formulative. I will have to use several different spells at once and even then, it may not work perfectly. You may not survive."

I don't know what to say. Before this wasn't even an option. A thought or a wish, but never a possibility. Is this actually what I want?

"Do I have to give you an answer today? Can this stay between us?"

"My mind," he says tapping the side of his head, "it's like a vault." His smile is soft and I know I can trust him. "The option is out there, if it is what you truly wish."

I can't sleep. Thoughts race through my head. I weight every option. Every choice. Every *feeling*. As heaviness weighs on my eyelids and my mind is threatened with sleep I wish would not come, I know what I wish. Tomorrow I will give Bairastyn my answer.

Chapter 24

ENZO

I don't know how the girls sit around all day reading these tomes. The history of our kingdoms is dreadfully boring and I find myself reading the same paragraph over and over again, lost in thought. I wanted to help find a way to bring down the pillar that connects The Banished Kingdom to Twilight Kingdom, but so far I have come up with nothing. It's like Aramot pulled a spell out of his butt and hoped it would work to repair the Bridge.

I was still a soldier when the War of Worlds ended, so I was never brought into the fold of how the pillar was brought down the first time. In present circumstances however, couldn't The Banished King simply sail across the expanse to get here? Would bringing the pillar down really matter that much?

Originally, it was imperative to take down the pillar because of the barrier around the island, but when the barrier dissipated the day Aliyah died, there is nothing stopping Tyros from taking over now. There isn't enough research in the world to make a difference for bringing down the pillar. Either way Tyros will have to cross the Twilight or sail to another kingdom. Which I suppose is why Kaleron is trying to buy an alliance with Captain Jonah. *Why did Kaleron have to come up with such a good plan?* I want to hate him so much, but I can't deny his battle skills are impeccable. Unfortunately, he was a huge help when we fought The Kalari in Rory's village. I know we will need him in the battle to come. *Dang it. This means I can't kill him...yet.*

How has Aliyah taken such a liking to him? Why can she forgive him so easily, but not me? He tried to kill her best friend! He tried to kill *her!* Yet, I am the one she cannot forgive. It's taking everything in me to give her the space she needs to work through her demons. All I want to do is fight them for her, to take away the darkness that plagues her mind.

I know she feels the pull of the bond as I do, yet she denies what is between us. It isn't anger that burns through my consciousness however, it's confusion. I knew what I felt for her the moment I laid eyes on her. I knew there was something special between us, how can she forget so easily?

"Think any harder and you'll pop a blood vessel." Gunnar claps me on the back before dropping into the couch opposite me, Duncan materializing next to him in an instant.

"He's brooding, don't you see the *dark and mysterious male persona* pouring off him in waves that will drown us all?" Duncan quips.

"So lovely to see you two banding together to point out my complete dismay over Aliyah." I roll my eyes, slamming the tome down beside me.

"Gosh, what did that book ever do to you?" Gunnar asks.

"What is the point in bringing down the pillar connecting The Banished Kingdom to Olyrium if Tyros can simply sail across? We know he still has allies in Olyrium, who is to say he won't use them to get ships?"

"Do you think we are wasting resources trying to find answers?" Duncan asks.

I stare into the fire before me, getting lost in the flames. "I don't know. What I do know is every day his army gets bigger and if we can't find allies of our own to bring him down, we are going to lose this war."

"So we forget the pillar and focus on building our own strength. Kaleron is already trying to convince Jonah to join, so hopefully he can find an enticing enough outcome that he agrees to work with us. We have recruits in Citrine and our numbers grow every day. Duncan has allies in Twilight who are waiting for his call to fight. What more can we do?" Gunnar asks.

"Jonah seems pretty *enticed* by Liliana." My eyes flick to Duncan to see his reaction.

"Enzo you savage," Gunnar laughs. "Don't push our little Duncan to such dark places. We all know he made a huge mistake but is too stubborn to admit it out loud to her."

"I did not make a mistake! I made a permanent solution to a temporary issue! I forgot how stubborn, thick-headed, irritating, and frustrating of a woman she can be!" Duncan booms.

"You're daft if you thought for one moment Liliana was going to do as you say. She loves this family, but she loves defying your wishes more. Liliana doesn't take direction from anyone," Gunnar laughs.

"Enough about Liliana! It's hard enough as it is..." Duncan trails off.

"Okay well one brooding male down, one to go. Enzo, why are you not fighting for Aliyah?" he asks.

"She doesn't want me to! She asked for space and that is exactly what I am giving to her!"

"You can't be serious? Enzo, of course she wants you to fight for her! Space to work out her troubles, fine, but she *loves* you man. If anything, all she ever wanted was for you to fight for her! You have to think about this from her perspective. She had no idea you were here trying to find a way to bring her back from the dead. All she knew is her screaming down the bond for you to come save her, and you ignored her," Gunnar adds.

"I did not ignore her!"

"Yes, Enzo, you did," Duncan says softly.

My power flares, poised right at my finger tips, begging to be unleashed upon them, but I made a vow when Aliyah came back that I would not hurt anyone else in her name. "I. Did. Not. Ignore. Her."

"Enzo, listen to me. Aliyah laid in a grave every day burning alive and when she got her wings, they protected her from daily death, but it left her to starve to death instead. Neither of you are in the wrong for how you feel. You were doing what you thought was best and she was hoping you would fight for her." Gunnar pauses, gauging if I was going to slaughter him or not.

He carefully continues. "Sometimes we do things without the intention to hurt someone we love, but it doesn't mean they won't get hurt in the end. From Aliyah's perspective, you left her. From your perspective, you were doing everything you could to bring her back. Neither one is wrong, but you *both* will have to work together to fix it. The question becomes, are you still willing to do whatever it takes to get her back?"

"I don't know how to give her space and fight for her." It pains me to admit my weakness, but if I am going to stand a chance in hell of getting her back, I know I need help. "I don't know what to do."

Duncan sighs, "don't ask me what to do. Apparently I've messed everything the hell up with the woman I love."

"You both just need to be the men they fell in love with! Open your eyes, people! They fell in love with you for a reason! Duncan, you let Liliana be free. You fought side by side with her in Twilight against Aramot and you saw how formidable she was on her own, but she was even stronger with you by her side. She is safe wherever you are because she knows you won't let anything happen to her." Gunnar knocks his shoulder into Duncan with a smile.

"And you! Aliyah fell in love with you because you were unapologetically in love with her! You freaking kidnapped her for Maker's sake! All because you knew how much you wanted her. You showed her your world and when you saw the trauma deep inside her, you didn't question her past, you didn't push her to share or be okay with what happened...you were just *there*. You loved her through it all. I watched you lay with her cold, dead body for hours because letting go was too painful. You have a second chance with her. Let her work through her troubles at her own pace, but for Maker's sake man, LOVE THE WOMAN OPENLY!"

"Maker, Gunnar! There is no need to yell about it! But what do I *do?!*"

"You both need to show your women how brightly your love burns for them! Duncan, tell Liliana you were wrong. Show her that every day for all your days, you will *choose her*. Enzo, stand by Aliyah's side. Be the rock she leans on when she needs it most. But most importantly, take every thread of love she will give you. Eventually you will be able to take all those threads and knit your future back together until it is whole again."

"Gunnar what the heck does that even mean?" Duncan quips.

"I don't know, but you know what I mean!" He laughs.

"How did we get to the point where Gunnar is giving us relationship advice?" I roll my eyes.

"I'm a married man now, my friends. I am officially the relationship expert of the group! Plus, I am the *master* of diabolical plans, and tonight, you will proposition your ladies and hope to hell they take your sorry butts back!"

"I am genuinely afraid of the plans you have for us," I cringe.

"Gentlemen!" Gunnar jumps onto the couch, standing above us, and throwing his fist in the air as if we are going into war. "Put on your finest suits and your best dancing shoes! For tonight, we are going into battle! We will fight for our women! Some of us may die, and victory is unlikely, but tonight we put it all on the line! Strap on your armor! Sharpen your swords! We are going to a ball!"

Chapter 25

KALERON

The gold buttons on my white suit glimmer in the candlelight from the chandeliers above us. Couples spin and dance on the ballroom floor, colors swirling together like the perfect paintings hung on the walls of the room. But it all drops away the moment I see her making her way through the room. Bright blue eyes sparkle with the promise of my downfall and a smile that could steal my breath away forever.

Aliyah's hair has been left down tonight, and the black exposed corseted dress clings to every curve of her body, but I don't miss the dagger strapped to her thigh which peeks out with each step through the slit of her dress. Her wings are on full display and she glides through the room as if walking on air. She looks *happy.*

Standing up from my throne, I make my way down the steps, pushing the crowd aside to have a direct path to her. My sister and Saraphena have their arms looped through hers, but if I don't feel her skin on mine in the next breath, my world may cease to exist.

"Dance with me," I say. Her eyes catch on mine, but it's my sister who responds.

"Yeah right, brother! She's ours for the night. You'll have to pry her from my cold, dead—"

"Sister, need I remind you that I can cut off your shopping allowance?"

"She's all yours!" Liliana pushes Aliyah in my direction, giving her an apologetic smile.

"Good to know what I'm worth to you, Lil," she laughs.

"My shopping allowance benefits both of us, so it's a lose-lose if he takes it away! Go have fun, we will find you later!" Lil calls back as she grabs Saraphena's hand and guides her across the room toward the buffet.

"You look absolutely delectable this evening," I say, my voice dropping so only she can hear.

"You clean up nice yourself, Your Majesty." Aliyah winks, running her fingers down the front of my suit. Her wings extend to their full width behind her and shutter. They are so large, everyone behind Aliyah is completely blocked out.

"You look lovely too, Sparky," I say, stepping into Aliyah's space to run my hand down her wing. They settle instantly, laying comfortably back down along her spine.

"You're going to give them a complex if you keep doing that," Aliyah says, stepping further into me so she has to look up at me when she speaks.

"The only thing more beautiful in this world than those wings are the woman they are attached to." I reach out, running my thumb along her bottom lip before moving my hand to grab the nape of her neck.

My other hand snakes along her lower back, feeling how her dress dips all the way down to the base of her spine, allowing my hand to connect with the soft flesh of her body. A low groan escapes my lips and my eyes flutter shut at the way her body arches into mine.

The music crescendos along with the beat of my heart. Pulling Aliyah into me, I swing her body to the side, still grasping the back of her neck as I pull her into a dip. Using my Maker-given strength, I hold her and her wings with no effort at all. Her head falls back as I deepen the move, and I can't help but lean in and run my nose along the length of her exposed neck.

As I pull her back up, I push her out into a spin before bringing her back in, her back pressed to my chest, her wings dropped low so I can speak into her ear.

"This takes me back to our first ball together."

"Only no one will be poisoned or beheaded tonight," she says, a playful, but serious tone to her voice.

"The night is still young," I wink. "Hopefully you won't be fleeing from me either."

"That all depends on if you behave yourself," she laughs. "Though tonight I am here with you under completely different circumstances. The first being of my own free will and not after being threatened. Destiny always seems to have a sense of humor."

"Stay with me tonight," I whisper.

"Kal, I—"

"Don't answer now. Think about it." I push her out once more, grasping her delicate fingers and lacing them through mine as I lead her through the dance. "There is no pressure, we can just sleep and add one more secret between us," I tease.

Her breath hitches. "You're the king," she breathes.

"And every inch of you is beautiful, every inch, every scar, every swirl."

"Kal, you have a kingdom to run."

"And I'm falling in love with you." I drag her into my body, her eyes wide as saucers.

"You can't say things like that, Kal." Aliyah begins to look around to make sure no one hears us, but I don't care if the world knows my feelings for Aliyah have grown. I use my thumb and forefinger to drag her chin back so she is looking at me.

"I thought we were stating obvious things," I smirk. "Tell me you don't feel this. Tell me I'm wrong and that there is nothing between us. Tell me you aren't falling in love with me too."

The room continues to spin around us, bodies moving on beat with the music flowing around us like a river around a rock in the stream.

"Kal, I—"

"Aliyah! Come on, you *have* to dance with us! This is my favorite song!" Liliana snatches Aliyah from my grasp and I watch as she gets pulled into the crowd. Our eyes connect across the room as she looks back at me one final time.

I leave the dance floor and make my way back toward the dais. My eyes can't leave her as she spins around the room with my sister and her best friend. I feel a slight tinge of guilt knowing that I've just lied to her, because I'm not just falling for Aliyah. I am completely, utterly, irrevocably in love with her.

Chapter 26

LILIANA

I always loved attending balls. The music, the laughter, the drinks, but most of all, I loved the dancing. The feeling of having the music envelop your soul and set you free within the rhythm, it's intoxicating. Saraphena's hand is clasped in mine and Aliyah's is held in the other. We spin in a circle, shoes forgotten, and let the music fuel our joy. *I can't believe we are all together again.*

My heart feels lighter than it has been in some time. I let my eyes drift around the room instinctively looking for him. I find him almost immediately, as if my heart knew the direction I would find him. He's wearing a smart black tunic shirt that is fitted perfectly to his body and his leather pants show off just how sculpted his thighs are. My mouth waters at the sight, remembering how his body used to feel under my touch. I shake my head and return to the moment. Tonight isn't about him, it's about being with my best friends.

The song ends, and as the musicians begin their next ministration, I take note of the slow tempo. Enzo approaches

Aliyah, whispering something in her ear. She gives a soft smile and they turn, finding a space together on the dance floor. Couples begin finding each other on the dance floor and I use this opportunity to take my leave.

"I'm going to go grab a drink," I say close to Saraphena's ear so she can hear me. She nods and when I step away, I turn back to see Gunnar spinning her in circles, a huge grin plastered on her face. I glance over to where Aliyah dances with Enzo. They look deep in conversation, yet she isn't angry or upset, just enraptured in all that is Enzo. She looks genuinely happy for the first time in a long time. Tonight, Aliyah's traumas don't haunt her. Tonight, my best friend is free.

I snag a bubbly drink off a passing tray and find my way to the edge of the crowd. Leaning against the wall, I shift my weight back and forth, giving my feet a break from dancing so long.

"She looks happy, doesn't she?" Duncan's voice caresses my ears.

I don't take my eyes off Aliyah for fear that I will lose myself in Duncan's gaze. Even now, even after everything, I still love him. I'll never admit it to him out loud, not until he chooses me *and* his kingdom, but he is still my King of Shadows.

"I hope she is. After everything she has been through, she deserves a night of peace." I take a sip of my drink, hoping to find some courage at the bottom of the glass.

"If you're not otherwise occupied, I would sell my soul for a dance with you, Sunshine."

"I thought I told you not to call me that anymore." I still can't bring myself to look at him.

His finger finds my chin and forces my eyes to gaze upon his. My lips part on a breath as I soak in his features. I haven't let myself look at him this way since that day in Jade's room when he said he wished we never met. I *can't* look at him this way. Not until he says the words.

"Dance with me, Princess Liliana."

"Ugh, that's even worse," I laugh. "But fine, I'll dance with you, *King* Duncan."

His eyes darken at my words, but he removes the glass from my hand and offers me his arm. "Shall we?"

He leads us through the throng of people. His broad shoulders creating space around us as we move through the crowd. When he turns, my knees turn to mush and something deep pulls in my chest. He bends at the waist and offers his hand. I curtsy in turn and take it before he spins me right into his chest. His smell wraps around me like a comforting blanket and suddenly, we are the only two people in the room.

His calloused hand engulfs mine and here, wrapped up in all that is Duncan, I'm safe. The bright light of SunSpark is no more and Duncan and I spin and twirl amongst the stars. Maybe the whole time I was never his sunshine, but instead, I was the comet in his night sky. No matter this chasm between us now, we are born of the cosmos. Born to burn brightly in the endless abyss forever. I feel it in my heart of hearts. Duncan is my forever, just like I promised him.

The ballroom comes back into focus around me and the reality of our relationship crashes in along with it. "Have you heard anything about how the Twilight Kingdom has been doing?"

Duncan's brow furrows as he looks down at me. "The village leaders who chose to come and live at the palace tell me things are going well, but they continue to urge me to claim the title officially."

"It sounds like the kingdom is ready to have you, whether you think they do or not," I smile.

"I know." The seriousness in Duncan's tone gives me pause. "Duncan—"

"No, Liliana. Not tonight. Tonight, I just want to be with you in this moment. I take back what I said about wishing we never met. That was cruel and I'm sorry, but tonight, can we just be *us?* Just for a little while longer."

I stare into his eyes for a moment, contemplating my answer. There is still so much left to be said between us, so much to fix. But I need this moment between us more than I thought I did. I swallow my pride and break every promise I've made to myself about Duncan.

"I choose you, Duncan. Time and time again, I will always choose you. No matter how long it takes, no matter how long you need, I will always be right here, choosing you."

Water brims in Duncan's eyes and for a moment, I think he is going to cry. I don't know when we stopped dancing, but it's as if the whole room is suspended in time as I wait for what he will say next.

"Liliana, your brother brought to light some things I denied the existence of before because I thought I was doing the right thing for you. I know I said I wanted to be just us tonight, but I want us to be *us* every night. I want to hold you in my arms as I fall asleep and I want to kiss away your nightmares as I wake. I want to stand before my people as king and then kneel in reverence as you take your place as queen beside me. I want to enter The Above and stand before the Maker and thank Him for allowing me a second chance at the love I never deserved after the things I've done. I want to dance amongst the stars with you for all eternity until the time comes for us to leave this world and take our place amongst the constellations. Even in death, others in love will look to the sky and see us burning for each other. I just. Want. You."

"I need to hear you say it."

"Liliana, I choose—"

Bright golden light bursts around us, the tether which will connect us for life snapping into place in my chest. A tear drips from my eye. I never knew someone could have two mates, but the Maker truly has blessed us with a second chance.

Duncan?

My heart stops as Duncan takes a step away from me, dropping his hands to his sides.

"What's wrong? Are you upset we are mates? I would never dream of replacing Zorellya, but maybe—" I don't understand his facial expression. He looks almost...in pain.

Voices mutter behind me and I spin around the room and watch as the crowd parts. I snap my head back in the direction of Duncan, but I'm met with his back facing me as he weaves his way through the crowd. I turn back, the bond between us is getting stronger as he walks away, but that doesn't make sense. He was about to choose me. He was going to say the words I desperately wanted to hear. We were about to have our second chance, but then...

Liliana, my unexpected mate.

A hand lands on my shoulder, turning me to face the one the crowd was parting for. He stands before me now, a broad smile across his face as he takes me in. I'm *his* mate.

"Jonah," I breathe.

Chapter 27

ALIYAH

"Dance with me," Enzo says into my ear.

I leave Saraphena and Liliana on the dance floor and let Enzo guide me to a spot of our own. "You look very handsome tonight."

"Thank you. It was Gunnar's suggestion we all look our best tonight," he smiles.

"Why?"

"I've been a fool, Aliyah. I didn't see things from your perspective and let my anger get the best of me. I didn't know how to show you love *and* give you space, but I'd like the chance to try. I want to be here for you Aliyah. I want to be there for you through the nightmares, to help you fight the darkness, and to fight for you now when I didn't fight for you before. I was stuck in my own perspective...I was wrong. Is there any hope for us?"

Guilt sits heavy on my chest as I think of the words Kal spoke to me. I can't sort out my feelings for him. Enzo is my mate, the man who loved me despite my past and accepted the dark corners of my mind and showed me that I can be loved. Yet now that love is tainted from months in the ground. Then there is Kal, the man who poisoned my best friend, killed Marigold to maintain appearances as King, but came for me when no one else did. Yet my feelings are as unclear for him as they are for Enzo. Am I starting to have feelings for Kal because I see a future for us, or was he simply the first person I latched onto after being alone all those months? If it had been Enzo who pulled me from the grave, would I still think of Kal?

The silence stretches between us as I war with the thoughts spinning in my brain. I do know one thing for certain, I need my head clear and my heart untethered to truly see clearly what future I want for myself.

"Enzo, my sweet, sweet ZoZo. I want there to be hope for us. It isn't that I don't accept your apology, or that I don't understand your motives for not coming for me. I think that's why it's so difficult for me to resist the bond between us, because there *is* hope for us, just not now. I have so much I need to sort out within myself."

"Then let me help you sort it out. I will do *anything* to make this right between us."

"Do you mean that? You would do anything?"

Without hesitation he replies. "Yes."

My resolve waivers, but only for a moment. Before I can respond, a bright light bursts through the room and I snap around to see who's mate bond has awoken. I see Liliana and Duncan standing facing each other and my heart explodes with joy that they are finally together. But when the light fades, Duncan is walking away. *Why is Duncan walking away?*

Jonah parts the crowd, walking toward Liliana. The breath leaves my lungs and I stumble into Enzo's arms as I realize what has happened.

"Jonah," Liliana mutters.

"In all the realms, I never thought my mate would be someone as beautiful as you. Maybe I should have come to SunSpark sooner and we could have had years together already." Jonah wipes the tears from Liliana's face and it's clear the horror she is feeling right now.

Enzo, do something. This can't be her mate. She is supposed to end up with Duncan.

There is nothing to be done, my dove. The mate bond is sealed for life.

I send a prayer up to the Maker to change her fate, to take back the bond between them. My wings shift behind me, crystalized feathers taking their place. "Not now, Sparky!" I mutter back to them.

Liliana turns and sprints from the ballroom, a soft sob on her lips as she goes. Kaleron appears next to me in an instant demanding to know what just happened.

"Liliana loves Duncan, but she bonded with Jonah. Do something, Kaleron. Please!" I beg. His soft eyes look into mine, confirming there is nothing to be done.

"I'm sorry, Aliyah. Even kings cannot control the bond." He gives my arm a light squeeze and Enzo steps up closer beside me, a growl on his lips as he wraps an arm around me protectively.

"Both of you stop. I don't have time to deal with this fight right now when Liliana is clearly hurting."

They both take a step back from me, but their eyes don't leave each other.

"King Kaleron!" Jonah makes his way toward us and the men around me are forced out of their contest to see who will back down first. "I know the terms of my alliance with SunSpark Kingdom against The Banished King."

"You've decided so quickly? You still have time to see the kingdom," Kaleron says hesitantly.

"I have seen all I need. I will send my ships to aid your Flying Legion against The Banished King whenever you call upon them. In return, I want a year's supply of seeds for The Islands of Loch, safe refuge for anyone coming from the islands should this war turn south, and lastly, when I return to my home...my mate to go with me, as my *wife*."

"Kaleron, this is insanity! We don't even know him! You know the kind of place The Islands of Loch can be! You cannot willingly send our sister back there!" Gunnar yells.

"What do you want me to do, Gunnar!? I don't like it either, but I have an entire kingdom to look out for!" Kaleron yells back.

Enzo, Kaleron, Gunnar, Saraphena, and I sit around the war table in Kaleron's council room. I'm still in shock over the events at the ball. Apparently we can never just have a normal evening which doesn't end in yelling or an all out brawl.

I haven't been able to find the words to describe how horrible this has become. I know what it is like to be confused over a bond with someone. To question if you should end up with them just because a magical tether told you to do so.

"Gunnar's right, we don't know anything about Captain Jonah, but we do know what kind of people come out of those islands," Saraphena adds.

"Jonah has shown us no signs of ill intent toward others. Sure, he may have grown up in a volatile place, but so did Aliyah, and Duncan, and Enzo, yet they all wouldn't lay a hand on someone they love," Kaleron says.

"Don't be so sure," Duncan grimaces. "Sometimes we are pushed into things we would never consider."

"Either way, I've done my research on Jonah. Everyone says he is a kind, confident, leader. Not a single bad word has been spoken about him. His father and mother raised two other boys alongside him and they never mentioned anything concerning."

"That should concern you even more! No one has spoken a single bad word about him? What if he pays them off to say nice things?!" Gunnar spirals.

"Gunnar, be rational. You're letting *what if's* take over. I have not agreed to his terms yet. I will place a clause in them that he must remain in SunSpark for the remaining days of our agreement and he must take time to get to know Liliana. This will give us a chance to see what his motives are," Kaleron says.

"That's not good enough!" Gunnar yells.

Enzo places his hand on his friend's knee in a show of comfort. "Gunnar, what is this really about?"

"It's about the fact he wants Duncan to end up with Liliana, but I have a kingdom to think about. I cannot think of only one person, even if it is my sister. I need to do what is best for SunSpark...what is best for *Olyrium.*" Kaleron paces in front of the fire and part of me feels bad for the weight of being a ruler that is thrust upon him. He has to make the hard decisions, even if no one else agrees with him.

"It just...it isn't fair," Gunnar says through his teeth.

"Enough." Liliana comes into the room, her eyes red and puffy from crying. Her voice is soft and filled with dread. "I agree with Kaleron. He has to think of his people...of *my* people. If I can help in ending this war before it has even begun, then I will do so. I was foolish to think I could escape the fate of a ruler. Sometimes we have to be pawns sacrificed for the long game. I'd like some time to get to know Jonah, so if he agrees, I accept the plan of him staying for the next several days. I will make an effort to get to know him. He is my mate after all."

"Liliana, you don't have to do this," Saraphena pleads.

"Yes I do," she says looking toward Duncan with a wince. "I must now choose my kingdom as Duncan chose his."

Saraphena stands, pulling Liliana into a tight embrace. I move to join them and the three of us stand there hugging, knowing our lives are forever altered. The others leave the room, but Kaleron lingers by the door.

"I'm going to go to my room. I think I just need to be alone," Liliana says. She gives Kaleron a nod as she steps into the hall. Saraphena gives my hand a squeeze before letting me know she is going to calm Gunnar down. I am left standing with Kaleron.

"I'm sorry I couldn't do more," he says.

"I know you have to do what is best for the kingdom, but I don't envy your position. I trust you, I'm just not sure I trust Jonah yet. I hope you're right about him."

"Me too." Kaleron sighs before continuing. "My mother has been away on a diplomatic mission and has just arrived home. She heard you were here and would like a word with you before you turn in for the night. She is in her room. Would you like me to escort you there?"

"I would love that," I smile. Kaleron leads me from the war room and through the hallways toward his mother's quarters. I have a strange sense of déjà vu.

"I never thanked you for sending that healer to my room. He was incredibly helpful."

"Always happy to be of assistance. Did he heal what ailed you most?"

"More like treating a symptom of a larger issue. Though I'm not sure the treatment will work, but I have to try."

"I'm here, whenever you need me," he smiles.

"I know. I wouldn't be here without you. You've done so much for me, Kaleron. I feel...safe...with you. And believe me, the irony of that is not lost on me. I'm forever grateful you found me that day and the friendship you have shown me ever since."

"I'm not just falling in love with you. I *am* in love with you, Aliyah."

"What?" We both stop walking, shock registering in my system. Surely I heard him wrong.

"I know you have a mate and I know you cannot give me that bond, but every day we move closer to a war I am not sure we can win. I needed you to know how I felt, even if you don't feel the same way right now. After watching my sister and Duncan be torn apart because he didn't express his feelings sooner, I know now what needs to be said."

"Kaleron, don't do this. Please don't take away the one place I feel safe right now. Let me sort out what is already in my mind first."

"I know the position I'm putting you in by admitting my feelings. I don't expect anything in return, but I need you to know that if ever given another fate, I would happily stand by your side as both friend...and lover."

"I can't do this right now. Please don't make me more confused than I already am. I'm trying to do what is best for *me* and I can't compromise that." I push on through the hall, wanting this conversation to be over as quickly as possible before he can ruin anything else between us.

"Then don't. Do what you need to do for you, but know that I will always love you. You are a part of me, Aliyah. I've seen it. What I said to you the night of the ball is still true, our futures are intertwined for life. When I lost you, I thought the fates might have been wrong about my future, but here you are. It has to mean something."

We arrive at his mothers room in perfect timing. "I'm sorry, Kaleron. I can't do this right now. I can't lose you as my friend, so please don't make me choose right now."

"I won't, but when you're ready, I'll be here."

Opening the door to his mother's room, I glance back at my safe haven. The only person who has made me feel normal in the past few weeks, the only person who wasn't complicated until recently. I close the door behind me and take a moment to pull my thoughts together. Meeting with Queen Starla always came with a twist, and I expect nothing less this time around.

"Aliyah? Is that you?"

"Hello, Queen Starla. How was your trip?" I ask, walking into her sitting room. The walls still sparkle with black gems, painting the room like the night sky of her home kingdom.

"Fine, fine. Do you still have the ring I gave you?" She asks hurriedly.

"Yes, I was buried with it. I haven't taken it off my finger since you gave it to me." My eyebrow quirks up in confusion.

"Thank the Maker. Aliyah you must *never* lose that ring. Is this how you came back from the grave? Did you use it to make a wish where you could never die?"

"What? No, I— Queen Starla, you aren't making any sense. My power is that of immortality. I die, but rise again from the grave. I didn't make a wish. It's just a ring, Your Majesty."

"That is not just any ring! That is the lost relic of Twilight! I assumed the Reflecting Pool showed me giving it to you because you would need it, but here you are not even knowing what you carried with you the whole time!"

"So you're saying I could have wished myself out of the grave?" How many times had I begged to be set free? Said the words *I wish for anything to get out of here.*

"Unless you had access to the heart of an innocent in that grave, you would have been unable to wish on it," she says flatly.

"Wait, what?" My brain is trying to put the pieces together, but she isn't making any sense. Queen Starla paces around the room, clearly in distress. "Why are you so panicked?"

"If that ring had fallen into the wrong hands. If The Banished King knew you possessed it...you mustn't tell anyone you have that ring Aliyah! Is that clear? I have spoken too much already...I assumed...I assumed you knew what you carried after your friends stole the pages from my collection."

"Your collection? Queen Starla, you aren't making any sense."

"Kaleron took the pages that detailed how the ring worked and all the rulers who did horrible things to grant their wishes. The thousands that died for riches or glory or compliance of the people. I took it. I took the ring when I left Twilight to stop it from falling into the wrong hands once more. I may not be the queen in Twilight, but those are still my people. They had suffered enough. I guarded that ring for hundreds of years. When I passed it onto you, I figured you must be capable of keeping it safe. No one must know of the ring you possess, do you understand me? Never let it out of your sight, not even for a moment. It was good they buried it with you."

"They...they didn't tell me they knew what the ring was. Enzo didn't say anything about it." My brain works double time to keep up with her words.

"That is for the best. Drop the subject all together, Aliyah. Do you understand me?" She shakes my shoulders, willing me to understand.

"I won't talk about it. I promise, but if my friends know, why can't I tell them I have it?"

"The ring...it corrupts you. This is why every ruler of Twilight has been the vile kings they were. The more you wish, the blacker your soul becomes. The ring craves the blood of the kill. It craves the chaos it creates in the mind of its owner. You must never use the ring and you must never let it fall into the hands of someone who would not hesitate to use it to get what they want. Duncan's father sought the ring day and night. Even the remnants of its magic can plague the mind of someone wicked and cruel. Why do you think The Banished King wanted to have Aramot under his thumb? *For the ring.*"

"How do you know all this? How could you know the workings of The Banished King?" Fear grips my chest wondering if she somehow has a history with him.

"I've been on several *diplomatic missions* over the years. I take it upon myself to personally investigate Tyros, to spy on his inner workings. Disguising oneself as a tree on the Banished's island is the perfect way to go about collecting information," she smiles.

"Why are you telling me all this?"

"Your future is bright, my girl. You will go on to do great things, while I know my time will come to an end. You are the perfect keeper for the ring as you can never die. Keep it safe from the grasp of those who would seek to destroy our home. Go now before anyone becomes suspicious of your absence. I will be gone for some time in the coming weeks. There are whispers The Banished King is in search of a new weapon and I am going to find out what. You will not see me for some time, but know that we stand with you Aliyah, when the time comes."

"Why me? You barely know me and the last time I was here, you were complicit in wanting me dead."

"There are many things you do not understand and plans that have yet to unfold. Stay safe, Aliyah. Harness your power and prepare for war, because it *is* coming."

Chapter 28

ALIYAH

I pace back and forth at the foot of my bed. I'm still shaken up at the conversation I had with Kaleron's mother. I was thankful when I left he was not waiting for me. I needed some time to clear my head before my conversation with Enzo. On my way back to my room I had reached out to him down the bond asking him to meet me.

He will be here any moment now and my heart flutters at the thought. I let my anxiety take over my mind just for a moment and I rehearse our impending conversation over and over again in my mind. I think about what I will say and then let my brain filter through each of his potential responses, finding an answer to each and every one of them so I'm not caught off guard.

A knock sounds at the door and my footsteps freeze along with my racing thoughts. I wring my hands together and take a steadying breath. *Here we go.*

"Come in."

Enzo's tall frame engulfs the room, a lump caught in my throat at the sight. I feel the tingle at my back as my wings decide if they want to shift to protect me, but I don't need them for this conversation. I need to do this on my own.

"Hi." His voice is breathless. He has been so understanding, so respectful, and our time during the dance almost made me back out of my decision, but I know my reasons are solid. I know in the long run, this is what is best for me. Though I fear his understanding tone is about to change.

"Thank you for coming. Would you like to sit down?" I gesture toward the high back chair placed in front of the roaring fireplace.

"I prefer to stand, if that's all right?"

Great. He already suspects this is bad news.

"Of course. I...I wanted to talk with you about something, but I need you to promise me you'll let me finish before responding."

I watch as his hands curl into tight fists at his side and his chest rises and falls with what I hope is a calming breath.

"I promise."

"I've been doing a lot of thinking recently." I resume my pacing, not daring to look him in the eye with what I'm about to say. "A lot has happened since we met...since I died. I've been wrestling with this new version of myself. I'm not sure who I'm supposed to be. I've been so...confused. My thoughts have been eating me up inside and I've been trying to process all of this new information. It's only been four months since my entire world was flipped upside down. Things are...going too fast. I think I need time to sort out what happened to me in that coffin...to sort out what happened between us.

"So I met with a healer. Someone who is a little more...um, experimental in their methods. He's been looking for a way to help me combat my demons and when he presented me with an option, I took some time to think heavily on it."

I risk a glance up at Enzo. He stands there, his face giving away no hint of what lies within his mind.

I look him straight in the eyes, he deserves that much. "I found a way to sever our mate bond and I'm going to do it."

A crack. A crack in his demeanor is all I get. His eyebrows curve down as a pained expression flashes across his face, but he doesn't say anything. He clears his throat, but still remains painfully silent. It is as if the room has stretched a thousand miles and we are standing on opposite ends.

"Say something."

"I wasn't sure I was allowed to speak."

"Please, tell me what you are thinking."

His weight shifts uncomfortably from one foot to the other, his hands opening and closing at his sides. I risk taking a step toward him. Then two. Then three. I move until I stand right before him and I reach out my hand to clasp his wrist. At the contact, Enzo shifts his eyes away from mine as he glances to the floor.

"Why?"

The question catches me off guard. In all the scenarios I played out in my head, the simplest one never occurred to me. But I had an answer all the same.

"Before I met you I had been searching for love all my life. I had lost my parents, was forced into a system overrun with children who all wanted the same thing, to find a family, and then everything happened with Cyrus. I had Saraphena, sure, but there was always something...missing. This ache in my heart that I knew in my soul would never be filled. Those days on the post, I wished for death. I told myself if I didn't wake up the next day, the world would spin on and I would finally be free of that hell.

"Then I met you. My heart was full for the first time and I found the family I had always been longing for, but despite finding my mate and the family I always wanted, there was still this crack that lay dormant in my heart. I didn't realize it was still there until I laid in that box day after day, praying to the Maker to let me die a final time and remain dead. My love for you wasn't enough to heal that deep fissure in my chest. It was in that box that I realized I never considered one crucial factor which would make me truly whole again. I never learned to love myself.

"I hated my childhood and the choices my parents made which left me without the two people who are supposed to show you what love really means. I hated the scars on my back because I was too poor to pay my rent and I was too proud to ever let a man take advantage of my circumstances. I hated how after Cyrus raped me, part of me never felt clean after that...like it was my fault because of my life circumstances that I was even in that situation. I hated that even when we met and fell in love, I knew I was never going to be of the proper status to be with you. I hated *myself*, Enzo.

"But most of all. I hated how I lacked the strength to heal the child inside me who was hurt so long ago. I know now that when my wings burst from my back in that iron coffin, protecting me from burning alive day after day, they were protecting the vulnerable child inside me ,screaming for help, for someone to save me. It's why I can't control whether they protect me or not, why they have a mind of their own. They are an outward expression of the protection I thought I needed from others, but really, it was inside me all along. Because it wasn't just about being in that box for all those months, it was that once again, I was alone, until they came."

I nod my head back toward my protectors and smile at the thought of what they have become for me. Another version of myself born out of the need to survive, to protect. These wings aren't separate from me at all...they *are* me, just in feather form. It wasn't until I learned to trust them that our bond was forged. I trusted them to catch me as I free fell through the sky, and I trust them now to know when I need protecting. I laugh lightly to myself before shaking my head and continuing.

"I need to learn to love myself, Enzo. But I don't think I can do that when I am constantly worrying about if I can truly forgive you or not. I know it isn't your fault, but I can't be focused on making sure we are okay all the time, because I'd neglect myself time and time again to help you. I know in my heart I will always care for you, that much has remained unchanged, but until I can love myself, I don't know if I can fully love you."

A long silence stretches between us. Enzo's eyes are still locked on the floor as my grip tightens around his wrist, willing him to understand.

"Would this make you happy?"

"I don't know if happiness is what this decision will grant me, but maybe apart, I can find a way to be whole."

"Then do what you must. I won't stand in your way."

"That's it? No bursting open doors, throwing items, or yelling? You're just okay with this?"

"Of course I'm not okay with this, Aliyah. I just told you that I was going to fight for you, but I also said I would stand by your side as you worked through your demons. If this is what that means, then I'm not going to stop you. If this gives us even the smallest chance of moving forward, then I'll support your decision."

Tears begin to well in my eyes, though with what emotion they are attached, I can't know.

"Thank you, Enzo."

"Be honest with me about one thing," he says, taking a step closer to me.

"Anything," I say, taking his hand in mine.

"I need to know if you are doing this so you can be with Kaleron without a tie to me?"

My answer is instant. "No."

His muscles visibly relax at my answer. "Okay," he sighs. "I'm not saying we won't still have things to work through after the bond is gone, but I hope we can work through them together."

"You trust me? Just like that, you just believe my answer even with everything going on between us?"

"No is a complete sentence, my dove. You explained why you wanted the bond gone and I have to trust that because if we lack the basic foundation of trusting what the other says, then there was never a future for us at all."

Enzo leans down and places a kiss to my cheek, lingering as he pulls away. He turns on his heel and leaves, shutting the door quietly as he goes. My emotions war in my chest. Was that the response I had wanted? Did I want him to give up so easily or did I want him to fight for us? What did I want him to say?

I huff out a breath and walk over to my bed, throwing myself amongst the pillows. I can't help the relief I feel in my chest. It's settled then. My bond with Enzo will be gone forever.

Chapter 29

KALERON

Maker she is beautiful.

I lean against the doorway to the training room watching her move through the training routines posted on the wall. I note the frustration on her face when she falls over from the weight of her wings shifting behind her. I can't imagine how aggravating it must be to accommodate something so huge jutting out from my back. But her determination is ever present with each slash of her dagger and thrust of her fist against the practice dummy. Her leather pants move with surprising ease through the motions, but it isn't her legs that keep my attention.

Her hair is pulled up into her favorite high pony tail and she blows it out of her face. The golden swirls down her body have me enraptured as they glisten in the shifting light. "Work with me, dang it! I thought we were finally on the same team here! I'm trying to work *with* you! Why do you keep working against me or worse, not at all?!" Aliyah talks to her wings as if they will speak back and I grin.

"Care for a real opponent?"

She whips around in shock, sweat dripping from her face, down her chest, and over the contours of her abs. "Hey, sorry, I didn't hear you come in. I can wrap it up if you're looking to train."

"No need. I could show you a few things if you'd like."

Aliyah's eyes narrow in suspicion as she takes me in. "Like what?"

"Your technique is good, not great, but good. Saraphena clearly taught you well, but you lack stability."

She huffs a breath. "How kind of you to notice," she smirks. Her wings shift behind her, moving around to shove at my chest, as if offended.

"Not what I meant, Sparky," I say, shifting her wing away from my sternum. "I mean that your wings are throwing you off balance. I could show you some ways to keep them steady behind you."

"You don't even have wings. How could you possibly help me?"

I stride across the room and stand before her, using my finger to draw a small circle in the air, signaling for her to turn around. She eyes me wearily before slowly turning her back to me. I watch as her back muscles shift uncomfortably. I place my palm ever so lightly on her back, right under the spot where her wing connects with her back. My fingers have craved the feel of her skin on mine since our last encounter. The sensation is like a drug I will never come down from. Her breath hitches in her lungs at the contact and I can't help but smile.

"How exactly is this supposed to help me?" she says, breathless.

I rest my other hand on the other side of her back, right under the other wing. "Move."

She begins to slowly go through the motions of one of the training routines and with each shift of her body, I help guide her wings in the opposite direction, balancing out her weight distribution. She doesn't lose her balance at all, and the strain on her back muscles lessens with the guidance of my hands.

We move together so perfectly. I let my mind drift to my vision from the pool. *Her chest pressed to mine, soft lush lips on my flesh. Her golden hair blowing around us—*

"Kaleron?" Aliyah has stopped moving, my hands still placed on her back.

"You did great," I smile. "Want to see if you can apply those motions to a real fight? An actual opponent won't let you get all the way through the routine before you change to another one."

"I know that," she frowns.

"So show me what you've got then."

Aliyah unsheathes a dagger from her thigh holster and falls into a fighting stance. "Don't take it easy on me."

"I didn't plan to," I smirk. I know I'll have to holster my strength, at least for the first round. Aliyah slashes at me with the dagger, but I catch her arm on the follow through and pull her into my body. I smile down at her, but she shoves back off my chest taking her stance.

A dagger comes flying at my head. I dodge at the last moment, but not fast enough to miss her fist connecting with my jaw. My head whips back, but I can't help the smirk crossing my face at her ferocity.

"Stop smiling during this! It's throwing me off," Aliyah says in frustration.

"How is smiling making this harder for you?"

"Because it makes you look like a cocky bastard," she laughs.

"I prefer the term confident," I wink.

"Ugh!" She throws her body into a blur of fists and daggers, each one missing the mark by mere inches. Frustration joins the fight and I can tell Aliyah is losing. I dodge each one of her combinations, and in a huff of anger, she growls and whips out her fist. I duck at the last second and when her fist connects with the training dummy behind me and a golden orb bursts from her fist, smashing the post into shards and lighting the pieces aflame.

She drops to her knees, a sob pulling at her throat. "Aliyah, what's wrong?"

"I feel so out of control. I need to be harnessing my powers, yet I feel like they control me instead of the other way around. If I can't use them to my advantage, how are we going to stop The Banished King?"

"Breathe, Aliyah. It has only been a few months since you came into your powers. Most fae have them for years before they begin to master them. You need to give yourself a little leeway here."

"I don't have time for this! I need to master them now! I need my mind clear so I can focus on the coming war. I need everything to be normal again!"

"Normal things never make it into the history books, Aliyah, and you are far from normal."

"Wow, Kaleron. How comforting. You really know how to brighten up someone's day."

"Have you tried *not* controlling your emotions?" I ask.

"Emotions make things unpredictable, Kal. That would go against everything they teach you about magical powers."

"Let me ask you something. When you first discovered your wings could turn into crystals, what did you feel?"

"Panicked."

"And when they could shoot out those crystalized feathers?"

"Scared."

"And when the golden orb exploded out of you for the first time?"

"Angry."

"So what I'm hearing is that every time your powers have come out, you've been *feeling* something."

"You know you—" She points her finger in my face with a look of irritation. "You just— Ugh! Your logic is infuriating. So you're saying I should just *feel* the power and use it?"

"I'm saying it's worth a shot," I smile. "Can we try something? A little experiment."

"What did you have in mind?"

A few moments later, after summoning Duncan to the training room, he materializes next to Aliyah.

"You *rang* King Kaleron." His dead pan face does nothing to hide the irritation.

Saraphena, Gunnar, and Liliana come walking into the training room.

"I'm just saying, if we could find a way to beat The Banished King and restore the island it would be a great vacation home!" Liliana says.

"We can't vacation there, Lil. It has like, bad luck, or something around that island. I couldn't see myself stepping foot on that island, let alone *vacationing* there," Saraphena shutters.

"I don't know! Maybe Lil is onto something! We do deserve a place to go after this is all over and frankly we did say we loved the islands when we were in Twilight." Gunnar saunters in, walking backwards so he can see the girls as he talks.

"You are literally the Prince of SunSpark. Buy any island you can find, just not that one," Saraphena says.

"But why buy what you can get for *free!*" Gunnar laughs.

"It isn't free— You know what, I'm just going to veto this entire conversation." Saraphena pushes past him, sticking her foot out to trip Gunnar as he turns around. He stumbles with a laugh and scoops his wife into his arms, placing a kiss to the top of her head.

"I see you brought the others," I say to Duncan.

"When they heard you called me to the training room they just started following me. Now are you going to tell me what we are doing here?"

"I'm running a little experiment with Aliyah. I am testing a theory that her powers are fueled by emotions, instead of control."

"And what does that have to do with him?" Aliyah asks.

"Simple," I reply. "Duncan, I want you to piss her off."

"What?!" Aliyah says at the same time Duncan replies "All right." Aliyah glares up at Duncan, her arms crossing over her chest.

"What if I hurt him?" Ali says, taking a step back.

"That's only if you can catch me," Duncan smirks.

"I just exploded that training dummy. I have no clue what my powers will do to you."

"I'd like to think I'm slightly more intelligent than a training dummy," Duncan says.

"Not by much, Dunca-doodle-doo!" Gunnar calls.

Duncan disappears and reappears behind Gunnar, smacking him on the back of the head before materializing next to Aliyah once more. Gunnar rubs the spot and leans over to Saraphena and whispers something that makes her giggle.

"Promise me you won't get hurt," Aliyah says to Duncan.

"I promise. Now give it your best shot." Duncan disappears, coming up behind Aliyah and shoving her in the back. Golden sparks flick down her wings as they crystalize, poised to strike.

Duncan appears again to her right, shoving her again. As she turns, her wing cuts out, but Duncan is already gone. He repeats his process again and again, popping in and out of existence, shoving Aliyah from side to side. She appears frustrated, and her wings unfurl to their full span, ready and lying in wait for the perfect opportunity.

"Get 'em, Aliyah! Show him who's the baddest fae of all!" Gunnar chants.

You can see Aliyah trying to reach for her power as she throws out her arms, trying to cast those golden spheres out, but nothing comes. I signal back to my sister, telling her to come to my side. I nod my head toward Saraphena as well to join us. Both women come to my side, and I whisper instructions to each of them before taking a step back.

Aliyah spins in a circle, but when her eyes catch on mine, I see tears tracking down her cheeks. The golden ring around her irises' shining in the light. A faint glow starts to radiate under her skin, illuminating the swirls on her arms. It starts at her finger tips, inching up her arm as each swirl begins to shimmer brighter and brighter. When the light reaches her eyes, I signal Saraphena.

Duncan continues to shove Aliyah from every direction. Liliana manipulating her emotions to make her feel sad, and now Saraphena jumping into the mix to hide herself and kicks in Aliyah's knee from behind, making it buckle. As her knee smashes to the ground, every inch of her golden swirls are glowing and her eyes are glimmering pure gold. The moment she throws out her hand again, a golden sphere shoots out of it, flying across the room and exploding across the white marble wall. Pieces fall around the giant hole she has caused.

Aliyah stills, Duncan coming up next to her, and Saraphena staring in awe at the carnage. "Wow!" Duncan says. It's the only thing he says before Aliyah's wing smacks him so hard in the chest he goes stumbling back. "*Oof*" he coughs, "I deserved that."

"Aliyah. How do you feel?"

"I'm not sure." She looks down at her hand and closes her eyes. Her finger tips start to illuminate once more and when she opens her eyes, a small sphere sits in her palm. Smiling, Aliyah whips her hand around to show us. "I'm doing it! Look! I'm doing it!"

"Whoa! Whoa!" Gunnar yells, jumping behind me. "You basically conjure up exploding balls of light! Keep that thing under control before you blow us all up!"

"Don't be such a baby, Gunnar." Aliyah walks toward me, Gunnar cowering behind me. "It's just a little orb!" She waves her hand around in Gunnar's face and he tucks himself tighter behind me.

"Maker let my brother's strength make him bomb proof!"

I step away from him and wrap Aliyah up in my arms. "I'm so proud of you! And you too, Sparky!" I run my hand down her wings and watch as they return to their feathery state. "What did you do to get it under control?"

"I just...felt it. I didn't think about controlling it. I just thought about Saraphena and our life together. About my friends and my family and let all my emotions flow through me and when I opened my eyes, there it was! Can I try something? How much do you care about that wall?"

"The only thing I care about is you, Ali."

She smiles, turning toward the wall with the gaping hole in it. Closing her eyes once more, she breathes in, then out. Faster this time, her fingertips start to glow, running up her forearm, bicep, neck, and then the swirls around her face. When her eyes open they glow like the brightest rays of sunlight. Conjuring up an orb in her hand, it grows in size until she throws it at the wall, an explosion going off on impact.

"Oh yeah, this is gonna be awesome," she says.

"Ah, King Kaleron, there you are!" One of my councilmen race after me, but I don't have time to stop.

"Do not ruin my mood, councilman." I never bothered to learn any of their names. They were all appointed by my father and I simply haven't had time to replace them, nor the desire. They only serve as a façade for men in power. A false perception there to appease the people into thinking they have representatives who have the ear of the king. The reality of politics is not as people wish it to be.

"Your Majesty, please! You have barely had time to attend any meetings and your kingdom needs you far more than some girl!"

I stop dead in my stride. My fists clench at my sides, anger shifting uncomfortably in my chest. I school my features into a deadly stare by the time I spin around to face him. His face pales as he gazes up at my expression. Malice rims my eyes, and for each step forward I take, he retreats back further until he is cornered.

"That *girl* is the future Queen of SunSpark. That *girl* is my future bride. That *girl* would crush you into a thousand pieces and I would stitch you back together again just for the chance of her obliterating you once more. That *girl* is the vision in my dreams, but will be your worst nightmare."

His eyes flick between mine, mercy begging from his gaze. "I meant no disrespect, Your Majesty. I only meant to warn that—"

"Don't. Walk away before I change my mind and am forced to have the help scrape your innards from the floor on which you stand."

I spin on my heel, stuffing my hands in my pockets to prevent me from doing anything I will have to explain myself for later.

"She won't choose you, Your Highness. She has a mate. No one can resist the bond." His voice quivers and the gulp is audible.

"You know what? You're right," I say laughing lightly, turning to face him once more. I rake a hand down my face, a smile splitting my face as I do.

"As one of the councilman, it is my duty to help guide you. If it costs me my life for speaking the truth, then so be it."

"Your bravery is noted, but it will not save you. You were right when you said my kingdom needs me more than she does. Aliyah is formidable, strong, relentless in her determination, and will never *need* anyone. She will choose me because she *wants* to, not because she *needs* to be with me. You slimy pit of fae filth, understand this, *she* is what true bravery looks like. She looked death in the face and told it to screw right the hell off and rose from the ashes of her enemies. If you are going to fear anyone in this kingdom, let it be the Queen of Ashes herself."

"I will fear no one in my final moments. Your father never would have let this stand. I was right to back him in his pursuit of eliminating this threat. No one should have the power she possesses and be allowed to live. She will never be the Queen of SunSpark so long as I still breathe." The councilman lifts his chin, choosing stupidity as his final act in life, turning his back on me.

"Then we shall remedy this situation quickly, for Aliyah will be my queen." With all my Maker-given strength, I shove my fist through his back, ripping his spine clean from his body. The lifeless carcass drops to the floor with a satisfying squelch like jelly and I relish in the sound knowing I've avenged my queen's honor. One less traitor standing in the way of her greatness.

As I drop the man's spine onto his body, a servant rounds the corner too quickly, slipping in the man's blood and landing on her backside with a thud. Her chest rises and falls rapidly as she takes in the scene before allowing her eyes to glance up at mine.

"Probably best to mop it up before anyone else slips." I spin on my heel, leaving the servant to her duties.

Chapter 30

LILIANA

I t's been a week since my bond awoke with Jonah. Seven days of hiding out in my room, praying to the Maker this isn't my reality. It was supposed to be Duncan. I was supposed to be able to choose my own fate. How can it be that my future is tied to the one person who has something to provide to our kingdom for the coming war? *Why did it have to be him?*

A soft knock comes at my door, but I don't answer. I never do. He comes at the same time every day, but never stays. After a few moments pass, I open the door and snatch up the familiar gift. A bushel of cut sunflowers and a small card. The same gift he leaves every day and every day I accept it, knowing I will soon need to see him face to face. His hazel and blue eyes flash in my mind. How warm his gaze had been the night in the ballroom when he found out I was his mate. I wanted to be strong, to save face and not hurt him, but my heart had other plans.

I agreed to take the time to get to know him, and that time was running out. Soon I would be whisked away to The Islands of Loch and I would be forced to leave my family behind in favor of a complete stranger. I place the sunflowers down on the mantle above the fireplace and open the seventh note as I crawl into bed.

Dearest Liliana,

I cannot begin to imagine how difficult this must be for you. Hoping to find love with another, only to be forced into a bond with a complete stranger. I know I may not be the man you wished for, but I hope in time we get the chance to know each other as deeply as mates are meant to. I may not have been your first choice, but I promise to be a devoted mate...and husband.

When you're ready, I will wait in the sunflower gardens each night until it is time for us to leave together and return to my home. I can't wait to show you The Islands. Hopefully you will love them as I have come to love you.

Yours with love,

Jonah

Guilt twists in my gut at his words. He's been so kind and understanding since our bond awoke. I huff out a breath of frustration, digging my fingers into the roots of my hair and pulling just until it hurts.

"Lil?" A soft, familiar voice comes from the other side of the door. Tears threaten to spill, my fist crumpling the paper in my hand. I lose control of my emotions, the one thing I'm supposed to be a master of. The doors open, two sets of arms wrap around me when my heart finally cracks open. I bury my face into the crook of Aliyah's neck, her wings wrapping the three of us protectively in their embrace. Saraphena pulls back first, wiping the tears from my eyes with her thumbs.

"Hey now, we've got you." Her warm smile brightens the room, filling the spaces where my own light once shown.

"What am I supposed to do, girls?" My voice cracks on the final word, a lump forming in my throat once more.

"What you have always done," Aliyah smiles. "You are going to do whatever the hell you want because you're Lili-freaking-ana who takes orders from no man, even if he is the king. You have always wanted to choose your own fate, and it might seem like that choice was taken from you, but it doesn't have to be. You can go, be with Duncan, reject the mate bond, and live a long happy life."

"Or?" I ask.

"Or, you can choose to give Jonah a chance. Hear him out at least and get to know him. Maybe he will surprise you," Saraphena says. She reaches up, brushing my wispy bangs out of my face.

"Two completely different perspectives. One serves my heart, but the other serves my kingdom. One is selfish, the other selfless. As much as my heart wars with itself, I know deep down what my choice needs to be." I make my way over to the bed, curling up beneath the covers, the girls joining me in stride. They crawl under the blankets with me on either side, Aliyah's wings flaring out behind her on the bed. They shift closer to me, trying to wrap around my shoulders. Aliyah scoffs at them.

"Do you mind switching with me? They aren't going to stop bothering us until they get what they want," she mumbles. A genuine smile crosses my lips and I shuffle to her other side so she is laying in the middle of the bed, her wings unfurling behind Saraphena and myself, pulling us in close.

"Aliyah, do you mind if I try something?" I ask.

"Touch at your own risk, Lil. That's all I can say about it."

Saraphena braces for the potential impact of Aliyah's wings shifting, sitting up slightly. I close my eyes and place the palm of my hand hesitantly to the feathers. Taking a measured breath, I throw out my power, searching for the energy of the wings. Pride slams into my chest, but Aliyah rolls her eyes as her wings act like a young alicanto. The plumes expand behind her back, larger and larger.

"Everyone brace yourself, I'm going to do something a little risky," I smirk. I push anger through my finger tips, imbuing the emotion into the feathers. Sparks cascade down Aliyah's back, sharp, crystal feathers replacing the previous lush ones. I snatch my hand back on instinct, but Saraphena yelps as she pats the sparks that landed on the bed, keeping it from igniting.

"Was that completely necessary, Lil?" Aliyah asks. "They are rather uncomfortable in this state."

"Hold on, hold on." Running my palm over the weapon once more, I coax out a peaceful feeling, a calming essence seeping from my touch. The wings return to their normal state, nudging me in the chest in fake annoyance as evidenced by the light-hearted feeling I sensed through my power.

"Well?" Saraphena's eyes are beaming as she waits to see what I did.

"I can feel them," I smile. "They are a completely different presence than your own! Your emotions differ from those of your wings!"

Silence settles over us as we lay back down together, all staring up at the canopy of my bed. After some time, Aliyah finally speaks. "So do you know what you want to do about Jonah?"

I sigh, contemplating what I feel. "Want and need are two different things for a ruler unfortunately. I know Duncan *wants* to be with me as I *want* to be with him, but what my kingdom *needs* is a different story. I'm going to do what is right for the future of our realm. I'm going to get to know Jonah, to give him a real chance, and at the end of his time here, I'll become his wife."

I feel the hesitation pouring off the girls, but their smiles betray nothing of their true feelings. "Well, I guess dresses are in order. Care for another day on the town?" Aliyah looks to Saraphena, a wicked smile pulling on her lips.

"You read my mind, but let's just promise no more taverns, the ole bird ball back here doesn't seem to care for the patrons," I wink.

"Oooooo! What about this one?!" I pull the pink silk dress from the rack, spinning around to face Aliyah sitting on a plush bench in the finest dress store SunSpark has to offer.

"Pink really isn't my color, Lil."

"She's into black now!" Saraphena calls from the dressing room.

"Black?!" I bark.

"Don't look at me. Sparky likes black. I think it matches her personality better. I've stopped fighting it," she laughs.

"Black it is," I smile. Turning back to the rack, I hear the dressing room curtain open behind me.

"Well? What do we think?!" Saraphena spins, the emerald green dress glistening in the sunlight streaming in from the front of the shop. The square neckline leads into chiffon sleeves that hang loosely around her arms before cuffing around her wrists. The material is light enough that she won't be warm in the light of SunSpark. It is a simple silk fabric with prominent boning in the bodice with beautiful lacing up the back, cinching it tight around her waist. Small diamond shaped cut-outs circle her waist before dropping into a flowing skirt, a small train trailing behind her.

"Absolutely brilliant! My brother is going to drop dead when he sees you!" I squeal. "Anything less and I'll be forced to take him out myself!"

"I'll be sure to hold him down while you do it," Aliyah laughs. "Well, shall we head out then?"

"What about you?" I ask, a frown pulling at my lips.

"I'm not going to find anything in this store that is going to work with my wings. I was actually hoping, if it isn't too much to ask, would you be willing to design me something?"

"Nothing would make me happier." I give Aliyah a hug, her wings caressing my arms in appreciation.

"We have one last stop we need to make," she says. Saraphena nods her head knowingly before stepping back into the dressing room.

"Where are we off to next?" I ask.

"You'll see. No more questions! Aliyah, lock down the excitement! I don't want her picking up on any hints through your emotions!"

"I wouldn't dare to use my powers for evil like that!" I say, feigning offense. Aliyah smacks me on the arm before taking my hand in hers. She leans in close so Saraphena can't hear.

"We have a surprise for you," she whispers.

"Aliyah!!!" Saraphena materializes directly behind us, scaring the sunlight right out of me. "I told you not to tell!"

"I didn't, I swear! You can even ask the bird ball! I didn't say a thing!"

The three of us laugh together, exiting the store front and making our way out onto the busy streets. Saraphena leads the group, swerving through the masses with precise skill. Aliyah trails behind me, apologizing to each patron that has to move out of her way.

"Almost there!" Saraphena calls back.

"Where are we going?!" Excitement bubbles in my chest and the feeling itches to burst out of me. "Just give me one hint!"

"No hints, Aliyah!" Saraphena addresses her. I glance back to see Aliyah roll her eyes.

"It's as if she thinks I can't keep a secret," she mutters.

"You can't!" Saraphena yells over the crowd.

"Do you suddenly have the hearing of a quayler up there?!" Ali calls.

"Don't even joke about that, Ali! That was arguably the scariest day of my life!"

"Yeah, so much so you peed in your pants a little!"

"I told you that in confidence!" Saraphena snaps her head back to glare at Ali before a huge smile breaks out across her face, her eyes narrowing at her best friend.

"If it makes you feel any better, I would have done more than just pee," I laugh.

"I'm never telling you two anything again! Thank goodness! We are here!" I glance up at the sign above the door. *Trydant Ink.*

"A body ink shop?" I question.

"You'll see!" Ali promises, taking my hand and pulling me inside. A small bell chimes above my head, signaling our entrance.

"Ladies! Welcome! I am so glad you could make it in! Do you have the sketches we discussed?" the shop keeper asks.

"Yes, we brought them! Thank you for being willing to get us in so quickly!" Saraphena smiles, handing the ink master a folded piece of parchment.

"Anything for the Princess of SunSpark and the mate of our prince!" he beams. Taking the piece of paper, he walks to the back of the small shop, signaling us to follow.

"Aliyah, I'm confused. What ink are we getting?"

"I'm getting my Soul Bond inked on my arm like I used to have with Saraphena," she smiles. "She got hers while I was gone and I loved it so much, I wanted to get mine again too." Aliyah takes a seat in the ink master's chair and he begins his work. A sinking feeling pulls in my chest. I don't know how this would have been a surprise for me, but I put a smile on my face regardless. I didn't have the bond these two had for 26 years.

I always considered Saraphena my best friend, but then she found Aliyah and had to leave me. I don't resent her for it, I know she did the right thing, but in finding Aliyah, I lost her along the way. I know I'll always be second in her heart when it comes to best friends. I try not to feel insecure in my friendship with them as I watch the ink master poke Aliyah's skin over and over, embedding the ink into her skin in the shape of a moon.

Aliyah beams down at the design and Saraphena gawks over the artwork, praising the ink master for his skill. "Lil!" Aliyah calls me over. I stand from the small chair I was waiting in. Aliyah shoves her arm in my direction, showing me her new ink.

"It's beautiful, Aliyah." I force a smile to my face as I stare down at the moon marked on her right forearm. "Aliyah, I think he missed something?" I question in confusion.

A knowing smile pulls at Aliyah's lips. "Did he?"

"Sir! You missed something on her design." I call the ink master back toward us, but he simply smiles. "Ali, you can't just leave the design incomplete."

"I'm not." Aliyah grasps my right hand and Saraphena snags my left. Dragging me over to the chair, the ink master pulls another folded design from his pocket. A star is sketched out on the paper, the same style star that once sat upon Aliyah's skin, marking her Soul Bond.

"I don't understand." I look to the girls in confusion.

"You were right that the design was incomplete. It was missing you," Saraphena smiles.

"Saraphena had only the sun, but I had the moon *and* the star. My soul was waiting to be split in three, Lil. Part of my heart was waiting until I met you." Aliyah grips my hand in hers, tears brimming in her eyes. "The moon can't shine without the sun, but the moon would also be nothing without the stars. She would be alone in her darkness, hanging in the endless abyss in the sky, but with the stars shining brightly beside her, she will always make it through the night to see the sun again."

My heart swells in my chest. I was never second in their lives, I was just here, keeping their home warm for when they returned to me again.

"A lot is going to change over the next few weeks, Lil," Saraphena starts. "But no matter where we end up in life, all we have to do is look up into the sky and know we are looking at the same sun, moon, and stars and we won't feel so far away from home."

A tear slips down my cheek and the three of us let the silence wash over us, all the unspoken words never needing to be voiced. Because one thing is for certain, no matter what comes our way, the three of us will survive it together, even if we are apart.

Chapter 31

LILIANA

I trace the new star inked on my arm as I make my way through the sunflower gardens. A warm breeze blows through the tall stems, green leaves with flashes of brown-ish yellow pulse with the waves of air heating my skin. My feet move instinctively through the fields, my mind numb to the storm of emotions brewing inside me. My nerves feel as if they are being consumed by the surface of the sun. The beat of my heart too fast, my breath shallow, the electrical signals my brain sends to my body telling it to panic fire in rapid succession. Why am I so nervous? He's just another man. I've flirted with men for as long as I could remember. Why did this one differ? *Just be yourself.*

His long red braid comes into view, his strong shoulders from years of living on The Islands bulging through his brown tunic shirt. Jonah's body is the outward expression of what it means to grow up in a place filled with the most brutal of fae. The stories I heard as a child were less than desirable. I remember the fear that used to feed my nightmares of what it would be like to spend even a single night there, but now I will be spending the rest of my life there. Night after night, away from my family...away from everything I know...everything I've come to love.

I swallow thickly, swearing the gulp could be heard for miles. "You're here," I say a little more quietly than I intend.

Jonah turns slowly, a huge smile spread across his face. He is nothing like the figures in my mind. His body may be formed one way, but his heart...it seems to be good.

"You came." He takes a step toward me, offering his hand for me to take. "Care to take a stroll and watch the lowering sun?"

Hesitation cripples my reach. *Give him a real chance.* "I'd like that." I place my hand in his, Jonah's grip is lighter than I anticipated. The next thing I know, I'm in a part of the garden I swear we hadn't been standing in before. Did we really walk so far already? Had I not been paying attention?

I look around at the garden, trying to sort out what happened. "Um...I...I have so many questions. Do you mind?" How I got to the garden doesn't matter I suppose.

"Is that not what we are here to do? Please, ask away." As we stroll through the gardens, I filter through the questions in my mind, selecting the ones that are most prominent.

"Do you have any powers?"

I swear I see Jonah's smile falter, but it returns so quickly I second guess if my mind truly saw it. "No, but where I come from, power is not found in abilities, it is found in brute strength. It is found in how strong your will is to survive. I would ask you the same, but I won't deny, I did some digging into your history when I found out we were mates. You're an empath, yes?"

I inadvertently reach out with my power to sense his emotions, the habit creeping in, but I don't feel anything in return. Maybe it doesn't work on mates? I've never heard of such a thing, but I've also never had a mate before.

"That's correct. I can feel another's emotions and—" I stop myself from finishing that sentence. I can't fully trust Jonah yet and I'm not sure I want him knowing I can influence the emotions of others.

He eyes me warily, a small crease forming between his brows, but he continues on. "Do you have any questions about The Islands?"

"So many," I admit. "But it isn't The Islands that worry me too much, though I have heard some...interesting...stories. However, I don't think my hesitation over going to The Islands matters too much. We are going regardless, so I suppose I will find out when I get there."

"True," he smiles. "But we don't have to stay there forever. Once we return home to secure my ships for the war, we can go wherever you like. We can even stay here in SunSpark if that is what you wish."

Hope blooms in my chest. "You mean that?" I might not have to leave my family after all! We can all stay together! Maybe Jonah would consider moving back to Citrine with us and taking a place as a trainer for the other recruits.

"You are my mate, the future love of my life, and soon to be wife. Where you go, I go." He lifts my hand and places a soft kiss to my knuckles. A blush creeps up my neck at the contact. His eyes lock on mine and my mouth goes dry in the heat of his gaze. His hand trails up my arm, his thumb circling the ink on my forearm, his eyes never leaving mine.

My tongue sticks to the roof of my mouth, scraping against the palate like sandpaper. Is he about to kiss me? Should I kiss him back? Is it too soon?

Jonah licks his lips, his sharp canines flashing in the setting sun's light. It's then that I see it...the *hunger* in his eyes as if he means to devour me. Guilt takes a seat in my heart...right next to desire. The bond sparkles between us, my heart surging forward trying to claw its way out of my chest and latch onto his. For a moment, when I look into Jonah's eyes, I don't see him staring back at me. Instead, jet black hair and deep emerald eyes bore into mine, but when I blink, the man I want vanishes.

"Jonah, I— AHH!" I snap my head back quickly, a bug hitting me square in the forehead, scaring the daylight out of me. I swat at my face, but Jonah simply laughs, snapping out his hand in a flash, he catches the bug by its wing. The insect struggles against his hold, flapping its other wing rapidly, squirming in his grasp.

"Scared of bugs are you?" He chuckles deeply, waiting for my response.

"I'm not fond of anything that hits me square in the face," I admit with a laugh of my own.

"Then let me avenge you! Die you vile creature!" Jonah gives a mock battle cry as he brings his hands together, squishing the insect between his palms. "You shall bother my mate no longer!"

The tension from before seems to dissipate as we continue walking through the garden. We share stories from our childhoods, how we came to meet the friends in our life, plans for the future, and laugh over silly jokes. By the time we reach the last row of sunflowers, my heart feels more at ease. I can see a life with Jonah. I don't yet know if that life is filled with love, but I know it will be filled with laughter, and right now, that doesn't seem like such a bad thing.

"Shall we meet again here tomorrow? We only have a few more days until we are to be wed. I'd like to continue getting to know you, Liliana, if you'll allow me." His mixed-matched eyes shine as he gazes down at me.

"I'd like that very much," I answer.

"Until tomorrow then...bug." Jonah winks at me before taking off in the direction of the palace. A genuine smile pulls at my lips. Life with Jonah might not be so bad after all.

I turn and start to make my way back to the palace myself, a smile still plastered to my face like an idiot. A shadow moves out from behind one of the garden statues.

"It's good to see you smiling again." Emerald eyes shine in the golden rays beaming from behind a head of jet black hair.

"No thanks to you." The insult comes out before I can stop myself. I let out a measured breath. "I'm sorry, I didn't mean it, I just—"

"You don't need to apologize. I know the choices I made for us. I know what I lost."

"You were going to choose me. You were going to say the words."

Silence settles between us, neither one of us daring to speak. Duncan huffs a frustrated breath and I take a step closer to him. He takes a step back. I won't deny the hurt that comes with the realization.

"I've made a lot of mistakes in my life, Liliana. Some worse than others. I don't mean to change your mind on marrying Jonah, I know the joys of having a mate and all that life can offer when you are with the one the Maker designed for you, but—"

"We can't do this now. My heart can't take it and...it isn't fair. I don't want to fight with you Duncan. I— I loved you. I *do* love you. But I have a duty now. You and I both know I never believed in mates or fate, I believed in love. I believed in...*us.* But you didn't and that's okay. That is the path you needed to choose for yourself, for your kingdom. Even if things were different the night of the ball and my bond didn't come into place, we will never know what could have been. It's too late now."

I take a step toward him and this time he doesn't back up. I close the space between us, placing my palm over his heart, feeling the steady beat beneath my touch. I let myself have one last moment with him because after this, I need to let him go once and for all. To give Jonah and I a real chance, I have to free myself from Duncan, even if it breaks me apart in the process. Maybe Jonah will be the one to put me back together.

"Every moment of every day I wanted to fight for us. I would have slain a hundred enemies to make my way back to you, but I never expected you to be the most formidable foe of all. You stood in the way of our future, and hard as I might have tried, I would never have been able to cut you down." My lip quivers when I see the tear slip from Duncan's eye. He stands there, literally blocking my path between me and my future waiting just inside. "You will always be a part of my story, Duncan, I just wish we didn't miss our chance at a happily ever after. You were right about one thing though...I wish we never met that day in SunSpark, because then I wouldn't have to try so hard to forget."

I push onto my tip-toes, placing a soft kiss to his cheek where another tear falls. I cup his jaw with my hand and gaze into those pools of green one last time. I memorize the lines of his face, the way his eyes search mine, and the feel of his skin on mine, because that is all he will be to me now...a memory.

I move around him, willing myself to walk toward my future, wishing I could turn back time and redo my past.

"Liliana, wait! Please—"

But I don't turn back. I keep walking, my own tears threatening to spill once more over a man I can never have. I open the doors to the palace and when I close them behind me, I also close the door on my past, on the heart break and on the broken version of myself. On this day, a new girl is forged. One of iron and steel. One that will not ever let a man break her again.

Chapter 32

JADE

Walking up to the palace ruins of The Banished Kingdom, I welcome the evil that spills from the stones around me. I breathe in the wicked stench of power I know belongs to me. Tyros said I would come back here when I was ready to accept my abilities. Back then I never thought I would be standing where I am, but the black stone walls of his...of *my*...fallen kingdom will be built back using the blood and bones of my enemies.

Tyros wanted to be my father, but I have no need for parental guidance. What I need now is a mentor who will help me harness the power he promised me. To be able to create someone's worst nightmare would give me the edge I need to take the retribution I am owed. I don't want my family back now. As far as I am concerned, they are already dead. What I want now is to see Aliyah *burn*.

I shove open the doors to the palace and listen as the resultant bang echoes through the halls of my inheritance. I am The

Banished King's daughter. The *Princess* of the Banished. The daughter of nightmares themselves.

Two of the Kalari guarding the entrance hall turn in surprise, spears raised as they move to attack me. I smirk, pulling my short swords from my back, and in two rapid slices, cut off the skulls from the Kalari and watch their bodies drop into a heap of bones on the floor, the magic holding them together dissipating.

"Tyros!" I call. I walk through the halls, heading for the throne room. I run the tips of my swords along the walls, watching as sparks light behind me, a vicious smile plastered onto my face.

When I reach the throne room, my gaze locks on The Banished King. Tyros, my father. He has a knowing smirk on his lips. His body is relaxed as he lounges on his throne, his elbow propped on the arm rest, his cheek pressed into his palm. "Daughter! To what do I owe this visit? Come for another bargain?"

"Aliyah is back from the dead. I want vengeance on her for what she took from me. I'm here to claim my power."

Tyros sits up, an arrogant smirk pulls on his lips. "I thought you were his true love?"

"How— How would you know about that?" My head tips in question.

"I've been keeping tabs on the little urchin," he sneers.

"Why is everyone so freaking obsessed with Aliyah?! Aliyah this, Aliyah that! She isn't special! She is just a poor girl from a rank village with no one who loves her! She is NOTHING!" I scream.

"How *did* she get out? It's the one thing I can't seem to figure out and my creatures are idiots with empty skulls."

"Kaleron. She showed up with Kaleron, but she's different now. She has these mutant wings and golden fire. I need my power to beat her into oblivion. I need to know how to kill someone who can't die."

"Kaleron can be dealt with easily enough, but wings? I did not expect that."

"How did you know about me being Enzo's true love?"

"Because I was the one who set the trap to make him think so." Tyros sits back in his seat, running a hand through his inky black hair, his tattooed face contorting as he pauses.

"The black veins. You cursed me. You tricked Enzo into thinking I was his true love, but it was all a sham, wasn't it?" I can't help the laugh in my voice.

Tyros huffs out a breath. "There are bigger things happening in this world than you and *your one true love,*" he mocks. "Though I have to admit, the plan was working perfectly if you could just learn to hold onto a man."

"Me?! I had him! He and I were going to be together until that monstrosity showed back up! How am I supposed to compete with his *mate?*"

"Aliyah must be dealt with. She cannot be allowed to live."

"Why are *you* so afraid of her? I would think a man of your capabilities would not be threatened by the likes of a stupid, blonde mutant."

"You know of the Reflecting Pool in SunSpark, yes?"

I nod.

"Before my father was banished, the rulers of SunSpark allowed my father and myself to float in the pool. My vision was of the future. A future in which Aliyah is my downfall."

"Then we need to wipe her off the map. Unlock my powers and let me get my revenge and save your coming reign."

"Unlocking your powers is not easily done. It will take a great sacrifice on your end."

"I will do whatever you ask of me so long as I can rip Aliyah's body limb from limb, starting with those monstrous wings."

"In that case, my child, I need your heart."

"Done."

PART IV:
IMPLEMENTATION

Chapter 33

ALIYAH

The sun beams overhead, the porch overlooking the garden bathed in golden rays of happiness. I sit with my eyes closed, my wings unfurled behind me, the plumes outstretched basking in the sunlight. I breathe in once...hold...and out. Today I am safe. Today I am out. Today...I am *free*. I conjure an orb to my finger tips, practicing holding it for as long as I can, and then conjuring a second in my other hand.

"Mind if I join you?"

The bucket of ice washing over me is a stark contrast to the warm wind that blows through my hair. I snap my hands closed, extinguishing the orbs. *Jonah.*

"I guess that would be okay," I say hesitantly. I don't know what it is about Jonah, but something shifts in my chest every time he's around. My wings take note of my unease, and lift from their relaxed position, poised to strike with the smallest shift in my emotions. Jonah moves around me, his hand landing on my shoulder, squeezing it slightly with a small smile on his face. I blink and Jonah is sitting on the stone porch across from me, both knees bent up so his elbows can rest there, hands clasped. Arrogance washes off him in waves, the utter example of relaxation across his face. When did he sit down?

"I wanted to speak with you about Liliana," he says.

"What about her? Saraphena has been her friend far longer than I have and she has two brothers who know her the best. It may be in your best interest to speak with any of them." I try to keep my eyes from shifting around, looking for a familiar face to come join this conversation. Unease washes over me, but my wings don't appear to be on high alert, so I try to relax, trusting their judgment.

"I think you are the exact person I need to be speaking with. I have sensed a...shift...in your relationship with the group. An outsider to the situation of course," he says, placing his hand on his chest in mocked understanding. "You've been gone for some time away from them, or so Liliana has told me in our conversations. A tragic story you have lived, Ali."

"It's Aliyah to you."

"Well, Ali, my bug has told me so many interesting tales of things that happened over these last few months and you weren't a part of any of them. Locked away so snug and tight. Aren't you upset they didn't come for you?" His head cocks to the side in question, but I don't miss the slightest lip twitch into a brief smile.

I do my best to have a passive face, but anger is shifting in the corners of my mind. "They had their reasons. Reasons that, as you have so eloquently pointed out, do not need to be explained to an *outsider.*"

"I won't be an outsider much longer, Ali. As Liliana's mate, you will all have to learn to accept me into your little...*family.*"

"Liliana will make her own choices about you, but rest assured, I will be *right* by her side...always." My eyes narrow, my body incapable of relaxing any longer, knowing where this conversation is headed but my wings still don't react.

"Speaking of, I think it's best my bug gets some distance from you. I wouldn't want you to *influence* her in any way. She needs time to grow accustomed to The Loch ways and that won't be possible with you hanging around her all the time. Besides, she won't be in SunSpark much longer. We return to The Islands as soon as our marital vows are complete. Better to cut all ties now."

"Liliana will never allow herself to be separated from us. She won't agree to just cut us all out!" I stand, my wings feeling heavy at my back, not a shift in sight. I try to hide my confusion as I continue. "As the mate of one of my best friends I will not hurt you unless you give me a reason to, but you are walking *dangerously* close to that line." I try to pull on my emotions to fuel my powers, but the space in my chest feels far away, almost dormant. It always picks the most inconvenient times to hide away.

"Oh sweet, sweet, Ali. The plans I have for Liliana and myself are already in motion. There is no stopping them." Jonah rises to his feet, the arrogance of indifference still painted across his smug face. Brushing off his pants, he continues. "You'd be wise to heed this warning. Stay away from Liliana."

"Hey! What's going on out here?" Lil comes bounding down the steps, but my eyes are locked with Jonah's, refusing to give in. "Ali, what's got you all in a huff?"

Finally breaking my eyes from his, I turn to Lil and pull her hand into mine, not forgetting to keep Jonah in my peripheral. "Lil, can I speak with you please?"

"Sure, we can head to your room! Saraphena was headed that way when I saw you out here. We can have another girl's night!" I move to pull Liliana inside, knowing my protector will slice into Jonah if need be, even if they don't appear threatened in this moment.

"Bug," Jonah says. "I thought we could spend some time together right now. It is far too close to our wedding day and there is still so much I don't know about you." A light smile graces his lips and my jaw aches from clenching it shut so hard.

"Lil, I *really* need to speak with you," I whisper, the plea in my voice clear.

Lil looks between Jonah and I. "Can it wait?" She bites her lip as if deciding between that monster or me is the hardest choice she will make today. I see the war going on in her mind.

"No."

"Liliana, please, my bug, walk with me through the gardens and leave Ali to some time with her best friend." Jonah outstretches his hand, a stupid sparkle in his eye.

"We can catch up later, Ali. I promise," she smiles. "I'll come find you as soon as I'm done! I love you." Lil squeezes my hand once and then walks away toward Jonah.

I watch as Jonah wraps an arm around Liliana's shoulder and leads her away from me. I try to pull on my power, but find it still oddly dormant. I don't even have time to question the feeling because Jonah turns his head to look over his shoulder and when his eyes lock with mine, a knowing smirk crosses his lips.

"I need to talk to you!" I say, bursting through my bedroom door.

Saraphena, Gunnar, Enzo, and Duncan all sit amongst the space in my room. Enzo has found a spot in the far corner of my room, his eyes never looking up from his gaze outside the window. Saraphena and Gunnar are piled onto the bed, and Duncan stands against the wall, arms crossed.

"What's going on?"

"You're going to break your bond with Enzo?" Saraphena questions, and I don't miss the fact that she reaches for Gunnar's hand.

"Yes." I look to Enzo who sits in the corner, still not looking up. Did he force them to come here? Did he tell them to talk me out of it?

"That's a really big decision, Aliyah. You're sure you've thought it through?" Duncan asks. Not in a judgmental way, but more, seeking understanding.

"Not that I have to justify my answers to you, but yes. I've thought this through. I know what I want...no...what I *need* in order to move *forward* with Enzo."

This is when he looks up, eyes latching onto mine. That's when I see it. The hurt and the hope written across his face.

"I know my reasons for wanting to break the bond and as messed up as you think it might be, it is with the hope that I can finally fix *myself* so that maybe Enzo and I can have a future together. This is so much more than just not wanting to be mated to him." I take a deep, steadying breath.

"I was alone. All those months I sat in that coffin, screaming for one of you to come and save me. I fought my demons *alone* in that box. I was trapped inside my own mind day in and day out, begging for one of you to come and save me from myself. I questioned my sanity, questioned if...if I even still wanted to be alive. I prayed to the Maker daily to let this be the time I didn't wake back up. I *needed* you all...and you weren't there.

That hurt, more than tearing away my flesh with my teeth. More than clawing away the strips of my skin trying to feel *something* instead of this pain inside my mind. More than beating my fists against the iron that burned my body day in and day out. But what hurt the most was that Enzo heard me. He heard me screaming and begging for him, *dying* waiting for him. Rory died trying to stay with me until his last breath.

"I know what Enzo did to try and bring me back. I know what all of you did to try and bring me back, but every day I have walked around these palace halls feeling *alone.* Sure, there were people there, all of you loving and supporting me along the way, but emotionally, I've been alone still dealing with the demons from my time in that box. Most of the time I'm still mentally there. But I've had to learn to become stronger than the iron grave that broke me. I'm becoming someone new. The Aliyah you knew died in that grave. I'm not that girl anymore, I *can't* be that girl anymore. I know I'm not the girl you recognize from before, and if I have to go through ripping out my bond alone too, then I will."

Saraphena stands first, moving toward me with tears dripping down her face. "I'm not going to pretend to understand what you went through, I don't think I ever will, but if this is what you truly need to do for you...then I'll stand by your side. I'm sorry for not coming for you, and I'm sorry you've felt so alone since coming back. You don't have to be alone anymore." She wraps me into her arms, tucking me in tight. Gunnar stands from the bed next.

"You deserved better, Ali. I'm sorry we never visited your grave. We should have made time, even if it hurt, even if it went against the plans to bring you back. We should have visited." Gunnar joins the hug, and the moment I feel his arms around me, the tears I'd been holding back finally fall.

Duncan rolls his eyes, pushing off the wall. In typical Duncan fashion, he doesn't say a word, but lets his actions speak for him. He moves around my left wing and wraps his arms around the group, pulling us all even tighter into each other. A moment passes before they let me go and exit the room, Saraphena promising to find me later. As I turn back after watching them go, Enzo still sits in the corner gazing out the window.

"I've been doing some thinking," he starts.

"Please don't try and talk me out of this."

"Dove, just listen." I make my way over to the bed, climbing in and waiting for him to continue. "I've been doing some thinking, and after hearing everything you just said, it only confirms what I had come here to talk about to begin with. I'm sorry you were bombarded by everyone, they followed me in here after I said I needed to talk to you about removing the bond. I assumed you would have told Saraphena, who naturally would have told Gunnar, and because Gunnar can't keep his mouth shut, would have told Duncan. I didn't realize you planned on going through this alone."

"It just didn't seem like it was anyone else's business what I did with our bond. The only person who needed to know was you."

He doesn't respond to that. Enzo breathes a heavy sigh before finally looking at me once more. "I'd like to be there when you do it."

"Enzo, you don't have to do that."

"No one should have to go through what you are alone. I know it's what you need to do, but it doesn't mean you have to endure that by yourself. I don't need to be there with you...I want to be. I wasn't there for you when you needed it most and I'll spend my entire life making it up to you, but this is one thing I can do for you."

"Can I admit something to you?" I ask.

"Always."

"I'm scared." Tears well in my eyes once more at the admittance of that. Enzo stands at the sight.

"What can I do?" Determination fills his tone as if that one simple question will fix all my problems. I might regret this. I might hate myself later for it, but I know what I need in this moment.

"Will you just...hold me? Take me away from this reality for just one more moment." Enzo moves around to the other side of the bed and pulls back the covers. I move my body toward the head board, making room to pull down the sheets on my side.

Climbing under, Enzo pulls the covers over our heads, just as before.

"The world can't get you in here, my dove." Here, in these brief moments, my world outside of Enzo doesn't exist once again. The sheets protect me from the demons waiting to consume me in the outside world, but here, as Enzo tucks me into his side and places a soft kiss on top of my head, I'm safe. I'm *me.* I'm not sure how much time passes, but I must have dozed off because when I wake, the sun is a deep amber shade mixed with the hues of orange light. For SunSpark, it's practically bedtime. The covers are still over our heads, and Enzo is looking at me like he holds the world in his hands.

"Are you ready?" He asks.

"I'm ready." Enzo leaves the room after I asked him for some time to compose myself. I wash my face, and when I look into the reflecting glass before me, I stare at the girl gazing back. The scar from the day we met peeks out above the top of my shirt. I run my finger down the raised flesh, feeling my heart beat under my touch. Gold and blue irises gaze back at me, my blonde hair cascading around my shoulders and down my back.

"So much has changed," I whisper to myself. Sparky takes note and feathers wrap around me in a comforting embrace. "I know with you I'll never truly be alone anymore." I pet the soft plumes, thankful for the solace I find in their embrace. Taking a final breath, I leave the washroom and head toward the next part of me that will change forever.

Chapter 34

ALIYAH

The walk to the healer's chambers feels like a death march. Placing one foot in front of the other, the walls around me feel cold, even amongst the heat of the SunSpark sun. Light streams in around me from the stained glass windows lining the walkway. These last few months have felt like an entire lifetime. Memories flash across my vision, playing out in front of me.

My village on fire, meeting Enzo for the first time. Feeling the way he wipes away the blood on my cheeks. The ring from the man who touched me in the bar. His hands wrapped tight around me as he pulled me from the Reflecting Pool. The promise that the next time we had a moment alone together I would be ready to take that next step with him...only to end up walking to a chamber where the very thing that binds us together will be physically ripped from my chest.

The threat of Tyros and The Kalari looms in the distance, creeping closer and closer every day. Liliana is marrying the man she was destined by the Maker to be with and yet something feels so entirely wrong about it. Saraphena and Gunnar found their way back to each other, but will this war rip them apart? Is it fair of me to ask them to fight by my side after everything they have been through?

I turn the final corner, the healer's chamber just at the end of the hall. Enzo waits outside the door, staring down the hall at me. I feel his pain ripple through the bond, but I try to block it out. I can only deal with one person's pain at a time and today, I'm choosing myself. I want Enzo to be my future, but first I need to put him in the past. Reaching him, I grasp the door handle, when Enzo's hand reaches out and stops my arm. "Aliyah. I need to say one last thing." I stare up at him, waiting for him to continue, hoping it won't make this moment even harder than it already is.

"There was a time when you asked me for total honesty and I feel like even now I owe you that. You've spent so long constantly thinking of others and what they needed from you. I ripped you from your life and threw you into this one. I don't regret it, not for a moment, because despite the damage I have caused over the last several months...it brought Saraphena back to Gunnar, and hell, even Duncan was able to see that he is capable of love again. You were the best decision I ever made, and I pray to the Maker one day you will come back to me by *your* choice, and no one else's. Even if we no longer have the mate bond, I know you are it for me."

I can't help the lump in my throat forming and deciding to make a permanent home in my throat. "I don't have the perfect words, Enzo. I know that I loved you and I know that I do love you now, I just need to sort out if I'm *in* love with you. So much has happened...but I don't regret it either. I came into my powers, which I never would have found until I died. I have a guardian on my back which never would have happened unless I was left in that box. Life has always happened *to* me though, and today I'm taking control."

"I know you don't need me to protect you anymore, Aliyah, but know that even though you might not need me, I'll still be here. Just because you can protect yourself, doesn't mean you should have to."

Nodding my head, I push open the door to the healer's chamber. Potions and poisons line the shelves of his small space along with thick, dusty tomes that can only be filled with spells and knowledge of years from harnessing his craft. I climb on the table, fear lacing my senses, but determination conquering the feeling.

"You're sure about this? Once the process has begun, there is no turning back. Picking out a piece of your soul...your bond...it will be excruciating."

"I'm sure. Once you have started, don't stop. Not for anything. Not for anyone. Do you understand?"

"Understood." The healer reaches up and locks my arms into iron shackles above my head. My wrists burn at the feeling, but I hold strong knowing this is what I need to do. I can't have this bond clouding my judgment any longer. I don't know how to truly forgive unless I have him out of my very soul. "Do you wish to have any medication for the pain? It will be truly horrible without it."

"No. I need to feel every moment of this. Let's begin." I feel the hot iron shackles wrap tight around my ankles. Completely immobile, I try to block out the pain burning at my wrists, knowing the pain to come will be far worse. A knife rips through the front of my tunic. I think back to those days in Mareen when I only had one shirt to spare. I would have cursed myself then for ruining another shirt, but I'm not that girl any longer. I feel his hand wrap around mine in the shackle and I instantly feel more calm. "Thank you."

"If you have a place in your mind that you feel most safe, I'd go there now." The healer's words come with a plea, but I need to be present for this moment. I'm not going to run from my decision. The cool tip of the knife rests at the top of my sternum, right over the crest of the scar from the ax that split open my chest not so long ago. *The ax that changed everything.*

"One last thing," Bairastyn starts. "This magic, it has never been done before. I am severing a piece of your soul, but I cannot guarantee it will last. The mate bond...it is a fickle thing. I cannot promise you it will not come back in the future."

"I understand. I'm willing to take that risk." I feel my skin split as he drags the knife through the scar tissue. I grit my teeth and suck in a harsh breath.

"Shhhh. It's okay. I've got you." Enzo's voice grounds me to the moment.

"If you plan to stay in the present moment, milady, don't close your eyes. You will only internalize the pain. Keep them open and breathe through it as best you can." The healer hesitates before beginning the next step of the procedure.

"I'm ready."

I hear the clamoring of tools as the healer picks up his next instrument. He rests it on the bone that covers my most precious organ and begins to saw. My grip tightens around Enzo's hand and I hear the distinct sound of my sternum cracking in two, exposing my heart and soul to the healer. It's ironic that someone who is meant to heal has to first cause so much pain. Sweat pours off me in buckets and I feel my hands slipping in the shackles. The chains pull and shake each time I try to rip my arms free.

"Hold her down for this next part."

Enzo's hands come on my shoulders, bracing himself against my body. I hear the crank of the tool as it cleaves my chest in two. Golden light breaks through the room as my power illuminates under my skin.

"Please try to contain the spark inside you. I do prefer my skin intact," Bairastyn quips and I try to reign in my ability, not letting my emotions take over. I feel my wings flex under my back, clearly uncomfortable with the pain I'm experiencing. *I need to know my love for him is real.* They calm at my back, but their hesitation is palpable. Blood pools around me and my chest is cracked in two, ready for a piece of my soul to be cut from my body. My breathing is ragged and I feel tears slipping from my eyes.

The soft words of an incantation fall from the healer's mouth. The spell that will bring my soul to a physical being and isolate the mate bond. My body thrashes as my soul takes form in my chest. I feel my heart beating wildly, but worse of all…I hear it. I hear it not inside my body, but in the room. It becomes painfully obvious that my chest is cracked in two and my entire set of organs is exposed to the world right now. I look down as the healer reaches inside my chest. Searing agony rips through me. I scream as loud as my throat allows, watching him pull a golden thread from inside my chest out of my body. There, between two small metal pinchers, is my bond with Enzo.

"Last chance. You're certain?"

"Cut it."

I love you, Aliyah. Even without this bond, I know you are my future. I will love you until the very breath in my lungs gives out and my heart is cleaved in two. I will always love—

Enzo's voice in my mind is cut off. Silence fills the space where that thread once lay. My bond with Enzo is no more.

Chapter 35

LILIANA

I race through the halls, fear ripping through me with every turn and I slip on the marble flooring. I hadn't realized how long I had been out in the gardens with Jonah. One moment we were walking away from Aliyah, and the next thing I knew the sun was transforming to its evening light. We were talking for so long I hadn't realized the time.

That's when Gunnar found me in the garden, telling me what Aliyah had done. Why didn't she ask for me? Why didn't she want me to be there with her? I'm— I'm the star to her moon.

I push open the door to her room and find her asleep on the bed. Enzo sits in the corner, his eyes red-rimmed, evidence of fresh tears having fallen.

"Enzo, what happened? How is she?" I ask, trying to catch my breath.

"Our bond is gone."

"What?! Enzo— How— What?!"

"It's okay, Liliana. It's what she needed."

"Are you...okay?" I try to reach out with my power to siphon off some of his pain, but it's as if the well of power inside of me has gone dry. How does this keep happening? I don't think I've been using my power that much recently. Maybe I have and I just don't realize it? There has been a lot going on emotionally for everyone.

"No. I'm not okay. But Aliyah can't know that. She did what was best for her and I just have to pray to the Maker it helps her come back to me one day. The healer gave her something to sleep it off for now. She will likely be asleep for the next few days. I'm sure she will be happy to know that you came to see her though."

"Of course I'm going to come and see her! Can I do anything? I can sit with her if—"

"Liliana, why don't we leave Aliyah to rest?" Jonah's hand lands on my lower back.

"Jonah, I didn't even hear you come in. I want to stay with her if that's okay."

"She should rest, bug. Let's just leave Enzo to care for his mate— I mean...his friend."

I pull back, intending to stay with Aliyah. "She is more than his friend. They love each other."

"I'm sure they do. All the more reason to let them be alone together now. They clearly need to sort some things out."

"Jonah, no, I want to stay. Enzo, tell him I can stay." I turn, searching Enzo's face, but his mind has drifted to another place as he stares out the window, tears streaking his cheeks. "Enzo—"

"It's better for them to be alone," Jonah says as we walk down the hall. I look around, not knowing when I left the room with him. His grip on my arm tightens slightly as he pulls me along.

"Jonah, let go of me."

"What?" He stops, looking down at me.

"I said let go of me."

His hand immediately releases from my arm and he steps back. "Bug, I'm so sorry. I didn't realize I had been holding you so tight. I just saw how upset Enzo was and he asked to be alone, but you were so upset over the situation, I had to bring you with me."

"No he didn't. I didn't hear him ask that, Jonah."

"Yes he did, Bug. You were standing right there when he said so."

"No, Jonah. He never said that."

"You were so upset over what Aliyah did, my bug. I'm sure you just blocked it out knowing how much you wanted to stay with her. But this is what is best for them. They just need some time, like we do."

"I— I really don't—"

"I don't want to fight about this tonight, okay? I just want to go back to the gardens with you and talk about *our* future. You get so wrapped up with everyone else, you barely have time for the two of us and we are about to be *married,* Bug. You need to start focusing on us and less on everyone else's drama."

"I— I'm sorry. I didn't realize you felt that way. I guess— Yeah, okay we can go back. But I'd like to check in on her later."

"Of course, Bug. Anything you want." Jonah leans down and places a soft kiss to my cheek before grasping my hand and walking us back toward the gardens. I turn my head to look back at the room where my best friend lies, but Jonah's hand snakes up to my neck, slowly turning it back toward the walkway ahead of us. Though, I'm starting to become unsure about him for another reason, it might just be too late.

Chapter 36

ENZO

The ache in my chest has become all consuming as I sit here and watch my ma— my love, sleep away the pain from the procedure. It's been three days since the bond has been taken out, and every fiber of my being is screaming against the empty feeling where the piece of her soul should be. But this pain is nothing compared to what she has been through. This is pain I can endure for *her*. She deserves so much better than what I can give her, but I'll be damned if I don't keep trying to show her how sorry I am.

Kaleron has been to visit her several times since the removal of her bond and I try to keep from thinking that he is trying to swoop in and be there for her in a way I cannot be. I know there is something between them, but I have to believe Aliyah when she said she was not removing the bond to be with him. If I can't trust her words, then we won't have a future together.

When we first met, I would have torn the world apart for Aliyah, I still would. But now I would only do it if she asks it of me. Aliyah is her own woman, strong, and formidable. She can tear the world apart for herself. She doesn't need me to be the fierce, over-protective, brute. She needs me to love her, to accept her. No longer will I stand in front of her as a shield, but by her side as an equal, and at her back when she rises up to claim her place in this world. My days of uncontrolled chaos are over...unless the situation truly calls for it.

A pained expression crosses her face as she twists and turns on the bed, coming out from the sleep the healer put her in. I race to her side, her wings shifting to crystal at my nearness. "Whoa there. I promise I don't want to hurt her. Just checking on her."

"They shifted because the pain hurts almost as bad as getting stabbed through the heart," she laughs.

"It's still too soon for that joke," I huff.

"As the person who was stabbed, I think I decide when it is too soon." Her eyes crack open and a smile forms on her lips while she sits up in bed. My hands hover close to her body just in case she needs help, but as per usual, she manages it all on her own.

"How do you feel?" I ask. I can't hide the nerves in my tone. I know what missing my bond feels like, and it isn't that I want her to regret her choices, but I have to know if she feels the same.

"Better," she smiles.

"Good." *Agony.* White hot pain lances through my heart at her words. I force a smile, knowing this was the choice *I* made. To be supportive, to be loving, to stand by her side no matter what. "I'm glad to hear it."

"You don't have to do that, Enzo. You don't have to pretend it doesn't hurt. I can see it written all over your face."

"Sorry. Yes, it does hurt, but it will pass in time," I smile.

"Where is everyone?" She asks, looking around the room as if they were supposed to be here the whole time. Saraphena and Gunnar came in and out during the last few days, but—

"Jonah has moved up his wedding date with Liliana. They are getting married today."

"What?! Enzo, we had more time! He can't just do that! He had a deal with Kaleron! I need to see him."

"I'll see if he is available." I stand, trying to reign in my power from letting loose at her words. Shutting the door behind me, I turn and run right into the man of the hour.

"Captain Jonah, so sorry. I didn't see you there. I was just on my way to find Kaleron. Excuse me."

"Not a problem! I was just checking in on Aliyah. I'll wait with her until you get back. Ensure she is healing after the procedure." Jonah claps me on the back and pushes through the door. I'm half way down the hall when I stop.

Where was I going again?

"Enzo! Come quick! Duncan's in trouble!" Gunnar grabs my arm and pulls me through the hallways to Duncan's room.

"Gunnar, I don't have time for this right now. I'm supposed to be on my way— I was supposed to be doing something right now."

"Okay well whatever it is it can wait. Duncan needs us!"

When we arrive at Duncan's room, it is clear that Gunnar was correct. Duncan does need help. His room is in complete darkness, every curtain drawn and not a candle to be found. "Duncan?"

"What am I going to do?" His voice is somber and the weight of his words lay heavy in the air. Duncan sits on the floor at the foot of his bed, his hands shoved into his hair.

"We can stop the wedding," Gunnar says.

"She doesn't want that. She has a mate now. She has Jonah." Duncan grits his teeth at his words.

"You know she loves you, man!" Gunnar implores.

"Don't. Don't say that. I messed everything up. I should have chosen her sooner. It's too late now. I ruined us."

"There is always time. We just have to —"

"Enough!" Duncan cuts Gunnar off. "Enough," he whispers.

"What can we do?" I ask. I move to sit on his right while Gunnar takes a seat on his left. Gunnar and I exchange a glance, worry etched into our expressions.

"Leave me be. I'll sit through the wedding and watch as the love of my life marries another, and then I'll go fight this stupid war if only for the distraction of not having to think of her with him. Who knows, maybe I'll die and all my problems will be solved. No becoming king, no hurt of losing my mate, no hurt of losing the only woman to love me since then. Just pure, empty, bliss."

"Duncan, you don't mean that," Gunnar says.

"Yes. I do. I'm no one's white knight. I can't save her from this. I've seen the way she looks at him and the way she looks at me. Jonah is her future now. She's made that clear. I will endure this, but after, I'm going back to Twilight to prepare for the war with The Banished King."

"You're— you're going to leave us?" I ask.

"Never. But I need to get the troops in Twilight ready to join the army in Citrine. This is a small problem in the grand scheme of everything else going on around us. The war isn't just going to wait while I grieve another loss."

"We will get through this, brother. Together," I say.

"Why is everything that happens to us something we actually have to deal with? Why are they never problems we can just ignore?" Duncan huffs out a light laugh.

"Because the choices others made long ago have created a ripple in the pond of life and we are dealing with the aftershock. There was never a way around this war," I sigh.

"Then we move into the next battle today...the battle of Liliana's wedding. I pray we all make it through," Gunnar winks.

Chapter 37

JONAH

"Hello, *dove.*" The frail creature before me looks so weak and pathetic. It's a miracle she's survived this long. The only redeeming quality about her is the beauty that adorns her back. Everything else is simply a *waste.*

"Don't call me that, Jonah. What do you want?" She sits up in bed, a pained expression across her face as she adjusts herself.

"I just came to check on you! As a friend of Liliana's, you are a friend of mine now too."

"I'm not really in the market for any more friends right now. Especially the likes of you."

"Now is that any way to treat your best friend's future husband?"

"I heard you managed to find a way to speed up your wedding date. What's your game, Jonah? What do you gain?"

"I have my reasons," I smile. "I know what you're going to get me as a wedding gift."

"If it's anything more than the dirt off my boots, you don't deserve it."

"Snarky little thing aren't you? But no. It is something *far* better and in reality, it is actually more of a gift for you." I can't help the wicked smile that plays across my face any longer. "I have to admit. I was really dreading this assignment. I mean, going after some small, frail, blonde, *barely* fae girl didn't seem like much of a treat. But getting to worm my way into your little family and tear it apart piece by piece? Now that has been far more enjoyable than I ever thought it would be."

I watch as Aliyah gets up from the bed, backing further into the corner of the room, wings crystalizing. She grips the wound on her chest. The scar has healed over already, but I'm sure the pain of losing her bond is deliciously dreadful.

"Don't come near me, Jonah. I mean it."

"Don't worry, I don't plan on coming anywhere near you...yet."

"When Liliana hears about this she isn't going to marry you. Mate or not, she won't stand for it. She will figure you out, and when she does, you best leave SunSpark and never come back or she will kill you. If Enzo doesn't get to you first for threatening me."

"Ah yes. *Enzo.* Your mate." I make sure I punctuate that last part with a tsk of disdain. "A silly concept if you ask me. As if being mated to someone is some glorious thing to be coveted by all. It isn't something to be celebrated. It's a chain around your neck. You were right to rip yours out. Maybe I'll make Liliana do the same after I bed her on our wedding night. Wouldn't that be fun?"

"You will not touch her. I'll be damned if I let you anywhere near her after this."

I watch as the swirls of gold on her arms shimmer in the dim light of her room.

"Time's up," I say.

"Time for—"

She doesn't even have a chance to react before she is pinned to the wall by her neck by my special little invention. I watch as she grapples at the iron chain around her neck, the spikes digging into her neck, severing her vocal cords. I know she can't die, but now she can't yell for help either. Her wings return to their natural state and slump behind her.

She tries to speak, straining against the prongs in her throat.

"Do you like it? I had it specially made for you." I walk up to her, knowing she is powerless against me now. I run my finger over the iron, watching as it sizzles against her skin. Her eyes are wide and filled with horror. *Perfect.*

"There is no use in trying to speak. The spikes have been specially designed to slice through your vocal cords without cutting off your airway. The chain, iron of course, because a little birdie told me that would hurt the most, and dipped in a coating laced with a power suppressant. That's why your wings, despite being a different part of you, are useless now. They were born as part of your power, therefore being suppressed by the same potion that makes you powerless. I was worried about how this was going to work with you being mated to Enzo, but you went ahead and took care of that problem for me!"

She continues to struggle fruitlessly like a helpless little sphinx lined up for slaughter.

"You're probably wondering why I'm doing this and the answer is quite simple. I hate Olyrium. They have always cast The Islands aside! Deemed us savages and unfit for society! Well I figure I might as well prove them right! See you're a little problem for a friend of mine and he knows to always call upon the best when dealing with annoying little things. Liliana being my mate was a happy coincidence, but it's no matter. She will be gone soon enough."

I reach around her, unhooking the fashioned spikes from the wall that hold her there and clasp the full chain around her neck. Reaching into my pack slung around my back, I pull out the leash attachment for the collar.

"You aren't mine to kill, but I certainly can't have you screwing up the wedding either and your wings were starting to give me away. I'll marry Liliana, kill King Kaleron and Gunnar in a *terrible* accident, and then take the SunSpark throne for myself as the rightful King. It's what is *owed* to me. Unfortunately for SunSpark, there were never going to be any ships. That was just my ploy to get information. How everything else played out was simply too good."

Aliyah continues to claw at the chain, desperately trying to pull it from around her throat, blood dripping down her hands at the contact with the iron.

"It's no use you simpering fool! Get it through your skull, Aliyah! You aren't getting out of that collar. Not until I've delivered you to the boss and he can do with you what he will! Come with me and I won't kill Enzo on the spot."

That makes her freeze. "Good. Now, we can't have you remembering all of this. Not yet anyways. The next time you wake up, you won't be in SunSpark anymore."

Laying my hand on her wrist, I push my power into her, erasing this conversation entirely from her mind.

Chapter 38

JADE

I look out over the horde of The Kalari kneeling before me. My father sits on his throne, ranting on about his coming reign and all the destruction he will bring with me at his side. I have no interest in his words, not these ones anyway, but the ones he will speak that will awaken my power. *The ones that will be the beginning of the end for Aliyah.* When I received news that Jonah was approaching the final stages of his plan, I knew my timeline was getting moved up.

"Daughter, Princess of Nightmares, are you ready to take your place at my side?" His voice booms over the army and they beat their spears against the stone floor in a rhythmic motion, signaling the beginning of the ceremony. My red silk dress swishes around my bare feet, the deep-cut front allowing access to where the first cut will start.

"Yes, father." My voice is even, not a hint of fear underlying my words, because I am not one who runs from fear...I am fear itself.

"Step forward and we shall begin." The Banished King lounges in his throne, pure power dripping from every inch of him. *Soon, that throne will be mine to inherit.* "Bring the dagger," he calls.

One of The Kalari walks up the three steps toward the dais and kneel, presenting a black dagger to me. Three crystals are embedded into the handle, two blood red, one pure and clear. Palming the dagger in my hand, I feel the hum of power in its hilt. A wicked smile breaks across my lips. *This is it.* Everything I've been waiting for, everything I've been *fighting* for, has led me to this moment. The others were only ever going to hold me back from what I was truly capable of.

"Blood of my blood, child of darkness, and thing of nightmares, bring me your heart and all the power in the world will run through your fingertips." Tyros stands, taking a place beside me as I prepare to fill the blood stone.

A soft chant falls from my fathers lips, the thundering of the spears connecting with the floor building my anticipation. I don't even flinch as I lift the dagger, plunging it into my chest. My breath catches, but I don't stop, pain never finding the hole in my gaping chest.

I work to bring the knife down and around, sawing a hole where my most precious organ lies. I know I won't die, father assured me of that. It's why I have no fear of what is to come. At the end of it all, I may not have a heart, but I will have something far more precious— Power.

Tyros continues chanting, the rhythmic beats from The Kalari get faster...I drop the dagger. Metal clatters on the cold stone floor, blood spurting from my chest. I should be horrified, but all I can do is smile. I dig my fingers deep into the hole of my ribs, that's when I feel it. The beating source of all my pain. Love is like a cancer, festering, consuming...and all you can do is the one thing to rid yourself of it forever. *Rip. It. Out.*

I pull, tissue tearing away, red blood running in streaks down my hands, over my forearm, and pooling onto the floor beneath my knees. I stare at the abomination in my palm. Finally...I'm free. I feel nothing except for the empty bliss of corruption. I slam the organ down, palming the dagger once more, its hilt slippery in my bloody hand. My father's hand strokes my hair and I look up at him.

Pride beams in his eyes and I focus on his words. "My father, your grandfather, was the first to perform this ritual. When he died, I took his place upon the throne and accepted my destiny, just as you are today. Join the generations that came before you, my child, and feed the dagger what it needs."

I clasp the hilt with both hands, bringing it up high above my head, letting every memory of Enzo flood my mind. Every touch, every kiss...every heart break. Every wishful thought, every moment of potential. Today, I will let it die. Today, I will find my retribution.

I slam the dagger into my still beating heart. My chest heaves as I release a flurry of stabs into the organ. *Again and again and again.* I scream, the sound ripping through the air, silencing the horde. Something takes over my body. I don't know if it's anger, fury, or something else entirely, but all I know is it consumes me. I watch as my blood swirls up the dagger, the once pure clear crystal now a deep shade of red.

The trails of blood that filled the crystal now slip out the other side in black tendrils of ooze. A familiar design slips beneath my skin, marking my body with blackness in my veins. I watch as it slithers up my hand, squeezing like a vice around my forearm, pain finally registering as it creeps through my body. I close my eyes, breathing through the searing agony that rips through my entire being.

I claw at my neck, feeling the burning sensation pouring through my veins and arteries. I fall forward, palms smacking against the stone, crushing it beneath my grip. I reach the end of the dais and clasp the edge of the step with my hands and squeeze. Stone shatters beneath my palms, my back arches like a feral feline, pure agony threatening to consume me fully.

My fingernails find my face, ripping into my skin with brutal strength as if I could strip the poison from beneath the surface. Black blood splatters onto the steps beneath me as I crawl toward the bottom, needing distance, needing space, needing anything but this feeling. My breaths are rabid, a low rumble unfurls in my chest as the beast inside me finally breaks free.

I remain staring at the ground, the crackle of pure, raw power pumping from where my heart once lay. A maniacal smile tugs at my lips, but I can only feel the right side pull up. Movement in front of me pulls me from my trance, something heavy being placed in front of me.

"I could not be more proud of you, daughter. Relish in this new power, but know our training has just begun. If it is vengeance you seek, then let us corrupt their peaceful little world." I look up to find my father standing behind a large reflecting glass, but as my eyes meet the woman reflecting back at me, I know I am going to claim everything I am owed...and more. She is truly a thing of nightmares.

Long onyx hair now pooling around her, ending at her elbows, blood-red streaks peaking through the oil like strands. Dark red eyes glow back at me, black power swimming in her gaze. The right side of her face is laced with inky veins creeping up her neck, cracking like lightning around her eye...but the left...the left side of her face was truly unique. From the center of her forehead, down the left side of her nose, through the center of her lips, and ending at the edge of her collar bone, a black skeleton shows through where the skin had been clawed away. She is beautiful and fierce, and nothing in this world will ever hurt her again.

Jade is dead...

Long live the Princess of Nightmares.

Chapter 39

LILIANA

"**A**re you ready?" Kaleron's voice ricochets through my mind as I stare at myself in the mirror. *This will be the happiest day of your life.* My mother's words, words meant to inspire joy, but instead are a stark reminder of my reality.

Lace sleeves cover my arms before swirling up and over my shoulders, dipping into a low V-shape before transforming into fitted silk that cascades down my legs into a pool around my feet. A long train sprawls out behind me, buttons lining up the middle before stopping just at the small of my back. The back of the dress is open, leaving me feeling exposed rather than beautiful.

Tears pull in my eyes. *It's not him out there waiting for you at the end of that aisle,* I remind myself. *He didn't choose you, Liliana.*

"Is he out there?"

Kaleron knows who I mean without having to ask. "Yes."

A tear slips down my cheek, leaving a line of exposed skin under my make-up in its wake. "I can't do this, Kaleron. I know...I know he is my...mate...but I can't do it."

"You have to, Lil." Kaleron laces his fingers through mine as we stand in front of the mirror together. "The deal is done. His ships for your hand. Mate or not, this is your future. I'm so sorry, Liliana."

I turn to look up at my brother. The King. "You can change this. Can't you? You're the king. Don't make me go through with this. I need more time."

"I wish I could, Liliana. As your brother, I would do it in a heartbeat, but as king...I have to think of our people."

"Jonah is a good man, right? He'll take care of me, won't he? These last few days I— I just have this feeling he isn't who he says he is."

"His advisors only have glowing things to say about him. A good leader of The Islands and his people seem to really love him."

"Okay." My heart feels pulled in two different directions. One toward darkness, a sky filled with stars that will forever shine, and the other across the sea, far away from everything I know...far from every one I love. "I'm ready."

As I make my way through the halls of SunSpark Palace, lady's maids hold my train up behind me. I pass through the glittering halls adorned with flowers of every variety. White and gold colors are strategically placed throughout the palace, reminding me how much I have grown to love the dark colors of night...the colors of *him.*

I shake my head to clear that thought from my mind. *He didn't choose you.* Over and over I remind myself of this fact.

The doors to the garden lay before me. The glass has been stained to hide me from my groom, like that will make a difference in the success of this union. My stomach does flips as I wait for the crescendo of the music outside. With each note cresting higher and higher so does my anxiety. I grip Kaleron's hand in mine.

I can't do this. I can't do this. I can't do this. Crippling fear creeps in. I don't *want* to do this!

"Lil." Saraphena steps up next to me. "I've got it from here, Kaleron." Her soft smile at my brother eases some of my nerves. Kaleron steps back from me and exits out the side door to join the others.

"Why aren't you out there?" I ask.

"If there was ever a time for you to need me, it would be now." Saraphena smiles, grabbing my hand.

"Where is Aliyah?" I ask.

"Last I knew she was still asleep. With the wedding being moved up— I don't know if she is going to be able to make it today, Lil."

"I don't want to do this. I keep thinking those doors are going to open and I'll find Duncan standing at the end of the aisle ready to sweep me away, but I know he won't be."

"Liliana, listen to me," Saraphena turns my head toward her. "I know this isn't what you imagined, or how you dreamed your wedding might go, but say the word and I will take you out of here right now. Contract be damned."

I bite my lower lip thinking over everything. Everything I've been through. Everything I've dreamed about this day. "No. I had given Duncan so many chances to choose me. Now I need to choose my people, just like he chose his. It may not be what I want, but it's what my people need. I made a commitment and who knows, maybe one day I'll end up loving Jonah too, despite what I feel now."

I can't wait for you to be mine forever, bug. My mate's voice filters through my mind. A weak smile pulls at my lips.

So I shall.

The doors open and the darkening orange of the sun spills over my dress causing the white silk to glow around me. The crowd stands and all eyes are on me, but there are only two that matter.

Duncan's eyes are wide as I start making my way down the aisle. Our gaze never leaves each other as I place one foot in front of the other. As I pass his row, I look down and see his hands clenched into two tight fists. I drag my eyes back up his body, over the tailored black shirt with a few buttons undone at the top revealing his tattoos and I watch as the wings around his throat constrict with his gulp.

I have to physically tear my eyes away from him to look at Jonah waiting for me at the end. His smile is bright and he has his hair styled perfectly, slicked back and tame. He wears a golden suit jacket with golden buttons and a crisp white shirt and pants. Everything about him screams SunSpark royalty.

Saraphena tightens her grip on me as I finally reach the end of the aisle before she leaves me to stand up here alone. I feel his eyes searing into my soul, not the man in front of me, but the one four rows back and three seats over.

Jonah reaches out his hand as I step forward. His palm is warm as it engulfs mine and I can't help but feel more grounded in the hands of my mate.

We face each other as Kaleron takes his place between us and begins speaking about the joys of marriage. *Like he would have a clue.*

You look so beautiful, bug.

Thank you. You clean up nice yourself.

When this is all over, I don't want to attend the party right away. I want you, Liliana. I want you to meet me in our bedroom directly after the ceremony.

I...I would but there are people to greet and thank. It isn't custom....

Liliana, my beautiful bug, do as you're told. He smirks at me with a twinkle in his eye and I can't help the blush that races up my cheeks at his words.

All right, but we can't stay away too long. I do have other duties to attend to. I wink at him across the way before focusing back on my brother's words.

"It is my honor to stand here today and join two kingdoms together, not only in politics, but in love. My baby sister was lucky enough not only to find a strong alliance, but her mate in the process. Not all of us are so lucky to find both. Do you have an exchange of vows prepared?"

"I um—"

"I do," Jonah smiles before pulling a small piece of parchment from his coat pocket. "Liliana, I promise to always keep you from the harm of others and I promise to love you as much as a man like myself can. I promise to always watch over you and I swear on my very soul that I will be with you until the end of my days."

The crowd's resounding *awww* signals me that it is my turn. "I um...Jonah I promise to always be a good wife and mate and I swear to you I will love you till the end of my days."

We recite the traditional words, binding our very souls together, and I feel the magic fusing us together for eternity.

"On that lovely note, you may now kiss your bride and join our kingdoms together forever," Kaleron declares.

Jonah's hand instantly comes around the back of my neck as he pulls me in close, his other hand finding my waist. His lips are cold and hard against mine. Nothing like— *Liliana, no.* I scold myself for even thinking that now. Jonah is my mate and my husband now. This is who I need to devote all of my time to.

He brings his lips to my ear in a warm embrace, but his words are nothing but ice. "Welcome to your worst nightmare, *wife*."

"Wha—" I'm cut off as he tugs away from me and drags me down the aisle in what looks like an excited fashion toward the back gate. As soon as we are clear from the crowd and out of sight, my entire world shatters.

His fist connects with my chin in one swift blow. "How dare you look at that piece of filth the entire walk down the aisle. *I* am your husband! *I* am your mate! You, bug, are *mine*. If you so much as set your eyes on another male again I will not hesitate to pluck them from your skull and say you had a horrible accident on our honeymoon. Am I clear?"

I can't speak. My body is frozen in horror. *What have I done?*

"Am. I. Clear?!" Jonah practically yells. I flinch at his words.

"Y— yes." I try to reach out my power to lower his anger, but I am met only with a hard stare.

He reaches out and wipes the small line of blood trickling away from my healing jaw. "Now, now. Let's get you cleaned up. We can't have you looking like a wreck as we make our debut!" He snags my hand and drags me back toward the garden where the chairs have been cleared and guests now mill about, grazing the table for food and sipping on expensive champagne, none the wiser to my husband's shift in mood.

He lights up the air as he moves through the crowd greeting guests and soaking up the compliments and congratulations on his new bride. Bile churns in my stomach as I feel those eyes searing through my mind again. I know he's watching me. *Duncan, please save me.* I wish I could reach out through a bond we shared. Something which is so special between two people, a life line.

But my tether is poisonous, a leach to my happiness. I don't dare look up. I do what is safe and look down at my shoes. The white tipped satin heels that peak out from under my silken dress.

Music plays in the grand hall connected to the gardens and guests filter inside to dance. I stand in the center with my mate alone now, but I still feel his eyes on me. Jonah's grip on my hand is crushing and I'm sure I'll have bruises where his fingers lie.

"Shall we dance?"

"Of course," I whisper.

"Speak up, *wife.*"

"I would love to dance," I say, raising my chin to meet his gaze.

As we spin around the dance floor, I note the smiles on everyone's faces as they watch us. I feel Jonah's fingers digging into the exposed skin of my back. "I can't wait to burn this dress into ash. If you ever wear something this revealing again, I'll make sure you never leave our rooms again."

Before I can respond, a dark figure appears in my peripheral. "Can I cut in?" Duncan's deep voice feels like a saving grace.

"Of course!" Jonah leans in to kiss my cheek before pulling away.

One glance at him and you will never see him again.

I keep my eyes fixed on the floor. I can't lose Duncan, not now, not ever. His life depends on me keeping my eyes on the ground.

"Liliana, look at me."

My lip trembles as we sway on the dance floor. Tears threaten to spill over, but I can't cry. If I do, he will know something is wrong.

"Excuse me," I say, pulling away from him. I keep my eyes trained on the floor as I scurry from the room. Out in the hall I finally let my sob break free. I lean up against a wall to steady myself and I clutch my stomach as dinner threatens to make a reappearance.

This can't be happening. Please let this all just be a nightmare I wake up from.

The golden walls and golden swirled floors suddenly seem too bright. Every time I catch a glimpse of gold, I flinch, remembering Jonah's golden jacket. Panic creeps into my veins. I could run. I could get Molly and fly far away from here. I could just leave forever and never come back.

Footsteps sound in the hall, getting closer to me. Full panic settles deep in my chest as I wait to see who it is that comes around the corner. "There you are!"

Jonah storms over to me and grabs me by the throat. "In such happy wedding bliss, you have been excused from the rest of the night, *bug*." He turns from me and tears threaten to spill over my lids once more. "Come on now. Time to seal our fates together forever."

I follow him up the steps toward our room. Each footfall sounding of dread and doom. Like with each step I am one closer to captivity. *I can still run.* As I place my next foot on the step, I let the shoe slip off my foot, and then the next. I won't make it far with my heels on. I glance back at the front hall, the doors to freedom lie just at the bottom. My heart races and blood pounds in my ears.

On three. One...two...three. I turn and sprint down the steps, Jonah screaming my name behind me. I hear his feet hitting the marble steps as he bounds after me.

I'm so close. So close to freedom.

I flip open the doors so hard they smack against the wall and almost break off the hinges. I sprint out the entrance and make a break for the sphinx fields.

"Molly! Molly!" I yell, trying to find her.

I turn back to see Jonah closing in on me. I can't find her anywhere! There isn't time. I hop on the back of another and the beast shoots into the sky, white wings flapping hard to push us toward the sky. Jonah yells after me to stop, but I can't. I can't go back now. My hair whips out of its style and I push it out of the way.

The sphinx climbs higher and higher, leaving my nightmare to be only a small dot standing in the field below me. Being a man of the sea, he wouldn't dream of getting on one of the sphinx. I hate to leave Molly behind, but I know she will find me again.

I urge the sphinx forward. I know where to go. I know Duncan will find me.

Chapter 40

LILIANA

I dangle my feet in the cool waters of the Reflecting Pool and stare down at my reflection as the sun's shade morphs into daybreak. My white dress, now covered in dirt and grime from the soil around me. *Please come for me Duncan.* What have I done? I've tied my life to a monster. This isn't like those morally gray men you read about in books who do questionable things, but you love them anyways. Jonah is a full-fledged monster through and through. His red flags are just that...*red.* Blood red, with no hints of green anywhere within them.

I knew he was too good to be true. Too loving. Too kind. Too *perfect.* I knew I never should have trusted him, yet duty and this stupid invisible tether convinced me to ignore my gut and follow blindly. I have to find a way out of this without severing the deal for his ships.

I hear the beating of wings before I see them. I shoot up from the ground, my dress pooling around my feet once more. I race over to the edge of the floating island and look down at my incoming savior. But it isn't Duncan who I find coming to my aid.

"Princess Liliana. Your presence is requested back at the palace. Your husband has been looking everywhere for you. He is worried sick!" Some of the SunSpark Flying Legion lands in front of me. Fear grips in my throat.

"I'm not going back. I am your princess and I order you to leave this place."

"Unfortunately, princess, the king himself has requested you back and we take our orders from him. Jonah has begged the king for his help in finding you. He is quite distraught over your disappearance," one of the legion says.

I look around the Reflecting Pool like someone is going to come out at any time and take me away from here, but once again, no one is coming to save me. "Okay, but I want to be taken to my brother straight away."

I climb on the back of one of the sphinx brought with them and the guard's arms wrap around me protectively as we take off into the sky. My heart lurches at the motion as we descend down through the sky, closer and closer to my new husband.

As we land in the field, I see Jonah standing by the fence, his strong body leaning against one of the posts, anger etched into his face. I gulp as I make my way over to him. His face morphs into the role of concerned husband, but I know I'm going to pay for my actions.

"Oh thank the Maker you're all right!" His strong arms wrap around me, but there is no warmth to his embrace. "I can't believe that sphinx just took off like that with you on its back! I have never seen such a wild creature before. Surely that beast must be dealt with."

"We will find the wild sphinx and get to the bottom of this. I am just as surprised as you are, sir."

"Please, call me Jonah. It is the least I can do to thank you for finding my wife. I thought I'd lost her forever! Come now, let's get back inside."

He grips my hand with bruising force, but I'm sure that to the Flying Legion it looks as if he is a loving mate. He plays his role perfectly.

Make one hint at the guards for help and it will be the last thing you do.

Death seems preferable at this point compared to another moment alone with you.

I will break you, wife. You will be the doting, loving, pliable, Princess you were born to be. You are mine now, body and soul. Even if you weren't my mate, you would still be mine, bound together forever in marriage and political gain. Without me you have no armies to man the seas.

A risk my brother is willing to take, I'm sure.

I wouldn't be so certain. He pulls me along at a crushing pace, my legs barely able to keep up as we stride toward the palace.

Gunnar stands at the front doors, concern flashing across his features. I shake my head quickly at him, not wanting Gunnar to get caught in the crossfire of my husband.

"Liliana, are you okay? Where were you?"

"Yes, I'm fine. A rogue sphinx is all. Nothing to worry about."

That's a good little wife. Now let's end this conversation.

"I do apologize, Gunnar, but Princess Liliana is very tired and I am certain very hungry." Jonah's words drip with concern, but I know his words are nothing but poisonous.

"I'd be happy to accompany her to breakfast. I could use the time to catch up with her anyways."

"No." Jonah's tone is clipped and his facade drops momentarily. I watch as small sparks play across my brother's fingers.

"Excuse me? Did you just—" Gunnar clenches his fists.

Dismiss your brother...now!

"Gunnar, it's all right. I want to spend time with my husband. It was terrifying to be away from him. A day in is exactly what I need. I'll find you later." I shake my head, panic swimming in my eyes.

Gunnar clenches and unclenches his fists and I note the sparks of fire threatening to come out. I plead to him with my eyes to stop.

"Apologies," he says.

"Forgiven. Now if you will excuse us." Jonah pushes past him, dragging me behind him. I risk a glance back at Gunnar, wishing to the Maker he was the one who could read emotions. *Please help me.* I want to scream it just as the doors to the palace shut, leaving Gunnar on the other side.

"You will change and then meet me for breakfast. No tricks, Liliana, or your *lover* will pay."

"Duncan is *not* my lover."

"Then you must take me for a fool, for which I am not. Bathe, dress, and meet me in my private room. I have prepared a special meal for your return." Jonah's smile is wicked and I can't help the nervousness that pools in my gut.

I walk into my room and head straight for the bathing chamber. I strip off the once-white wedding gown and watch it pool around my ankles. I step into the shower and let the warm water wash over me, praying it washes away the fear along with it. I scrub my skin practically raw, hoping to erase the feeling of his touch on me.

How am I going to survive this night? A light knock comes at the door. I quickly wrap myself in my robe and tie it off just as the door to my room swings open.

"Duncan," I whisper. "Duncan! You can't be here. You need to leave!" I push at his chest, trying to get him to leave.

"Liliana tell me what's going on. Why did you run away?"

"I—" Tears well up in my eyes. I want to tell him everything. How Jonah hit me, threatened him and the rest of my family, but I can't. I won't put anyone at risk for my own safety. I can handle Jonah on my own. "Nothing. It's nothing."

"Liliana, I can see it isn't nothing. I know despite everything we have been through— You can trust me."

My eyes snap to his. I won't risk him. "Get out Duncan. You didn't choose me. You left me. You made your choice. You made *our* choice and I've made mine. I'm with Jonah now. I just got cold feet earlier, but I want to be with Jonah. Get out of my room and never come back."

"I know you, Liliana. I *see* you. I know you aren't okay. I will leave you now, but believe me when I say, I will find out what is going on here." Just like that, Duncan teleports out of my room. Relief washes over me at his absence. I don't want him involved in this. I don't know what Jonah will do to him, but I do know what I will do to Jonah. I'm going to make his life a living hell. I'm going to make him regret ever laying a hand on me.

"This is quite the spread you have laid out for me," I quip. "It's almost as if you care for me."

"Oh wife, I care quite deeply for you actually. I can't have my favorite play toy break on my first day with it. Sit, eat."

"I'm actually not very hungry." I rap my fingers on the table as I watch his jaw muscles flicker with annoyance.

"You will eat."

"Nah, I don't think I will."

Jonah looks to his men who stand behind me in Jonah's private dining chamber. They come up on either side of me and grip my wrists forcefully.

"Hey! Let go of me!"

Iron cuffs wrap around the bottom of the arm of the chair and clamp around my wrists. I grit my teeth and spit a large, wet wad on one of the goons faces. He doesn't even flinch. He simply wipes it away and continues shackling me to my chair.

"Well congratulations. You've trapped me into sitting in a chair I was already sitting in. I'm still not going to eat." I push out my power, attempting to sooth some of his anger. As if Jonah can sense my intentions, his eyes flare up with anger.

He shoves his chair back and picks something up off the table I hadn't noticed was there before. He storms over to my side of the table and in one swift motion, stabs a small needle into my neck. I wince at the burn as I feel the needle extract from my neck muscle.

"What the hell was that!?"

"I won't have you using your powers on me, or anyone else for that matter. This was a special little concoction made just for you. It will stop you from being able to use your abilities. You'll receive a daily dose, whether by choice, or by force." Jonah's grin is anything but sincere.

"I don't need my powers to make your life miserable. You will never lay a hand on me again."

"I don't need to lay a hand on you to control you, bug. I have many other ways of making you compliant."

"Stop calling me bug!"

"But that is what you are. A little bug that interests me for the time being, until I am ready to squash you. Now, eat."

"No."

Jonah lets out a long sigh. "Men, my wife is clearly too tired to eat on her own. Please see to it that she is fed."

Jonah's goons swarm me once more and I try to jerk away from them. One claps his hand over my forehead and shoves my head backwards against the back of the chair. A thick strap is produced by the other lackey and it is securely buckled around my forehead, forcing my head into an immobile position. I jerk in the chair trying to find any form of movement I can.

One of the goons begins cutting a large slab of meat in front of me. It is so undercooked, blood pools at the bottom of the plate. Bile churns in my throat at the sight. I try to turn my head away as he produces a piece in front of my mouth. I clamp my lips together so hard, my skin breaks at the contact.

The other dickwad wrenches open my mouth and right as his finger gets too close to my teeth, I bite down hard. He screams as he whips his hand back, connecting it with my face in one swift motion. Blood pools in my mouth from my cut lip, but I won't let that break my determination.

He reaches for my jaw again, this time keeping his hands clear of my teeth. His thumb and forefinger lay on either side of my jaw and he presses hard, forcing my joints to cave and open. The goon in front of me shoves a piece of meat into my mouth and I gag at the flavor. It is like no meat I have ever tasted before. Dickwad #1 forces my jaw closed while Dickwad #2 pinches my nose shut, forcing me to swallow the wretched meat.

Dickwad #1 and #2 continue to force feed me pieces of meat until my entire plate is clear. Finally they unbuckle the strap around my head and I sag in my chair. My body may be exhausted, but my mind is in a fit of fury.

"You better count your days, Jonah. When I get out of here, I'm going to find Molly and disappear. The next time you see me, will be the day you die."

"Hmmm. I don't think you will."

"Will what?"

"Find Molly."

"Wha— What have you done with her?"

"She's right in the other room, bug. Please feel free to visit her any time you wish, but she will be staying with me from now on."

"Over my dead body." I storm into the attached bedroom and shove open the doors. Horror grips my chest as I look to the ceiling above the bed. There, splayed out are two giant white wings, nailed to the ceiling and Molly's head mounted on a black wooden slab, bolted to the ceiling in the center of her wings.

"NOO! You monster! What have you done!? What have you done to her?!" I scream at the top of my lungs as I collapse onto the ground, sobs wracking my body.

"Fear not, little bug. I am a good hunter. I never let my spoils go to waste. Molly will forever be a part of you now. Well, at least for the next few hours when your body is done digesting her. But after that you can gaze upon her every night. You're welcome, bug." Jonah leans down and pets my head as I lay it on the floor, letting my sobs consume me.

Let this be a lesson. Run from me again, and one day you'll have no one to come back to. Imagine how glorious Duncan's head would look added to my collection.

Chapter 41

SARAPHENA

I race through the halls of SunSpark Palace, my feet beating against the ground with each step. My breathing is ragged and my mind is whirling at what I saw. I push open the door to Gunnar's room and find Duncan, Enzo, and Gunnar sitting on his bed, anxiously waiting for my return.

Duncan shoots up from the bed. "Well?"

"He— Duncan. I don't even know where to start! He—"

"Spit it out!" Duncan yells.

"He killed Molly! He killed Molly and then— He made her—" My gut churns at the thought. I sprint away toward the bathing chamber and the distinct sound of vomiting carries through the small space. Gunnar is behind me in a second.

"Shhhhh. It's okay. I've got you. Get it all out." His hand rubs soothing circles on my back while the other holds my long curly hair out of my face. The entirety of my stomach comes up at the thought of telling them.

"I'm okay now." I sit back and take a few deep breaths before making my way back out to the bedroom. "He made her eat Molly."

"What do you mean he *made* her?" Duncan's voice is low.

"He had his minions strap her to the chair and literally force feed her the sphinx, but she didn't know it was Molly at the time. It wasn't until— Oh Gunnar it was horrible." He moves over to wrap me up in his arms. I let my sobs get absorbed into his chest for a few moments before wiping the snot away on the hem of my sleeve. "He nailed Molly's wings to the ceiling right above the bed and mounted her head right in the center of them."

"He's a monster." Enzo's soft voice rings through the silence of the room. "A monster that needs to be put down."

"Agreed. He needs to go. Now." Duncan moves to teleport, but not before Enzo grabs his wrist.

"Wait. We need to be strategic about this. If we just outright kill Jonah, SunSpark will lose the ships he promised to bring during the war. We can't lose those ships or his army. We need to find a way to eliminate him without anyone finding out it was us."

"Enzo is right," I say, wiping my nose once more. "We need to protect Liliana as best we can while we figure out a plan."

"I have a plan! Kill him. It's that simple. He cannot live for what he has done." Duncan grits his teeth and I swear I see fire in his eyes.

"Duncan I know you want him dead like...right now...but we have to be rational about this. We need a plan," I say.

"Leave it to me," Gunnar smirks. A collective groan rings throughout the group. "What?!" Gunnar says, shocked.

"Oh, baby. Listen, I love you, but your plans...well, they aren't always the best," I say, patting him on the back.

"How can you say that?! My plan to chlorofae Enzo worked perfectly!"

"Well, we lost Jade as the strategist of the group. I suppose that position does need to be filled at some point. Let's hear what you got," Enzo smiles.

Gunnar leans in close so his voice is just above a whisper. "So here's the plan."

"That's a stupid idea, Gunnar," Duncan deadpans.

"It is not! We have a problem, I have a solution," Gunnar says with pride.

"A stupid solution..." I mutter under my breath.

"Baby, come on! You believe in me right?!" Gunnar beams at me.

"Gunnar you are talented at so many things, but this plan is...complex. Everything has to fall into place literally perfectly and when has that ever happened to us?" I say calmly.

"Okay so let's take a vote then! All in favor of Saraphena sneaking into each of the crew members' rooms and killing them while Duncan teleports them to their ship before we let it set sail with a bomb on board to explode when they get out to sea, say I!"

Gunnar waits anxiously while we all look around to each other, hoping someone else has a better plan.

"You all have no faith in me," Gunnar sighs. "It will work! I know we can do it! There is only like fourteen of his men here. We can totally pull this off!"

"This is such a bad idea," Enzo says. "But I don't see many other options besides outright slaughtering all of them. I guess this is the best plan."

"Great! So Enzo and I will keep lookout outside each of the rooms while Saraphena and Duncan sneak in to do the dirty work!" Gunnar claps.

"So happy to help, honey," I sneer.

"You're gonna do great, babe!"

"Should we get Aliyah for this? She can't possibly still be sleeping right?" I ask. "Enzo, you were with her last."

"I— She was still sleeping...I think. I can't really— I can't remember actually. But the healer did send one of his trainees to find me with a note before the wedding to tell me that he had to put her into a deeper sleep because she was not taking to the procedure well. I intended to visit her afterward but— I don't remember why I didn't," Enzo says, confusion in his tone.

"The healer doesn't have any trainees," Gunnar says. "He never wanted to take anyone else on because his practices were so experimental in nature he didn't want anyone getting in trouble because of him if things went wrong."

"No but he— the boy— I could have sworn. UGH! Why can't I remember?" Enzo yells.

"Okay, new plan. We will go check on Aliyah, then head to the crew's rooms, and then kill Jonah." Gunnar starts making his way to Aliyah's room. When Enzo pushes open the door, we all peer in around him when he stops dead in his tracks.

"Where is she?" I ask.

"I— I don't know." Enzo races to the bedside table where a small note is left. Reading it over, Enzo throws the note down on the bed, storming out. Gunnar plucks it off the bed and holds it out for us to see.

Dearest Enzo,

I'm sorry to have to do this to you, but after waking up without the bond, I knew I didn't want to be with you any longer. I couldn't face you to say goodbye, or find a way to explain to the others. Don't come looking for me. There is no future here.

Aliyah

"Enzo, wait up!" I call. "This doesn't make any sense! She wouldn't do this. She wouldn't leave you behind."

"Yes, she would. But that isn't what bothers me. She wouldn't leave *you* behind. I remember now. Aliyah woke up and the last person she saw was Jonah."

Chapter 42

ENZO

"**Y**ou're a dead man walking, *Captain* Jonah!" I storm through the halls, Duncan and the others hot on my heels. I throw open the doors to the wing housing Jonah and his men.

A door to the right opens and out steps one of his crew. "Where is he?" I ask.

"You'll never find—" *Snap.* The crewman's head falls to the side at an odd angle.

Two more doors open down the hall, three of the crew come into view. Duncan materializes behind one of them, a dagger splitting through the fae's throat, severing his spinal cord in the process. A fire ball flies through the air as Saraphena makes herself visible behind one of the others, forcing his mouth open to swallow the fire thrown by her husband. The man burns from the inside out.

The final one stands. "Where is Jonah?"

Pee trickles down the fae's trousers. "Now that's just sad," Gunnar laughs.

With a flick of my wrist, the man's spine twists in a full circle, snapping on impact.

"WHERE IS JONAH?" I yell.

"There's no need to shout." The man in question steps into the hall, Liliana chained to his side, a dagger to her throat. Tears stream from her eyes.

Duncan seethes. "Brother, not yet. He needs to tell us where Aliyah is and then he can die," I say, trying to quell his anger.

"By the time you reach her, she won't be in one piece anymore," Jonah laughs. "I've already sent my remaining crew members off with her hours ago. She should be reaching the shores of His Majesty in a few day's time."

"You snake. You planned this all along," Saraphena spits.

"In truth, yes. There were a few happy coincidences, but unfortunately, our time together has come to an end. I knew this little façade couldn't last forever. But my wife and I must be on our way now. One move and she dies." Jonah's true nature comes out in the wicked smile that breaks across his face.

"You're not going anywhere with her," Duncan fires off.

"And who's going to stop me?" Jonah winks.

I hear the zing right before the pain spikes through my neck. I stumble, feeling the power drain out of me. The others find their balance, likely feeling the same. The remaining doors open around us in the hall, revealing four of Jonah's men, long, hollow poles in their hands, loading another poison tipped dart into the barrel.

"You think I need powers to kill you?" Duncan says between gritted teeth. "I'll happily end you here and now without a drop of power in me."

"I'd like to see you try." Jonah backs into the room, Liliana in tow, closing it behind him. I hear the faint click of the lock before the fight breaks out. I watch as one of the men grab Saraphena from behind, trying to put his hand over her mouth before she bites his palm, ripping out a large chunk. Blood spurts down her face as she begins her attack.

Duncan gets hit in the head by a metal rod, but it doesn't deter him. A fury of kicks and punches breaks out. Vases are smashed, priceless paintings torn from the walls. My own opponent tries, and epically fails to subdue me.

"You may be from The Islands of Loch where savages are made, but I was *born* to destroy." My knuckles crack as they connect with his mouth, several teeth falling to the ground. He stumbles back and I take the opportunity to grip his head in both my hands, smashing it into the wall behind him, rendering him unconscious.

"I'd kill you, but I really am trying to lower my body count as a promise I made to my dove when she came back to me." I step over his limp body, intent on helping Saraphena. She ducks as her opponent swings at her face, and pulling a dagger from her boot, slams it into the ribcage of the crewman.

"I made no such promise," she quips. She wipes the blood from her chin, a savage smile on her face.

"And take that! And take that!" Gunnar is kicking his opponent who clearly has already been incapacitated.

"Gunnar, I think you got him," Saraphena laughs.

"Yeah but I think his stupid face deserved a few more kicks. It looks better that way!" He smiles.

"Duncan how we doing over—"

Duncan lifts a screaming opponent in the air before bringing down his back, breaking it over his knee. "I'll be better when Jonah is dead."

Stepping over the fallen bodies, Duncan lifts his foot, kicking down the bedroom door. Liliana is inside, chained to the window, a gag keeping her from speaking.

Jonah's sword comes cutting through the air. Duncan's hand snatches Jonah's wrist at the last moment, snapping it over so it hangs limp attached to his arm. The sword clamors to the floor.

He must realize how much trouble he is in, because Jonah starts to back up. The look of utter destruction storming through Duncan's gaze is enough to strike fear into any fae's heart. Even I shutter a little bit at the sight. Duncan stalks after Jonah, who is now tripping over his feet to get away from him.

"You have no idea what he will do to Aliyah. You need me. You can bargain with him! My life for hers!" Jonah simpers.

"You are meaningless to him. He has what he wants. You are of no consequence to him now. Your life is worthless," Duncan states.

Reaching him, Duncan lifts Jonah up from the floor by his long, red braid. Shoving him up against the wall by his throat, I watch as Jonah moves to reach for Duncan.

"Not so fast. I don't know what your powers are exactly, but I know if you touch him he will falter and I can't let that happen." I snatch both of Jonah's wrists and place them above his head.

"Gunnar, you always wanted in on this stuff. Still want your turn?"

"For what he's done to my sister, it would be my pleasure." Gunnar steps up, unsheathing his knife. "Turn around, babe, I don't want you to see this."

"Not a chance," Saraphena says as she unhooks Liliana's shackles from around her neck and wrists. She helps Liliana stand, and pulls her into a tight embrace.

In one swift movement, Gunnar brings his knife down onto Jonah's wrists. Blood splatters onto the wall and rains down over us, his hands falling to the floor. Duncan, Gunnar, and I stand there soaked in his blood as his screams fill the air.

"What are they planning to do with Aliyah?" I ask.

"You won't get to her in time. He has plans for her and with his new weapon at his side, you'll never see her again. She won't stand for it," Jonah cries.

"WHO!?" Duncan yells.

"The Banished King and his new pet. The Princess of Nightmares he calls her."

"What is he planning to do with Aliyah?" Saraphena asks.

"I don't know. I swear I don't know," Jonah pleads.

"Then you're of no use to us anymore," Duncan states. "Liliana?"

"I'm here. I'm okay." Liliana comes up and lays her hand on Duncan's shoulder.

"This is your kill, sunshine."

"No. He isn't even worth the effort. He is *nothing* to me," she says.

"How can I make this right for you?" Duncan asks.

Liliana stands there contemplating for a moment. A wicked smile comes across her face before she gives her answer.

"You are nothing but a pest that has infested my home. One could say you are nothing but a *bug*. And do you know what we do with bugs?" Liliana asks, stepping up to Jonah who cowers away from her. "We *squash* them."

Without hesitation, Duncan grips both sides of Jonah's head and squeezes...*hard.* And just like that, the once formidable Captain of The Island's most ruthless crew is reduced to nothing more than a fractured skull and spilled blood.

As we pile out of the room, blood splattered across our skin and clothes, there is a moment of accomplishment that settles over the group. Liliana is freed from an abusive, evil man. Duncan might just get *another* chance to do the right thing with her. We have inside knowledge of The Banished King's new weapon and where exactly we can find Aliyah. For just this brief moment, things are finally looking up.

"What in the *hell* is going on around here?!"

Our brief moment of reprieve is over as *King Kaleron* steps into the entry way of the recently deceased Captain's wing.

"There is a totally reasonable explanation for this, I swear," Gunnar says.

"Save it brother. I don't want to hear whatever excuse you have to say. You all have risked the safety of this kingdom and all of Olyrium by your actions here today. Where is Captain Jonah so I can at least try to salvage the negotiations while I still can?"

"Ummm, about that," Gunnar chimes in once more.

Kaleron searches our faces for the truth of the situation. "You're joking. You have to absolutely be kidding me! You killed him, didn't you? Why? Why can't I leave you all for *one moment* without someone being killed?"

"In their defense, they did what you weren't allowed to do as king," Liliana says.

"Jonah was a good—"

"No. He wasn't a good man," Liliana cuts off. "He hit me, shackled me to a chair, force fed me Molly, and then kept me chained to the wall. He was *not* a good man."

"Lil, I— I had no idea," Kaleron says.

"I know. You only knew what he showed you, what he showed the world. But sometimes the kindest mask hides the most rotten of souls. He walked around with a smile on his face and warmth in his touch, but the moment the doors closed, the real monster came out. I would have found a way out of it eventually, but luckily I didn't have to. I know your hands were tied, but their's weren't. Don't punish them for saving me from my situation," Liliana pleads.

"I never wanted to put you in this position, Lil. I'm so sorry. If I had known the kind of man he was, I never would have allowed you to marry him. Contract be damned."

"I know. I don't have any ill feelings toward you, Kaleron. We're good," she smiles.

"There is just one more problem," I start. "Jonah shipped Aliyah off to The Banished King."

Kaleron's eyes widen. "He what?! When? I will get the Flying Legion on it as fast as I can."

"With all due respect, I will be the one to rid this world of Tyros. We will get her back," I say.

"I'm coming with you," Kaleron says. I nod my head knowing we can use all the help we can get. "But first, we need to deal with this situation."

"There is nothing to deal with, Kaleron. Jonah told me there were never any ships coming. He was always working for Tyros. He was never going to work with us against him. Jonah is a traitor and a liar. You may have to deal with some diplomatic crap when The Islands find out he has been killed, but...it is worth it," Liliana says.

"What was the original plan you had here?" Kaleron asks.

"We were going to kill them one by one and have Duncan teleport them to their boat with a bomb on board to die at sea," Gunnar beams with pride in his plan. I roll my eyes.

"You see how well that worked out," I say.

"Not the most solid of plans, but it can still work here. Help me get them loaded onto their boat and we will send them to their watery grave," Kaleron smiles.

The six of us spend the rest of the time cleaning the hall and bedroom of any signs of foul play and when we push the boat off the dock headed for The Islands, Gunnar tosses out a fireball onto the ship. Watching it burn and sink into the sea brings a new sense of purpose to our mission. I will watch the entire world burn if that is what it takes to get Aliyah back...starting with the Princess of Nightmares, whoever she may be.

Part V:
Retribution

Chapter 43

LILIANA

"Enzo you oaf, we can't just pack up and walk up to The Banished King's doorstep!" Saraphena's voice snaps me out of the trance I've been floating in for the last several minutes. Flashes of my Molly being shoved down my throat as bloody meat causes my heart rate to spike. I blink, trying to clear the images, but in the darkness behind my eyelids, more visions come.

"Lil?" Duncan's eyes fill with concern as they meet mine across the table. "You okay?"

"Fine." The lie slips out so easily, so...practiced. I suppose it has been after all these years of pretending like I'm *fine* day in and day out. "But Saraphena is right, we can't just go up and say *hey Tyros, we'd like to come in now.* He'd kill us, or worse, turn our minds into puddles, before we even got a chance to save Aliyah."

"Tyros is not a king, only a false ruler built on the backs of our people's sacrifice. We have two legitimate Kings sitting in this room. Something can be done." Kaleron crosses his arms over his chest with a huff and nods to Duncan.

Impassive as always, Duncan's eyes haven't left mine. "Twilight has not yet accepted me as their King."

"The people of Twilight do not get to just decide who is King. It is your blood right and therefore you can make decisions for your people. Call upon the soldiers who are willing to fight back. We should gather everyone we can and then end this once and for all," Kaleron sneers.

"That will take too much time! Aliyah is facing who knows what right now and the only reason why I am sitting here this very moment and not ripping apart his *castle* brick by brick is because I've gone up against Tyros before and he bent my mind a million different ways."

"I will go and get her. I can be in and out, undetected," Saraphena offers.

"No mate of mine will be going anywhere alone," Gunnar notes.

"Um, excuse me, but I don't think going in there fireballs-a-blazing is going to help us out here, *mate,* so why don't you pipe down as if you could stop me from going anyways!" Saraphena smacks the back of Gunnar's head and I can't help the small smile that cracks on my face.

"There she is." Duncan's voice barely registers to the others, but I hear him loud and clear, a blush creeping up my cheeks. We haven't had much time to talk since everything happened with

Jonah. I've wanted to go to him so many times, tell him how I feel, and tell him how I never meant what I said in the garden. But I saw the look on his face the day Jonah was revealed as my mate.

"Why are we sitting here acting like we aren't about to go and rescue her as a group anyways and ignore the diplomatic part in all of this?" Gunnar asks.

Silence.

"Right, so when do we leave?" Gunnar pushes back his chair, bringing Saraphena up with him. "Because I am going to need at least an hour with my mate before we leave in case we die in a horrible mind-bending way."

"What could possibly take an hour to— You know what, never mind. I don't want to know," I laugh.

"I will head to the kitchens to get us packed for the journey and everyone is taking a sphinx so we can get there as fast as possible. Saraphena, you should fly in first and do some recon. We need to know what's happening on the ground. Enzo, you hover close by to wipe out any incoming Kalari she doesn't see and the rest of us will wait for the signal. We leave from the front gates in a half hour. Let's get a move on people!" Kaleron bellows.

Gunnar and Kaleron start arguing over not having a full hour before they need to leave. As the rest of the team files out of the room, I hang back to collect myself before heading back to my room. I turn back to the council table, laughing softly to myself that a room meant for war council members only has become the sanctuary in which my found family gathers to once again save someone we love.

I run my hand over the smooth finish of the mahogany, feeling the cool, gold inlays beneath my palm. I close my eyes, feeling the warm sun crest over my face. The smell of sweat and blood lingers in the air from Jonah and his crew, whose blood marked all of our bodies. I listen intently to the sounds around me; Gunnar and the others still arguing down the hall over our departure. I center myself in this moment. I'm safe. I'm alive. I'm *free.* The words I heard Aliyah speak to herself time and time again since getting out of her own prison. I thought I would be in mine forever.

A strong hand runs down my arm, startling me for a moment until the familiar feeling of me in his arms comes crashing back to me. I move to turn around, but Duncan holds me firm with my back to his chest.

"Stay with me in this moment." His voice is low and soothing like a thick blanket around my shoulders keeping me warm and safe. His fingers reach mine and interlock, pressing my palm into the imprint on the wood. I lay my head back on his shoulder, fusing our bodies together in every way possible.

I know it's illogical to trust someone so quickly after everything I've been through, but Duncan is different. Jonah— Jonah was a blip on the map compared to the journey that stretches before me. A journey I want Duncan to be by my side for.

His breath on my neck as he speaks sends goosebumps down my spine. "I know you have suffered a great loss with Molly, and I can't begin to imagine what that must be like for you. Jonah's death will never be enough to fix what he broke, but I'll be damned if I'm not the one to crawl across the pieces of your shattered bond and bleed for you. Let me suffer the death of a thousand cuts, the jaws of the fiercest monster, or the wrath of The Banished King for just a chance at reversing my greatest regret in losing you. Let my heart be torn from my chest and I bleed out on this floor in front of you if it means a chance at giving you the world."

"Duncan," I breathe, reaching my other hand up and around his neck as he places a soft kiss to the side of mine. "Don't say things you don't mean. Don't play with my emotions or make promises you have no intent on keeping. If you choose this now, there is no more backing out. I will swim across the largest oceans, tear down any enemy that dares stand in my way, all to ensure you remain by my side forever. I choose you, Duncan. I always have, and I always will."

"You are my choice, Princess Liliana, and I will never waiver in that decision again." Duncan's hand clasps around my neck, my eyes softly opening for the first time, daring to lock in our fates forever.

"I'll never be your mate..." My eyes search his for any hesitation, not trusting my power to give me the real answer I seek.

"But you'll always be *mine*." His lips meet mine in a swift and passionate flurry of kisses. His hands move to the center of my tunic and with the force of a thousand swords, tears it straight down the middle until it is nothing but a forgotten piece of scrap on the floor. The heat in the room intensifies, even with the magic keeping the palace cool from the scorching sun outside.

Impatient hands push and pull until Duncan's bare skin meets mine. He lays me gently back on the war room table, a place where treaties have been crafted, alliances forged, and today, fates sealed for eternity. The cool wood and golden inlays send a wave of shivers down my back, but the fervor in Duncan's lips on my skin is like a salve to my soul, healing with each pass of his touch.

Duncan is the other half to my soul, mate or not, and no matter what comes next, I'll know that everything we suffered was what drove us to find each other. Him and I are enviable, in this life and the next, and I plan to savor every second with him available, because I know as we move to take on The Banished King, life is not guaranteed. The moment Duncan joins his body with mine, I realize we might need that full hour after all.

Chapter 44

ENZO

We ready our sphinx to take us to the gates of The Banished King's door, a tension hanging in the air knowing this may all be for nothing. Aliyah might already be dead.

"Don't think like that." Liliana shoves me in the chest as she tightens the saddle on the beast before me.

"Get out of my emotions, Liliana." I gaze out over the village of SunSpark, the undisturbed rays of the sun cast an orange glow over the rows of sunflowers lining the streets.

"I would, but you're basically broadcasting them for the world. Aliyah isn't dead, she literally can't die. Her wings will protect her at the very least, and I don't know if you've noticed, but she is more than capable of taking care of herself these days. I'm sure by the time we get there she will be slaughtering The Kalari left and right and wearing The Banished King's fingers as a necklace."

"That's a horrifying image, Lil," Saraphena says with a look of disgust on her face.

"But nothing less than the truth," Liliana shrugs. "Our girl has this handled. I'm sure of it."

"Let's hope you're right," I say, my gaze drifting over the far side of the village. A disruption in the sun's rays catches my eye.

"Enzo? What's up?" Gunnar asks, stepping up to my side.

"Did you see that?" I ask.

"See what?" Duncan adds.

"I'm sure it was nothing. Let's get going. I don't want to waste any more time." I swing my leg up and over the back of the sphinx, the large mane engulfing my hands as they take grip. I remember the first time I ever flew with Aliyah. The look of freedom on her face, pure joy radiating from her. It feels like so long ago that we were simply searching for her family and not fighting a losing battle time and time again.

The sphinx shifts beneath me, unease washing over the space between us all. The others mount their sphinx alike, a look passing between us in the sudden shift of air.

"Something's wrong," Saraphena says.

"Aliyah is missing, kidnapped, and possibly tortured," Kaleron quips. "That's what's wrong."

"No. Saraphena's right. I can feel it. Something...dark." Liliana closes her eyes, a look of concentration crossing her features as she throws her power out to the world around us.

"Steady, beast," I whisper to the sphinx. "Don't get jumpy on me now." I run my hand down the mane. Waiting. *Watching.*

"Enzo!" A voice breaks through the silence, the person heard, but not yet seen. "Enzo! Run!"

"Jade?"

Her short brown hair blows back behind her as she sprints toward us. "Run! The Kalari! They're coming! We're under attack!"

"That cannot be. The SunSpark Flying Legion would have given me a report that Tyros was moving his hoard of filth across the land or sea." Kaleron jumps down from his sphinx. The rest of us dismount in turn. "I will speak with my advisors immediately and summon my troops if this news is true." Kaleron turns and strides into the palace.

"Jade, why— how are you here? Who is with the recruits?" I ask.

"Enzo, you need to listen to me. The Kalari are coming. I saw them! You have to believe me." Jade stops before us, breathing in deeply, in and out.

"How do you know this?" Duncan asks, a sense of urgency in his voice.

"I saw them! They are coming through the village, they will be here any moment!" Jade waves her arm around, gesturing to the quiet village.

"I don't see anyone or hear anything like what they normally do to villages, Jade. We need to leave. I'm sure if anything comes this way, Kaleron's army can deal with it, but for now we need to go. I still want answers as to why you aren't back in Citrine with the recruits, but we can talk about that later. There is a lot you need to get caught up on, but right now we need to go. I can explain on the way." I move to get back on the sphinx, but Jade huffs, catching me off guard.

"There isn't time to save her, Enzo! We're about to be under attack!"

"How do you— Jade, what's going on?" Liliana's lip quivers slightly as realization hits her in the chest. "Jade...why do you feel so...empty?"

Jade begins taking a few steps back, her eyes never leaving mine, but her expression morphs into something sinister. Her lips spread into a wicked smile, her eyes burning a shimmering shade of emerald green, as if glowing within her irises.

"The charade had to end sometime, but I do wish I could have had a bit more fun before the work began," she sneers.

Tears pour down Liliana's face, Saraphena clasps Gunnar's hand, and Duncan clenches his fists, ready to fight.

"What happened to you, Jade?"

"I got what I deserved, Enzo! You all sat here and saw me as less than you because I was not born with an ability! But who's laughing now? ME! You are all less than the dirt on my boots!" The Kalari appear behind Jade, swarming around her, but waiting with a calm I haven't seen before. Waiting...for a *command.*

"Don't do this. Whatever you've gotten yourself into, we can fix it." I put my hands out in front of me, a coaxing tone to my voice. Hundreds...no...*thousands* of The Kalari appear along the streets of SunSpark. Far too many for me to take out alone without burning out, and far too many for us to walk away from this alive. If this battle begins, we will lose everything. I can't use my power like before to level that village. No more innocent lives will be lost on this day.

"You know, I thought about it. I thought about coming to you, leaving the past where it belonged, but then I realized...retribution is far more fulfilling. Besides, I realized that only by removing the *pests* of Olyrium will true balance and power be restored. And oh, how many pests there are." Jade reaches out to one of The Kalari standing beside her, a sack dripping red is passed into her clutches. My heart stops. *Please don't be Aliyah.*

Pulling off the bag, Jade rolls the head across the ground, the open eyes and mouth of her victim agape in horror from their last moments alive. "Ugh, finally. She was starting to smell really bad and lugging her head around was beginning to grow tiresome," Jade drawls.

Liliana drops to her knees, her hand outstretched toward the head, a sob catching in her throat. Duncan drops beside her, wrapping her in his arms as she takes in the sight before her. Gunnar and Kaleron stare on, blank expressions on their faces as they take in the horror of this moment.

"You will regret this, Jade. Mark my words. Today, you will take your last breath," Kaleron promises. I take one last look at

Queen Starla's severed head on the ground before snapping into the role of General.

"Enough of this foolishness! You need to stand down, now! I will not ask again," I yell. Jade simply smiles.

"Oh sweet, sweet ZoZo. I'm just getting started." With a snap of her fingers, a group of The Kalari standing at the front of the hoard reveal their own death sentences. Severed heads of sphinx and Flying Legion members all roll forward on the stone, joining their leader with their own look of horror on their faces and maws.

A moment of silence passes over the chasm between us. My once best friend, now turned enemy, stands across from me, but I don't recognize her. She steps back into the hoard, disappearing into them, and it's in this moment I know we are done talking. The next battle has begun and I pray to the Maker Aliyah can hold on a little while longer.

Chapter 45

LILIANA

Duncan rips my sword from its sheath and shoves it into my hand. "I'm so sorry you will not have time to grieve her death, but right now I need you to fight for your life. I need you to fight for us and our future, and all the moments we have yet to share."

I snap out of my stupor and look him in the eyes, lost in the love that is pleading for me to understand. "Don't you dare die, Duncan, or I will kill you myself." I pull him in by his neck, smashing our lips together in one last kiss before Enzo is shouting orders over us, directing us on how to stay alive for the longest amount of time.

I turn my focus on The Kalari, throwing out my power to sense any part of their soul to tap into their emotions and turn them to dust, but I feel...nothing. Jade's laughter rings loud across the battle ground and I'm suddenly very angry that we ever tried to include her in our family when she would turn so easily to another, more evil, man. I let the rage I have been holding back flood my veins and set my sights on The Kalari before me.

"That's my girl. Let them see your wrath," Duncan smirks before turning his back and facing his own demons. Sweat pours down my back as I cut through each one of the enemies in my path, but for every one I cut down, two more appear.

"Where are they coming from?!" I call out over the sound of clashing swords.

"Just keep fighting! Do not yield!" Duncan yells back. Streaks of red cover his body from wounds already healed. I keep him in my peripheral, always making sure he is there. I fight for us, just like he said. I fight for kisses we haven't yet shared, stories we have yet to weave, a kingdom to rebuild and pass on to our children.

Slices to my own skin sting as The Kalari close in around me, the rest of my family lost to the sea of rotten skin and black bones. My breath is labored and I feel myself waning. I don't know how much longer I can keep this up. No matter how many I cut down, they just...keep...coming.

I turn, searching for Duncan, ensuring his heart still beats. I don't see him though. Panic ripples through my bones. I spin around, trying to find the direction I just came from where I last saw him. The world spins as I try to find my direction, but I'm completely surrounded.

"Duncan!" I call. "Duncan, where are you?"

"On your left! I've got you, Princess! Don't worry, you're not going to get rid of me that easily!"

I ease at his words, working my way back to him, cutting down the mass of creatures before me as I go. Finally, I see him. "Duncan!"

His head snaps my way, the briefest of moments. "Look out!" I scream, shoving myself through the hoard. Duncan blocks the axe coming toward his right, but he doesn't even see the other threat coming.

A scream rips through the air as an arrow pierces through his neck and comes out the front of his throat. "NO!" I try to push and fight my way through, but I'm completely surrounded. A cut to the back of my thigh causes me to stumble, my eyes locked on the blood pooling around Duncan's fallen body, his eyes never leaving mine as his body spasms with his last breath.

"Duncan! Please! Get up! You have to get up! You can't leave—"

My scream pours out of me, but it never passes my lips. The sound escapes through the slice across my throat and as my face smashes onto the blood stained cobble stone, my eyes find Duncan, his hand outstretched toward me. I reach for him, feeling the last few beats of my pulse spurting my blood out of my body. We're so close to finding each other amongst the carnage, but as my vision turns black, I know we never made it back to one another.

Chapter 46

SARAPHENA

There's too many of them. We can't keep doing this much longer. I can feel my power burning out.

Keep going for as long as you can. If The Kalari turn their focus away from us, they will attack this village. We cannot let that happen. Right now Jade has them completely focused on us and Enzo. I think this is what they were talking about when they made up that saying about a woman scorned.

Please don't take this as an opportunity to make jokes. You need to be focusing.

What's a battle without a little bit of humor?

I smile to myself, vanishing in and out of sight to escape blows from The Kalari. Gunnar stands at my back, fire flaring up all around us as he lights up the changing sun with his own glowing embers.

I hear Lil scream, my head snapping in her direction as I watch Duncan fall. I move to work my way toward them, knowing Liliana will be on her own now.

Don't. You can't help them. We are surrounded and there is no way you are getting to them alive. I love them, but I love you more.

Gunnar's voice speaks reason into my natural reaction, but I know he is right. I would never make it to Duncan in time. When I turn again, I look for her black hair amongst the crowd. Bile creeps up in my throat when I see it. One of The Kalari is running toward us, Liliana's scalp and hair flowing over his black skull.

Don't look. You don't need to see that.

They're dead. Tears blur my vision, but I wipe them away quickly, not wanting my own death to follow. I watch Enzo plow through a section of The Kalari, his path clear and set.

Enzo is going after Jade. We should help him.

Baby, I don't know if you've noticed this, but we aren't exactly doing so hot ourselves. Let's just try and get out of this alive, okay?

No one else is dying here today, you hear me? Let's work our way toward Enzo at least so we can help him if we can. He can't take on Jade alone. She's...different.

You mean like how she betrayed everything she knows and loves different or like how she has gone completely bad shit crazy and is clearly working with the enemy different?

Both.

I push my way through the hoard, trying to get myself closer to Enzo in case he needs help taking Jade down.

Saraphena, wait! I'm getting separated from you. Hold up.

I turn, watching as Gunnar breaks through the bones of our enemies one by one. My eyes snag on a movement to my right. The Kalari part, making way for a beast no one could predict. The monster's skull, deformed and cracked, bulges to the size of a small horse. Its shoulders broad, on *both* sets of arms. The first set appearing at a normal placement, but the second sit below, protruding from its waist. Its body is thick and corded with muscles. Three sets of eyes line its head, saliva dripping from the rows of teeth sticking out from its mouth. But the most horrifying thing of all, is that it's headed straight for Gunnar.

Don't worry, babe. I got this. No sweat.

Gunnar, don't! Just come with me! It's too big and we can't fight something like that! Please, just run!

I watch as Gunnar ignores my pleas and launches himself into the air at the beast. I swing around, my sword catching on another of The Kalari's. I work to fight the ones around me, panic in my chest as I watch Gunnar poke and prod at the monster before him, nearly missing his colossal fists.

I've got him right where I want him! I told you I got—

The beast grabs his torso, pinning Gunnar's arms to his sides. In one swift motion, the monster grabs Gunnar's legs and I turn, not wanting to see what comes next. I feel his blood splatter across the back of my body, The Kalari cheering as Gunnar is ripped in half. Every part of my soul dies. The creature bellows into the sky, claiming his victory over my mate. The crunch of blood and bones rushes into my ears and even though I want to slam my hands over them to block out the sound, I know I have to keep fighting, even as my heart shatters into a million pieces.

My Soul Bond has been kidnapped, my best friend and her mate slaughtered, and the love of my life has been ripped apart. My very being has been shredded into ribbons, and I know exactly who to blame. *This ends now, Jade.*

Chapter 47

ENZO

I feel my power reserves emptying with each passing second as I cut my way through The Kalari to get to Jade. I never thought in all our years together we would be standing on opposite sides of the battlefield, and yet here we are. I don't have the time or energy to allow myself to go into the spiral of losing one of my family members to the enemy. If I let myself start down that road, there is no telling what kind of carnage I'll leave behind.

My instincts kick in and I am fully the General I was molded into by my father; ruthless, driven, heartless, *fearless*. With each slash of my battle axe, I am one step closer to ending this madness. As much as it pains me, Jade needs to die. Every fiber of my being is screaming not to end her here and now, but to show mercy for my friend. I will hold onto that feeling until she gives me no other choice.

The streets of SunSpark are flooded with vile creatures, yet none of them turn on the villagers. Confusion takes hold in my mind as I turn, searching to see if any of the homes have been destroyed. A scream pulls my attention and I watch as Duncan and Liliana fall to their deaths. Horror grips my heart, but when I try to move toward them, another swarm of The Kalari push me back. They climb over each other, piling on top of one another, all to get to me, driven by pure ravenous evil not easily satisfied.

A beast like no other strides toward Gunnar and Saraphena. I yell to Gunnar to run, to stand down, but he can't hear me over the chittering of the skeleton jaws and war cries from the hoard. I don't let myself look away when I see Gunnar being torn apart. My family is falling, being ripped from this earth piece by piece in the most horrific way. I need them, all of them.

Visions of Gunnar and Duncan holding me while I wept for Aliyah with every failed attempt to end my life and join her flash through my mind. Saraphena and Gunnar getting married, a ceremony crafted by Liliana in an attempt to get Aliyah and I to work through our issues, as if Liliana thought I didn't know what she was trying to do. Duncan leaving that ballroom when Liliana found her mate in Jonah, only to find his way back to her. For each amazing thing that has happened in our time together, something equally horrific has followed.

The slices across my body increase as my attention is pulled back into the moment, thankful my instincts to continue fighting even as my mind waivers in and out of reality. A break in the path reveals Jade, propped on the edge of a fountain at the center square, one leg crossed over the other, picking at her nails as if this entire situation is a bore. People she has known her entire life are being slaughtered around her, yet she sits there unbothered. Fury rages in my veins at her relaxed demeanor. How can she sit there when she is the cause of all this destruction?

"Jade!" I bellow, shoving my way through the hoard to get to her. She finally looks up, and when her eyes lock on mine, a wicked smile pulls across her face as she stands. With one wave of her hand, The Kalari around me part, a direct line to her opening. I don't question. I don't think. I just charge.

As I reach the last row of the creatures, I raise my axe, ready to strike. From seemingly out of nowhere, Jade draws a sword from behind her back. A flicker of something...odd...flashes across Jade's features, but when my axe collides with her weapon, the only thing left standing between her and death is our history.

Chapter 48

JADE

"Don't do this, Jade!" Enzo yells as my sword clashes with his battle ax.

"I have to! It's what I'm owed after what you did to me!"

"What *I* did to *you*?! You manipulated me in my grief! You used our history and my past to fabricate feelings for you! Nothing we had was ever real!"

The ringing of steel reverberates through the air with each continued blow. "Don't let your ego do the talking here, Enzo! You never loved me! Ever! You would always put me second. Second to the war, second to your brothers, second to that winged creature you call a mate! Deep down you knew you'd never choose me! You always held your father's death over my head, even if you didn't say it! You never forgave me no matter how many times I made up for it!"

"I did forgive you, Jade! I forgave you a long time ago for that, but what you are doing now...this is what would be unforgivable! Look around you! You've lost your mind! I don't want you to lose your life too. Just give this up, Jade! Give up

The Banished King's malicious plans and come back to us. We can be a family again!"

My arm is fully cocked, ready to land my next blow, but his words give me pause. "As if I would ever believe anything you say. You would do anything for Aliyah and if she were here now and drove a sword through my neck you would forgive her in a heart beat or less! But I save you from an abusive father and what do I get?"

"You made a decision that wasn't yours to make! I knew what he was. I knew the monster he was turning me into, but you took the choice away from me to fight my own battles."

"You know what, *ZoZo,* this conversation is beginning to bore me and I have a new toy at home waiting to be broken and ripped into pieces, so let's wrap this up shall we?"

I attack him with everything I have. Every blow is packed with the force of revenge. He is going to pay for everything he has done to me. He made me believe we had a future together. That true love would conquer all. He made me *hope.* His battle ax swings and collides with my sword, the force pushing me back slightly. I just need to get close enough to— *There.* His ax is a near miss as it swings down to the right side of my body, leaving his face exposed, and in one quick motion, I pull the powder from the small bag tied around my hip. Gripping the fine dust in my hand, I blow it into Enzo's face before staggering back a few steps, just in case it takes a few moments to affect him.

"Jade— Wha— What did you ju— just—"

Enzo drops to the ground, dust flying up around him upon impact. "I did what I had to do. You took everything from me, so I took away the one thing you love most."

His gaze is glazed over as he stares up at the blazing sun. Sweat coats his brow and his body is slick with the wet sheen of battle. I stride over to him and kneel in the dirt next to his body. I lean over so his eyesight rests upon my face.

"Your body is completely immobile thanks to the larkspurs flower I used on you. It is a powerful sedative, and if contact is made with a high enough dosage, can cause complete paralysis. Combined with the spell Tyros gave me, your magic is useless. I assume it worked the same on Aliyah so that pesky immortality power won't work either. Hopefully The Banished King doesn't end her before you have a chance to see me have my fun."

Enzo's eyes widen in horror, but his body is completely at my will.

"I could end you right here and now if I wished, but I want you to watch her suffer before I end her life once and for all. You don't deserve a quick death. I want you to suffer the way I have. I want you to watch as I torture and rip apart your *mate* limb from limb, starting with those ugly wings. I have watched you for *years.* I watched you fall apart after your father's death, watched you fight in battle, watched you fall in love, and I suffered through the entire thing. I know that watching me break your precious dove will make you suffer just a fraction of how I have suffered."

My mind relaxes as I let the illusion drop away, piece by piece, but I let one image remain. I leave an image in place just for *them*. The battlefield goes quiet. The Kalari around me burst into strings of smoke as they return to the place in my mind which conjures the nightmares of others. My power feels depleted after having held up this mirage for so long. I let my true form show, knowing he will be deliciously horrified by the powerful force I have grown into.

His face shows the realization of who I really am, shock registering in every feature he shows. But one thing shines brighter than the rest...horror.

"Jade, what have you done to yourself?" He gasps.

"It's a shame I'm no longer your strategist because this plan was once again flawless. It was the perfect ploy and one that cost me nothing. I lost no soldiers today, no weapons, no family, no friends, and yet you lost everything."

"Enzo!" Saraphena yells as her gaze turns my way, the bodies of her beloved friends and mate strewn on the ground around her. I know I only have a few moments before she is upon me. I look up and meet her gaze, a wicked smile on my face.

"Tootles," I wink at her before whispering the words to bring me back home...back to my real family and Enzo is coming with me.

EPILOGUE
ALIYAH

My eyes feel like lead as I try to open them. My head lolls backwards as the sensation of burning at my wrists brings me back fully. I try to yank my arms away from the feeling, but the sound of heavy chains ripples through the still air.

"Where—Where am I?" I blink a few more times as the room clears around me. Black stone walls surround me and the high ceiling above me sparkles with the flames of candle light. "Hello!"

I look up and see my hands cuffed in iron shackles above my head and a large stone slab juts up behind me with the chain bolted into it. "You've gotta be fu—"

"Whoa now! No need for that sort of profanity in my home. It isn't decent for a lady to say such things. Though, upon further inspection, it seems you are no lady at all, but simply an enigma among the fae." His eyes roam over the wings protruding from my back.

I don't recognize the man before me, but his face is tattooed with half a skull and his inky black hair is slicked back in a way that is oddly sophisticated. It screams power.

"Who are you?" I ask, my mind clearly more fuzzy than I realized.

"I'm sure you have heard of me, though I don't believe we have been formally introduced. My name is Tyros, but you may know me as The Banished King, and you, my disgusting little creature, need to go back to your grave...permanently."

ACKNOWLEDGEMENTS

Holy crap! Another book is completed! This book has truly been one of my favorites to write! With only one more book to write in this series, I don't know how I am going to feel when it is all over. There are so many thank you's to go around, but there are a few I want to point out specifically.

First, thank you once again to my amazing husband. Without your dedicated love and support to continue pursuing my dreams, I don't know that I could have done it. You have taken care of me every step of the way while dealing with Lyme Disease and making sure I'm fed when spending hours in front of the computer writing this story. The love you have for me rivals all the love stories we find in books!

Second, a huge thank you to my best friend, Jacque. Knowing you are reading every chapter and version that comes out during this process and loving every one of them warms my heart. You are truly the best friend anyone could ask for and I can't wait to see where life takes us! You are truly the Saraphena to my Aliyah. 'Til the end.

Third, once again, to my amazing dad for reading story after story and helping me make them perfect. I know this book has been a long time coming, so thank you for waiting and being willing to jump right back in! For always wearing my t-shirts at book events and going into random book stores to tell them about my stories. The real MVP. To my mom, who keeps pushing me to write and show my stories to the world. For attending my book events and cheering me on, even when I don't feel like writing. I love you to the moon and back momma.

Fourth, to the group chat. You know who you are! Thank you for always hyping me up and making me feel like more than just an author, but your friend. You are the OG group of supporters and I wouldn't be here without you! You will always and forever be the Survivors of Jane's Wrath and #1 fans of the Soul Snatcher 3000, even when I break your heart time and time again! I hope I made you proud in this book and can't wait for you to finish out the series alongside me!

Last, but certainly not least, to you. The reader. Without you and your support I wouldn't have the drive to keep breaking hearts! I hope you found something in this story to connect with and love the inner versions of yourself along the way. I can't wait to see you in the next book: Enemies & Endings. Until then, go pick your jaw up off the floor with this ending and settle into that book slump.

With love, Jane.

About the Author

Jane has a love for Dark Romantic Fantasy and being able to bring about justice through fiction. In her spare time, Jane helps other indie authors with graphic design creations and hosting Tales as Dark as Time, an all indie author book signing event. Jane has been overwhelmed with the joy and love readers have for her books and knows that absolutely none of this would be possible without *you!*

Follow along on social medias: @janerose_thebookbesties

ALSO BY JANE

Broken Realms Series

Banished & Broken

Anguish & Anarchy

Standalone Books

Secrets of Sòlas (Coming in 2026)

www.ingramcontent.com/pod-product-compliance
Lightning Source LLC
Chambersburg PA
CBHW070208310726
48976CB00001B/250